# ADVERSITY

## REN BROWNE

DIVERSITY
ENTERTAINMENT

# CONTENT NOTES

The story you are about to read is a fast-paced old west adventure with high stakes gun fights, bad guys that need killin', and three outlaws who can't keep their hands off each other. As a result, there are a number of mature themes in this story, including detailed sex scenes involving multiple partners and dynamics, on-page violence and death, references to domestic violence and sexual assault, depictions of hunger and poverty, representations of mental health struggles, scenes where a main character is being held captive and hurt, and use of derogatory language that may be triggering for some readers.

If you would like to view a more comprehensive list of triggers and tropes before proceeding, please visit **RenBrowne.com**. If you're good to go, then by all means, ride on.

# THE MIDNIGHT GANG SERIES

## ADVERSITY

## PROVIDENCE

# PLAYLIST

Cowboy Take Me Away — The Chicks

Kalahari Down — Orville Peck

The Devil Wears a Suit and Tie — Colter Wall

The Outlaw Josey Wales — Zella Day

Saddle Tramp — Marty Robbins

Moonrise — Anne Buckle

Red Right Hand — Nick Cave and the Bad Seeds

Worst Way  — Riley Green

Wild One — Faith Hill

Francesca — Hozier

Can I Get It — Adele

Wild as You — Cody Johnson

Moonshiners — Goodnight, Texas

Wild Dogs — Colter Wall

Another Man's Grave — Amigo the Devil

Devil's Backbone — The Civil Wars

Everything — Alex Warren

Work Song — Hozier

Me and the Devil — Soap&Skin

Carry You Home — Alex Warren

In Your Love — Tyler Childers

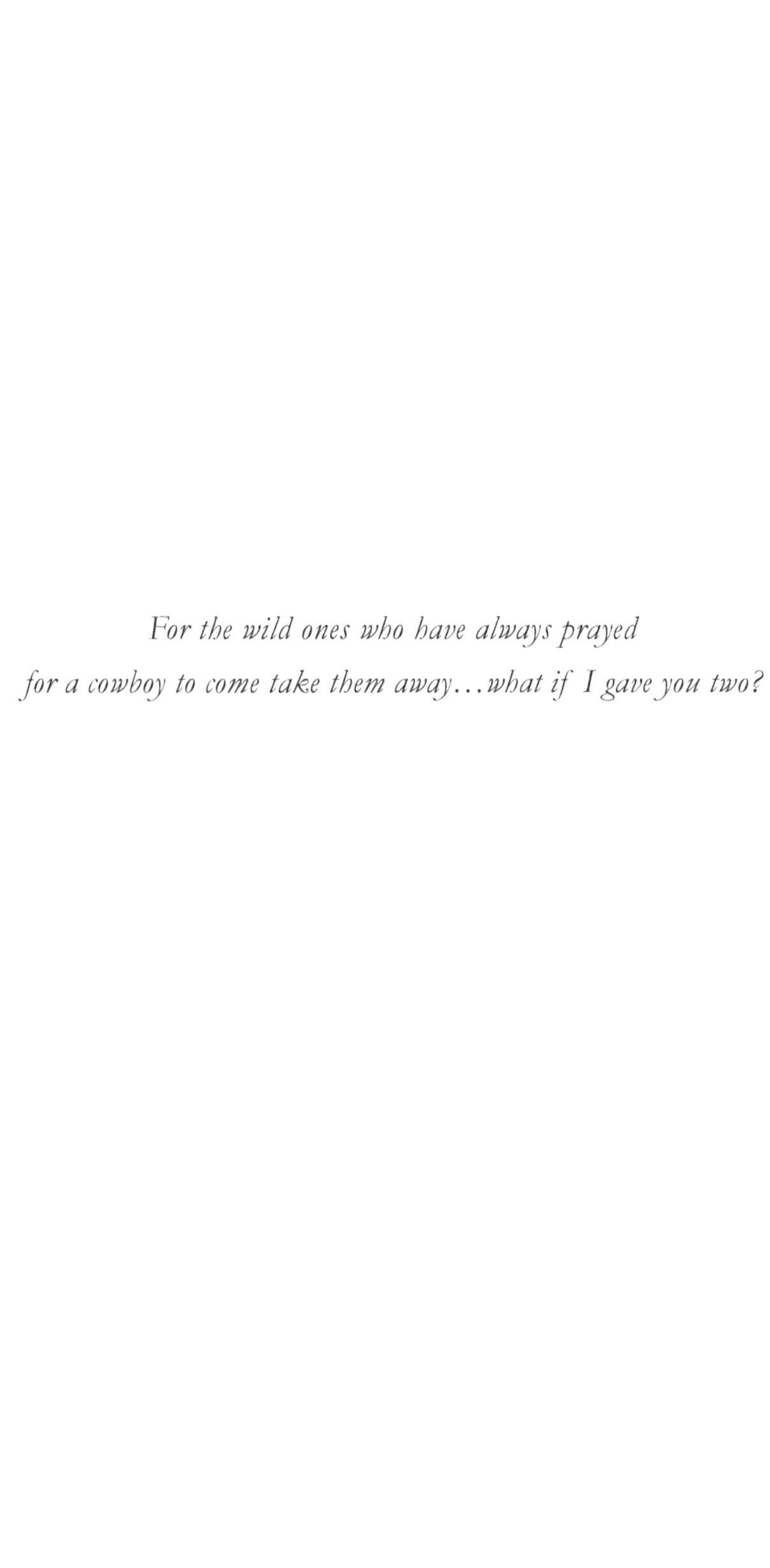

*For the wild ones who have always prayed
for a cowboy to come take them away…what if I gave you two?*

# CHAPTER 1
## CORA

I bury him on a hill.

A peaceful spot beneath the desert sky, the kind of place where he liked to sit as time passed him by alongside his remaining chances. Given the last few days, it's hard for me not to feel that my father had squandered both, just as it's hard for me not to feel angry with him as I carry the stones for his grave all the way up from the dry creek bed. The rock pile and the wooden cross serving as perhaps the only real marks he managed to leave on this world.

Maybe he would have better luck in the next one. But then again, maybe not, since I had barely scraped together enough to fetch a coffin. Let alone a priest.

All he has is me, stumbling over his favorite passages from the Bible while I try to stop fresh tears from falling onto the worn pages, try to look away from the violent crimson stains that no amount of scrubbing has been able to lift from the light gray hem of the only dress I have left that can still be considered nice.

Truthfully, the worst part had been the waiting. Standing on that hill until the encroaching chill of night seemed poised to swallow me up. Until all I could rely on was the falling sun and the rising moon to help me on the slow walk back to the house, becoming more and more resigned with each step I took that I would make the journey alone.

I had not expected my mother to come. Not really. Why would she, when she had hardly spoken to my father in life and seemed ready to hold to that in death? Any remaining allotments of compassion she had were already overspent during this last year of barely surviving as Arizona settlers.

*Must be a misunderstanding,* my father had said when we arrived off the wagon train with all we had left to our name. Dust covered and sun scorched, surveying the dismal future that we'd been promised would make the last seven months on the trail worth it. *This can't be right. The man in Boston, he told me…*

The man in Boston had likely seen my father coming from miles away. They always did, which is why the still untamed land beneath my feet is just the most recent of his promises of paradise that turned out to be a mirage, the poster he kept in his pocket of rolling green hills and shimmering lakes drying up faster than the ink could set on his purchase of one hundred acres of barren dirt.

My mother hadn't even raised her voice. Instead, she simply placed my eight-year-old sisters back in the wagon and took them to town for the day, their long blonde braids swaying with the rock of the departing wagon while I was left behind to make what I could of things.

I'd had more hope then, I think. Despite what I'd learned to expect, I'd still had hope we would be able to make something out here. That all the fractured pieces of my family might finally find a way to knit themselves together with a fresh start.

How fitting, then, that our cornerstone cracked almost as soon as we'd laid it. Right down the center, and so deep that it is visible in the low guiding light of the lantern left in our front window, the deceptively welcoming glow enough to get me over the threshold, though not much farther.

When I walk in, my mother is seated at the kitchen table. Her spotless white dress free of wrinkles and her hair pinned up, as if she had been expected for a luncheon instead of a wake. She glances up from her Bible to acknowledge me only once I've stood too long right in front of her, determined not to move until I've said my final piece.

"You could've at least brought the girls," I begin, my voice kept soft so as not to wake them where they sleep in their cot in the corner. "I could have—*they* could have had a chance to say their goodbyes. He was their father."

"A distinction he did not deserve," she responds coolly, eyes already back on her gospel. "They've been through enough. I didn't see any point in upsetting them further."

"No, of course," I mutter with an unwise edge to my voice. "Why should any of us be upset at all? You clearly are not."

"That's not true." She calmly turns a page. "I am *beside myself* that he had the opportunity to drag us out to this godforsaken country in the first place. If only he had met his untimely end sooner."

I wince. Even for her, the cruelty is sharp, but she offers no apology.

Rather, she sighs, her shoulders sagging as she sinks back in her chair. "Don't ask me to mourn him. I said my goodbyes to the man I believed he was a long while ago. Too long ago to pretend otherwise."

Not for the first time, I wish I'd known what they had been like back then. Wish that I could have known the versions of them that had loved each other.

That could have loved me differently.

*What does she see when she looks at me now?* I wonder. Now that I am not just a reminder of her dead aspirations but also her dead husband. His green in my eyes instead of her blue. His auburn tint to my hair instead of her golden waves. His freckles across my nose…and his blood on my hands.

As if to hide the evidence of my guilt, I clasp my palms tightly behind my back, my fresh blisters biting as I assure her, "I'm not asking you to mourn him. I'm only asking you to—"

"*No,*" she replies, standing and setting her book to the side with a snap. "I've told you I'm not going to see the law. It's not necessary."

"But I've already tried going on my own. Perhaps if they saw that he also had a wife and young children, then—"

"Then *nothing.* Why should they care? This territory is practically lawless. What is done is done. The best thing for us to do is to go on with our lives." She looks toward the opposite corner of the cabin, her expression temporarily easing, and I follow her gaze to the neatly packed trunks. "No one has been foolish enough to take the land. But I did get some money for the rest of the animals today from the neighboring farms. And we'll get more in the morning when we sell the horses in town."

"In the morning?" I feel sick again as she speaks. That same rising sense of panic I'd felt as I watched my father fade away in that street, as I stood up on that hill earlier and thought about what would happen next. "Do we have to leave so soon?"

"Be *sensible*," my mother insists, her face pinching into a frustrated frown at my clear lack of corresponding enthusiasm. "We cannot stay here. Even if we make it to the fall without someone coming to collect, we will never make it through the winter. I won't die out here. I won't let my girls die out here, either." Her attention shifts away from me as she makes that declaration, back to the still sleeping forms of my sisters. "They deserve better."

I can't argue with her. Not convincingly. Not after what happened. Soon enough, the vultures will begin circling, swooping in to pick off what little meat remains on our bones. I told my father as much myself the day he died. I'd been *so* angry with him. I'd walked away from him in that street and then… I can still see the shock on his face. The way he simply crumpled right where he stood before the sound of the shot had even faded. Before I'd been able to get to him. I should never have left him alone.

"Do you think it's been easy for me? Do you think I enjoy having to always rely on *charity*?" My mother spits the word out as if the taste of it is sour, shaking her head at me in censure. "Do you realize how shameful it is? How *sinful*? We are lucky that my sister's husband is gracious enough to take us in at all."

*Lucky* is not the word I would use. Although, since my uncle only comes home when no one will have him elsewhere, I doubt he will even notice additional occupants unless he is short on someone to bellow at.

Say what people would about my father, but at least what he lacked in dependability, he made up for in other ways. He had been kind. He had believed in things. Believed too much, maybe. In the end.

"We can only impose so much on them for so long. The sooner we can get you married off, the better," my mother continues. "In Sarah's last letter, she wrote that she thought she might have found someone. Given your age—and with nothing to offer—it wasn't easy, Lord knows." Her upper lip curls slightly as she surveys me head to toe. "We'll have to hope he will take you before he has time to realize you're half wild."

*Half wild.* This is one of my mother's favorite judgments to throw at me. Its origin rooted in her belief that, especially now at twenty-three, I am simply too old and too unruly to be groomed into the type of respectable lady who could make her proud.

"You should be grateful that she's willing to do this for you when it should have fallen to your father. A good situation for you, all things considered. A widower, lost his wife of thirty years to the fever last spring. His children are grown but he needs someone to mind his house. To be useful to him."

She has already told me all this many times, though I don't dare point that out. As soon as the letter arrived weeks ago, it became a constant topic between us, but I had taken solace in the fact that she couldn't so easily give me to a man who was half a country away. Not when my father was still here to shake his head and ask why they would send me back when they needed hands at home.

Never mind that I simply didn't want to go. Didn't want to spend my days trapped in another house that wouldn't feel like mine, little more than another fixture for someone to deem *useful.*

"I don't—" I start to say, looking her in the eyes. "I don't want—" My mother steps forward and slaps me across the face, hard enough that I hold my hand against my cheek to try to stop both the stinging and the tears as my gaze goes to the floor.

"Listen to me, stupid girl," she hisses. "You are the daughter of a man who has left you with no options and no money. You have no say in this, and if I were you, I would be thankful that I don't leave you out there with him. I will not allow you to be a burden on my sister's household the way you've been on mine, do you understand?"

Before I can attempt to respond, she steps away, sweeping over to check that my sisters haven't been disturbed. I wonder if they can feel her there as they sleep. The sensation of someone looking over them, looking out *for* them, watchful and protective so that they don't come to harm. What would that feel like?

"Pack your things then get some rest," she tells me, polished and polite again as she straightens. "We are leaving this place by sunup."

I only nod, not bothering to say anything else while I dutifully gather my few belongings from around the cabin into a sack: my clothes from the corner, my father's Bible, my thin bedroll from the loft, a few days' worth of hardtack.

I wait for her to fall asleep before I also take my father's pocket watch. And the small knife he kept tucked in his boot. And the gun from the war that he still wore proudly at his hip. I try not to make a sound with any of it, don't even trust a backward glance as I slip back out into the night and sprint for the barn.

I needn't have worried. No one comes looking for me.

# CHAPTER 2
## CORA

"As I've explained, it won't be a simple matter to track down the man who killed your father. You must understand that these things take time…"

*Three months.* Three months I have been coming to this office, and somehow every time it is the same. The same endless excuses. The same sympathetic sighs. The same stagnant summer air. The same empty cells.

*These things take time. You must be reasonable in your expectations. Difficult with no names. No witnesses.*

"*I* am a witness," I remind Sheriff Mathews when he starts to amble down that familiar path again. "I saw the man who shot him clearly. I've described him to you."

The sheriff gives me a well-aged and weary stare from behind his desk, a look that is a far cry from the polite smile and warm handshake with which he used to greet my appearance. These days, he rarely even gets up, only gestures toward the open chair so that we can get straight to business. Suits me fine, although it would suit me even better to have him actually do *something* about my father's murder.

"Tan hair," I offer again. "Short beard. Light eyes. A powder burn—"

"We remember your description, Miss," reassures the younger man standing near the large front window, no doubt wishing he was on the other side of it. "It does not match anyone from town."

"He's not *from* town," I reply, unable to keep the frustration out of my tone at the mention of a second point that we have already discussed. I shift in my seat slightly to face Zeke Mathews, the sheriff's only deputy and his only son, which makes him the shining apple of his father's bloodshot eye. "If he was local, he likely would have been far more concerned about being recognized while shooting someone in broad daylight. Not to mention that I would have seen him myself by now if he was still around."

So far untouched by the population booms that other parts of the Arizona territory have seen thanks to the promise of copper and cattle, Preston is a tiny town, but rich all the same due to the constant stream of settlers passing through with a pressing need to resupply. So much so that, over the last decade, the town has become a regular stop on the trail even if all it has to offer is a general store, a stable, a saloon, and a boarding house as the largest share of its main street. And, of course, a sheriff's office as the largest share of my wasted time.

"I saw him flee northwest," I continue, pointing that direction for emphasis. As if it will actually help. "Someone needs to go after him."

"I'm afraid that will not be possible." As he speaks, Sheriff Mathews pulls a clean cloth from his vest to polish his badge, the symbol feeling far more like a taunt than a promise. "Even if there was something more to go on, we could not be the ones to pursue him for you. Our jurisdiction only extends so far, and we both have responsibilities to attend to here."

"Surely those responsibilities include justice for someone who was murdered in your town?" I say back. "Not fifteen yards from where we sit."

"A very regrettable occurrence. And a far too common one at that. All this bloodshed these days…" He sighs. "I pray on it nightly. That we might see a return to people's good sense in this world."

"Right," I say tightly. "And should God not decide to intervene… what then?"

Out of the corner of my eye, I see Zeke's mouth twitch, although his father does not seem remotely as amused. "Miss, I can appreciate that you are upset and trying to do right by your father, I really can," he says, his tone stern. "However, given the circumstances…"

"Why stay here when you could be heading back to Boston?" cuts in Zeke, quickly checking out the window again before granting me his focus. As he turns, his honey-colored hair shines in the sun, his white linen suit still as neat and clean as when he put it on this morning.

"Surely you must miss the city's distractions? Far more exciting than anything we have here. We will write to you if anything turns up." He smiles reassuringly, the same smile I've seen him use a thousand times while he strolls down the main street as if he's the prince of Preston. I suppose he is. "You have my word that we will continue to pursue this."

"Just not outside the county?"

Zeke lets out a long breath, and even if he's kept his kindness with me longer than his father, I suspect that it's soon to run out. "You have— Miss, you've admitted your father took on debts. *Substantial* debts. I'm sorry to say it, but he should have understood the risks."

"The *risks?*" I repeat, also not for the first time. "He was conned into buying a worthless piece of land in exchange for a sizeable down payment and an outrageous yearly sum. Those men knew full well he would never be able to produce enough to pay them back. And then when he couldn't, they—"

"Young lady." The sheriff holds up a hand to silence me. "What my son is getting at is that your father made a bargain, and regardless of if he made it with a devil, his inability to keep his side will not be as easily overlooked here as it may have been back east. Out here, men take issue with such things, and your father is not the only one to have learned that the hard way. Why, the sheer number of settlers we've had turn back in the last year *alone…*"

"For the best," Zeke finishes for him, hooking his thumbs in his belt as he shakes his head sadly. "Not everyone has what it takes to survive out here. A shame that some don't come to that conclusion before it's too late."

*Too late.* He's talking about my father's fate, but I know he would just as easily assign it to mine. Just as easily deem it *too late* for me, and I'm more furious than hurt that they're proving my mother right. *They really don't care.*

"So that's it, then?" I ask when I trust my voice again. "He deserved what was coming to him so the man who killed him deserves no punishment?" There's a long pause, neither man offering a rebuttal, so I offer one instead. "I wonder if the U.S. Marshals would feel the same way. Perhaps if I were to write to the Attorney General? Let him know how things are being handled *out here?*"

Zeke's mouth presses into a thin line, but it's his father who blusters out, "Miss, I was elected by the people of Preston. I do not answer to U.S. Marshals."

"They might disagree. After what happened in Tombstone," I press, repeating almost word for word what I had read in a discarded newspaper earlier this week and tucked away for such an occasion. "They're promising a return to order. To make things safer."

He laughs bitterly, the sound clawing at any optimism I might have felt in my latest attempt to inspire action. "To make things safer for their railroad, perhaps. For their own business interests to flourish without them ever having to step a toe into this territory. Miss, if you are under the impression that a marshal is going to come in here and tell me how to handle things in *my* town simply because you've written them a letter about your papa, you are sorely mistaken." He reaches for the tin of tobacco on his desk, angrily shoving a large wad into his cheek. "I can tell you from tremendous personal experience that, should you write to them for assistance, you will be months waiting on a reply. *If* they reply at all. Isn't that right, son? Have you ever received an answer to the letters we sent last year?"

Zeke shakes his head before looking out the window again, but I barely register his disinterest. Too busy fighting the desolation I feel at even the suggestion of more *months* spent waiting, and, judging by the look on the sheriff's face, he knows it.

"I have tried to be patient with you on this, but I need you to understand." He gestures behind me toward the crowded wall of wanted posters vying for attention near the door. Stagecoach robbers. Cattle rustlers. Serial murderers. Dozens of men with prices on their heads but none of them the one I want found.

"It's not that your father doesn't deserve justice, it's simply that it's in short supply. My son's right. You belong back with your kin. During times like this, family is so comforting."

A nearly hysterical laugh almost escapes me, and all I can think is that I'm certain he wouldn't say so if he'd had the opportunity to meet mine. "There has to be something else."

"I'm afraid not. At least, not without the money for a reward or for a bounty hunter—"

*Money… It always comes back to money.* The only real power, the only true separation between people. It's money, and whether or not you have it. And I never have.

"How much?" I say, even as the rational part of my brain wonders why I am even bothering to ask. "How much would it take?"

"To get someone to pick up your job?" The sheriff chews it over along with the tobacco, pausing to spit onto the floor and making my stomach turn before he answers, "At least a hundred dollars. Half when they accept. Half when it's done."

*A hundred dollars.* Might as well be a thousand, but I still find myself saying, "I'll get it."

"Even if you were to come up with the wages"—he courteously leaves off the *somehow*—"there's still no guarantee someone will want the job. This country is bigger and more perilous than you can possibly imagine. And your trail's gone cold."

I bite my tongue to keep myself from asking where he thinks the guilt for that might lie. "How long would it take you to find someone?"

"Depends. How long would it take you to pull together the money?"

"I have some savings," I reply, skirting the question, and I see the way the sheriff looks to his son. When I follow his gaze, Zeke sighs and looks at the ground.

"If that's the way you'd prefer to proceed…" he says.

"It is." I stand at last, trying to escape before the last of my false bravado can abandon me completely. "I do appreciate your assistance. I'll get the money together and—"

"Young lady." The sheriff gets up, too, before I can make it to the door. "I want you to think long and hard before you agree to this. These bounty hunters that Zeke works with are often as dangerous as the men they're tracking, and I'd hate to see you get involved in something that you'll come to regret. Don't make your father's same mistakes."

My chest tightens, the image of him lying in the street flashing through my mind. "I understand."

"You understand, too, then, that you'll likely be sending someone out to kill a man regardless of if you want him brought in alive? I know that's an ugly thing for a woman to have to consider, but I've been in this position long enough to know that if they bring him back at all, it'll be for the bounty and a burial. Not for a trial."

"I understand," I say again, giving him a tight smile. "Thank you, Sheriff. Honestly, it would come as a relief." He looks surprised, but his expression sours again when I say before stepping out the door, "I'm afraid that I've already experienced as much of this town's legal system as I can stand."

# CHAPTER 3
## CORA

I use my hand to shield my eyes from the sun before stepping out into the street, careful to dodge the number of pedestrians, horses, and wagons who are making their way just as I am. Once across, I climb up onto the weathered sidewalk planks and head east, considering again the possibility of scraping together a hundred dollars to afford a hired gun when I can't even scrape together enough to afford a proper meal.

Since the night I ran away, I have prided myself on the fact that I have never once asked for charity. Nor have I given anyone less than everything I have in whatever odd work they throw my way before shooing me off. In a town this small, it's not just the sheriff who tends to take care of his own, and it has been made clear to me again and again that I am not their *own*. I am a stranger, one who is beginning to look more ghost than girl.

A passing glance at my reflection in the general store front window reveals no color left in my cheeks. A dullness to my hair. Frayed patches on a worn-out brown dress that hangs on me just as well as an empty flour sack. Still, I walk into the store with what I hope is an appeasing smile fixed on my face, my head bent slightly and my hands clasped as soon as I'm in the door so as not to appear as impertinent as my mother always believed me to be. Not sure what difference it makes, though, when people don't even bother to look.

"Nothing for you," says the tidy man behind the counter, his eyes remaining on his ledger, though he does pause his scribbling long enough to ask, "Unless you have something to sell?"

I don't. Not since I sold him my father's pocket watch when I got to town, swearing that I'd buy it right back up until the day it disappeared from the display case and into its new owner's pocket. I had consoled myself over the loss with the certainty that I hadn't had another choice. Without steady work, the earnings from that sale have been the majority of what I've had to live on, since my remaining sense of self-preservation keeps me from selling either my father's knife or his gun. My hope that I will someday leave this place also keeps me from selling the brown and white mare he named Tess.

After I'd fled, I admittedly felt a sizable twinge of remorse for taking her and the money she would have brought my mother and sisters, but it had quickly dissipated the following morning when I watched from a nearby alley as they boarded the stagecoach that would take them back to Boston without missing a step. In truth, when my mother had woken to find me gone, she probably considered the trade-off between the price of the mare and the price of my ongoing company and believed she had gotten the better end of the deal.

"Young lady?" The shopkeeper is leaning against the counter now, his eyes finally peering over the top of his spectacles in annoyance. "You have something to sell?"

"No," I admit. "Not today."

"Looking to buy, then?"

"No," I repeat, refusing to let myself even glance at the shelf of food to my left. "Not today. But I *can* work."

He waves me off before going back to his books, and after a few more unsuccessful attempts to get him to reconsider, I leave to try the house next door. And the one next to it. And the one next to that one. On down the street until the boarding house near the stable is my last option.

I raise my hand to knock, already believing that this is likely not the place where my fate will turn, but I experience a moment of suspended possibility when the door opens almost as soon as my knuckles strike the wood.

"Hello, welcome to…" The older woman's words trail off, her expression dropping like a stone along with my hopes. "Oh, it's you."

"Hello, Mrs. Jensen," I say, brushing off the lackluster greeting. "I was wondering—"

"No," she says quickly, stepping out onto the porch in her best church clothes and looking up and down the street with her carefully set gray curls bobbing. Apparently not finding what she is seeking, she takes the time to step back inside before turning her disappointment back on me. "Off with you. I'm expecting guests."

She shuts the door in my face without another word, which results in me being already halfway back down the front steps and nowhere close to knowing what to do when it opens again.

"Wait," Mrs. Jensen calls after me, and I can tell by the look on her face that she is already regretting whatever she is about to say. "Can you cook?"

I turn, clasping my hands at my waist. "Yes, ma'am."

"You can clean? Make beds?"

"Yes, ma'am."

She looks my dress up and down. "Laundry?"

"Yes, ma'am."

She sighs, folding her arms and shifting from side to side. "I've got a party coming this evening, but my daughter just had my new grandson yesterday. She lives outside town, and I haven't had a chance to make it over to see them with everything needing to be done. If you are able to help take care of some things tomorrow, perhaps I could make it over for at least a couple hours."

"I can help," I say quickly. "Anything you need."

Her eyes are piercing as she looks me over again. "You have something else to wear?"

My hands press tighter together. "Yes, ma'am."

"All right then. Be at the back door first thing in the morning. Don't you be coming to the front again. And don't you be late."

She shuts the door, and I wait long enough to hear the lock slide into place before I fly down the rest of the stairs, running for the stable as fast as my feet can carry me.

# CHAPTER 4
## CORA

From what I've been able to put together through my limited interactions with him, the bedraggled, young man named Elliot who runs the stable on the outskirts of town does not do it for the love of it. He does it because it is what his father did, and his father's father, and now here he is to carry on the legacy whenever he can be bothered to put down the bottle. Which is rarely.

Generally preferring the company of the bar to the company of horses, I'm fortunate in that our paths usually only cross when board is due and I have no choice but to talk to him. A whiskey bottle tight in his left fist and his eyes practically floating in his skull as he seems to debate whether to make a grab for me or for the money in my outstretched hand. Which is why, on any other occasion that I hear him coming, I quickly find my way to one of the plentiful hiding spots amongst the debris that litters the grounds or the hay bales that fill the loft. The latter spot the one I had sequestered myself to on that first night and all the nights that have followed.

Perhaps when I said I hadn't asked anyone for charity I should have considered this an exception, but given that I *am* paying him for boarding Tess *and* taking care of the other boarded horses more often than he does, I am choosing not to feel shame for it. At least, not until the day when I can no longer afford to keep Tess here, which is fast approaching based on the few remaining dollars I manage to pull from the old tin I tucked up in the rafters.

My so-called *savings* are proof of how unlikely it is that I will be able to provide a bounty hunter's wage. Even if Mrs. Jensen is impressed enough with me tomorrow to keep me on for a time, it would take me *weeks* to put together even a quarter of the required amount. Then likely far longer for someone to track and apprehend the man who killed my father. Both irrelevant unless I can come up with a better place to stay.

As hot as the days can run in this part of the country, the nights are cold enough to make you wish the heat had stayed, especially during the oncoming fall and winter months when a body needs a fire as much as a warm meal.

Setting the tin aside, I pull my small sack from its spot next, steeling myself for the sight of my ruined gray dress inside. Even the idea of wearing it makes me feel ill, but I examine it closer anyway, folding up the hem until the now brown-black splotches are successfully hidden from sight. The adjusted length won't exactly be fashionable. It will actually come dangerously close to obscene, but I figure that a potential peek of stockings will be better than a certain view of bloodstains.

I sew fast, trying not to add more blood to the dress as I jab my fingers in the dwindling light of the day. After the last stitch, I hang it from a nail in the rafters in hopes that some of the wrinkles will also fall away overnight, and that it will remain free of the random bits of hay that always manage to cling to my clothes no matter how careful I am to stay on my bedroll.

Finished with my task, I give the dress a satisfied nod before stepping toward the hayloft hatch, falling back into my usual routine as I pull it up to go check on Tess in her stall now that she's in for the night. Instead, I immediately drop to the hayloft floor, too surprised to stop the *thump* of the hatch closing again or to even pray that I hadn't been seen by the figure below.

I hadn't heard him come in, a dead giveaway that this isn't Elliot swaying his way through the aisle while he belts whatever songs the girls had sung at the saloon. And if that hadn't already been enough to convince me, the blinding speed and steady aim with which this man pulled a gun certainly would have been.

*Oh, God. Oh, God.* I am frozen in place, too afraid to reach for the knife I have hidden under my skirt or to crawl for the gun still tucked away in my sack. *No. God, please not like this.*

"I know you're up there. Best show yourself," a deep voice barks out from beneath me, and I can't breathe as I listen to him step closer to the ladder leading up to the hatch. "I'll give you to the count of three."

He is directly below me now, but I still can't get myself to move. "One." The ladder creaks when he sets his weight on it. "Two."

*Move,* I will myself. *Move. Don't just let him kill you.* There is a long pause, as if he is waiting for me to act as much as I am. Or, maybe by some miracle, he has simply dismissed me as unimportant and gone on his way?

My answer comes with the sudden upward explosion of the hatch door, lantern light spilling in as I startle backward and find myself squinting down the barrel of a gun.

"I haven't done anything," I say, the first defense that comes to mind as my spine hits the bale of hay behind me. "*Please*, I haven't done anything."

The lantern lowers slowly, enough that I can make out the man who is holding it. Beneath a well-worn black hat, he stares at me from a pair of deep brown eyes set above a strong nose and jaw. A few days' worth of dark whiskers and a mustache marking an undeniably handsome face that is likely only a few years younger than my father's had been. Although he looks like he's lived an entirely different kind of life in that time.

The man cocks his head, appearing as caught off guard to find me up here as I was to find him down below, but after a few more seconds, he lowers his weapon. "Christ, you're— you're just a girl…" I hear him mutter. I sit up straighter at the offense while he takes a quick look around, still with little more than his upper body through the opening. A pretty tight fit given the breadth of him. When his search pauses on my dress hanging in the rafters, he looks back at me, and color rushes to my cheeks.

"You alone up here? Or you got a beau who is planning to be stupid?"

"A beau?" My blush deepens. "No, no one else is up here." I feel a pulse of fear at the realization that I just admitted to being alone, sharp enough that I do reach for my knife now, disentangling it from my dress and gripping the handle of the blade tightly as I hold it out in his direction.

"Little late for that, don't you think?" he says, enough of a gentleman to avoid looking too long at the place where I had undoubtedly revealed an actually obscene flash of my undergarments as I'd gone for my weapon. "Don't you have a gun?"

I glance toward the corner.

"Christ," he mutters again, before ducking back down the ladder. "Put that can opener away and come down here. I won't hurt ya."

*Can opener?* I stare at the knife in my hand, my body still stuck in place until he whistles up at me. "You comin'? Or do I need to haul you down?"

"I can manage," I mutter, scooting over with my heart pounding and crawling down the ladder against my better judgment. However, I don't get the impression that I have much say in the matter. "No need to be so pushy about it."

He lets out a half-laugh, the unexpected sound making me slip on the first rung almost as soon as I've stepped onto it. His hand snaps out to catch my waist to steady me, but he releases me the second I have my feet on the ground.

Now that we are both standing on the stable floor, I have a chance to fully appreciate the size of my would-be opponent. He towers over me so much that I have to tilt my chin up to meet his eyes as he stands with a strong pair of arms banded across an equally strong chest.

*Good God.* For some reason, my mouth has gone dry, and I look down to swallow in hopes that it will help me speak. But all it does is help me take in the rest of him. His dark clothes with a fair share of trail dust and dirt on them, his scarred-up brown leather chaps and scuffed-up boots that look like they have survived several years of hard use. The shiniest thing on him is the gun at his hip, which looks decades newer than my own now that I can see it properly. And now that it isn't being aimed at my face.

"I'm not gonna hurt ya," he repeats, his voice kinder this time. He holds his palms up as if to prove it before briefly lifting his hat to push back loose brown waves in need of a trim. "As long as you don't go messin' with what's mine."

"What's yours?" I question. "What precisely is it that you think I'm going to take?"

He pivots, pointing toward the only other horses stabled along with Tess, one a curious but regal black stallion and the other a buckskin mustang with a dark streak down its back like a snake lying in the sand. The antsy toss of its head suggests it would throw me just as soon as look at me. That one must be his.

"Why would you assume…" I start to say, turning my attention back to its owner and doing my best to draw myself up to my full height, because really, *why* is he so big? So overwhelming when each breath I take in carries the scent of simmering campfire and aged leather? "Fine. I won't go *messin'* with what's yours." I narrow my eyes as I meet his gaze and point my finger at him, my best imitation of a threat in an attempt to recover from my initial reaction. "But you have to do the same."

He glances up in the direction of the hayloft, and I correct him by pointing in Tess's direction. His eyes flick between me and her. "The brown and white paint there?"

He walks away from me without waiting for an answer, heading straight for her stall to look her over. Tess—sweet, trusting girl that she is—sticks her head out at once to greet him, nosing at his pockets until he produces an apple. I cough to cover the way my stomach pipes up in envy.

"She looks well." He gives her forehead a friendly scratch. "You take good care of her." He says it as a statement of fact, and a small part of me lights up with the praise, because I *have* been doing my best to take care of Tess. Isn't her fault she is stuck with me.

He gives her a final pat before turning to me again, his eyes lingering on my face for what feels like a heartbeat too long before he bends to pick up the rucksack at his feet. "Next time someone threatens you, don't hesitate," he directs, as he begins to rifle through its contents. "You either fight or flee right then, you hear me? Don't wait for someone to choose for you."

I nod, so distracted by the streaks of amber in his brown eyes that I don't even manage a protest when he places a tied-up cloth in my hand. He gives me one last long look before returning my nod. Then he's gone, disappearing out the front doors and into the night as quietly as he had appeared.

Later, when I have returned to the hayloft, I open the small parcel to find another apple along with several soft biscuits and strips of deer jerky, and I'm unable to keep myself from groaning at the taste when I bite into the fruit. Undeniably my first bit of charity, but that night as I fall asleep still thinking about his eyes instead of my empty stomach, the last thing it feels like is a sin.

# CHAPTER 5
## CORA

I arrive at the back stoop of the boarding house before Mrs. Jensen's rooster even has a chance to crow. My hair braided and my skin scrubbed as clean as I could manage without catching my death in the cold water of the nearby stream. My teeth are still chattering, the last bits of the biscuits and jerky rattling around in my stomach like my body no longer knows what to do with such a feast.

Still, I do my best to look the part when Mrs. Jensen opens the door, which is why her immediate scowl makes me touch the few small flowers I placed in my hair before inspecting my dress for my mistake. The hem did indeed turn out a little high, but the dress hangs so loosely on me that I had convinced myself no one would really notice.

"Change of plans," she tells me, seeming put out by having to communicate this to me. "Don't need you anymore."

She goes to shut the door, but I quickly jam my foot in the way, wincing at the pain that reverberates through my thin shoes. "Wait, I—"

"I told you, I don't need you," she says crossly, purposefully eyeing my intruding foot. "Turned out to only be one guest. I had assumed that he wouldn't be traveling alone when he requested the whole place, but I suppose if he wants to be a fool with his money I certainly won't complain." She shakes her head as if she still might like to. "I'll have no trouble handling him on my own."

"Yes, but neither would I," I offer hastily through the still-stalled door. "If it's only one guest, I could take care of everything for you. Then you could spend the whole day with your daughter and the new baby. Not just a few hours."

This makes her pause, but she quickly shrugs off the notion. "You don't know how things are done. I can't leave you on your own."

"I'm a quick learner. And I promise I won't mess anything up. If I do, you don't even have to pay me." As soon as I say it, I know it's a terrible thing to offer, but desperation tends to have that effect on people. And if she sees that I can be trusted… "I'm only asking for a chance."

She stares me down, waiting for me to whither under her gaze. When I don't, she begrudgingly eases the door back open, blessedly allowing the feeling to rush back into my foot. "All right, but *one* thing out of place, and you're out."

Once I make it inside, the early morning passes quickly, and though it has been a few months since I spent time in a real home, my mother taught me things in a way that is hard to forget. Even Mrs. Jensen seems begrudgingly impressed with how neatly the linens are pressed, with how the dishes shine, with how efficiently I fry up the salted pork and potatoes for breakfast. Soon enough, she goes from hovering over my shoulder to aimlessly drifting about the house, straightening knickknacks and dusting shelves.

More than once I offer for her to go ahead and leave for her daughter's house, but she refuses each time, determined to make her guest feel welcome when he finally emerges from his room. "Wouldn't be suitable," she keeps muttering, eyes switching between the parlor clock and the stairs. "Wealthy man like that will want to be greeted by the owner."

When we finally hear the first steps from upstairs, it is nearly mid-morning, and Mrs. Jensen hurriedly directs me back to the kitchen to warm up breakfast with a frantic wave of her hand before she goes to stand by the dining room table. Observing how she pinches her cheeks for color and smooths down her hair, I automatically do the same after tucking myself out of sight.

Back at the stove, I wonder for a brief moment if this man could be the same one I encountered last night. After all, he'd made a point to tell me to steer clear of his horse. Maybe he takes the same approach for his lodgings. If it *is* him, what would I say to him? What would *he* say? I should thank him for the food, but what if he tells Mrs. Jensen about me staying at the stable?

I am about to risk an anxious peek into the room when I hear her guest speak, his voice low and smooth and more…polished than the one I'd heard last night.

"I can assure you everything has been satisfactory. One of the nicest beds I've ever had the fortune to fall into, which is why you must forgive me for the late hour."

No, not the man from the night before, although perhaps equally as unexpected. The longer I eavesdrop on their small talk, the more I can't help but notice that there is something unusual about the way he speaks. *Polished* isn't the right word for it. His cadence is almost melodic, his accent unlike anything else I have heard this far west. Although I wouldn't necessarily place him with the gentlemen back east either.

"Well, if you're sure there is nothing more I can do for you," I finally hear Mrs. Jensen say as I am making up his plate, her voice now higher and friendlier than the one she used with me all morning. "I'll be heading out for a while to see my daughter and new grandson, but my girl is here. You let her know if there's anything you need."

I am so busy tamping down my excitement over the fact she referred to me as *her* girl I nearly miss his insistence that she is surely not old enough to have a grandson, along with the resulting *giggle* from Mrs. Jensen. I roll my eyes. *God*, he is laying it on thick, and I wonder why he bothers when I am certain his finances are already plenty charming on his behalf.

"I'll have your breakfast brought out straight away, sir." Mrs. Jensen's voice grows closer. "Enjoy your stay. I'll be back to check on you this evening."

Mrs. Jensen rounds the corner into the kitchen, her warm and cheerful façade immediately fading as she speaks to me without bothering to lower her voice. "Remember our bargain. *One* thing out of place."

"Yes, ma'am," I reassure her, carefully placing the breakfast plate on a clean tray along with a mug of coffee and a side of fresh bread. "I'll take care of everything. I do hope you enjoy your visit." She nods, but she also casts one last critical eye over the food before she leaves through the front door, and it makes me give everything a second look myself before I set off toward the dining room.

When I walk in, I expect to find her guest seated, but instead he's up and pacing, his left hand *tap, tap, tapping* against his leg. I clear my throat gently to get his attention, wondering if I have already misstepped by making him impatient. He turns abruptly at the sound, but the creases in his forehead ease as he takes me in with quick, clever eyes that hold no apparent ill intent. On the contrary, he grins, humming the beginning of a song to himself before murmuring, "She appears."

"I'm sorry to have kept you waiting." I smile back, hoping that it will help convince him to pass compliments of me on to Mrs. Jensen rather than any complaints on my tardiness. "I have your breakfast."

Since he is looking at me, I take the opportunity to do the same, able to determine at a glance that he is in his late thirties. Similar in age to the man I met last night, but that is where the similarities end.

Everything about this one seems *precise*, from his long tailored suit coat to his short coal-black hair to his neatly trimmed mustache and close shave. All of it makes me think again of the high society men back in Boston, although, as I step closer, the shifting daylight from the windows reveals several thin, pale scars on his face and neck. Rather than diminish his handsomeness, the evidence of an existence that has been lived outside the comfortable confines of dining rooms and parlors only makes him look more striking.

Maybe not so different from the other man after all, then…

I set the plate at the head of the table, but he makes no immediate move to try his food or even to sit. Instead, he keeps his crystalline blue eyes focused on me in a way that feels like he's expecting something.

"Will there be anything else?" I ask, starting to fidget. "I could see if Mrs. Jensen has a copy of the latest newspaper."

"That's all right." He rests his tall, lean frame against the back of his chair. "I would rather prefer some company for a while, if you wouldn't mind? I don't tend to do very well with solitary confinement."

The frankness of his confession surprises me, so much so that I don't catch myself before I ask, "If that's the case, why rent out the whole place so that you're alone?"

He grins again. "But I'm not alone."

"I'm only here to help should you need something."

"And as it happens, I am in need of a breakfast companion." He straightens, gesturing toward the kitchen. "Fetch yourself a plate. We will eat together."

I pale, thinking of Mrs. Jensen and what she would say about me eating her food. "I'm not sure if I should…"

"I would consider it a great personal favor," he tries again. "It's boring as well as unhealthy to eat alone."

"Is it?"

"Quite."

I stand in place for a few more moments, debating, until I decide that Mrs. Jensen would likely prefer her guest happy even if it means I sit myself for breakfast. Resolved, I disappear back into the kitchen for a plate and a slice of bread.

When I return, he is standing at the opposite head of the table with a dining chair pulled out, indicating with a nod that I am to sit. Still not wanting to upset him, I do so, my heart rate ticking up when he so easily pushes in the chair once I'm seated. I expect him to walk away then but instead he crouches, picking up one of the small white flowers that must have come loose from my hair. He holds it up to me in the center of his wide palm, holding my gaze at the same time, and I take it back with a quiet, "Thank you," as he straightens with an easy smile.

*He must think I'm someone else,* I think, setting the fallen flower next to my plate as he heads for his own place at the table. Perhaps he had misunderstood Mrs. Jensen when she said I was her girl. Believes I'm family instead of simply the help. I should correct him. I should. I open my mouth to speak, but as I stare down at the full plate of food before me, I find I can't quite get the words out that might take away a meal.

Instead, I make a quick sign of the cross, pretending that my moment of hesitation was nothing more than my usual recitation of The Lord's Prayer before eating. When I look back up, I expect to see him doing the same now that he's taken his chair, but his eyes are still on me.

"What is your name?"

"My name?" I nibble a bit at the bread while I politely but impatiently wait for him to start eating his own food. "It's Cora."

"How fitting for a Catholic." That grin again. "Is it a family name? A remembrance?"

"No. Or well, I don't think so," I tell him, trying to think if anyone had ever mentioned anything remarkable about my name before. "My parents were young when they had me, and their families…" I clear my throat before accidentally confessing a story that would certainly give me away if he really does think I'm someone that I'm not. "They must have simply heard it and picked it."

"Whispered to them by the stars, perhaps," he ventures.

I outright laugh at the idea before replying, "Maybe to my father. But not to my mother."

"She doesn't make a habit of talking to stars?"

"She does not."

"Do you?"

"Do I what?"

"Converse with the constellations?"

I consider him again, trying to determine if he is poking fun at me, but his expression holds only an earnest curiosity.

"I can't say that I do," I admit. "Why would I?"

"You pray," he points out, making it sound like a counterargument rather than a simple observation.

"Yes. To God."

"To *your* God?"

To *my* God? Has it ever felt like he's mine? My mother's surely. My father's at times. But mine? As if he can hear the direction of my thoughts, my breakfast companion continues, "You could always choose a new one."

"A new what?"

"A new God."

"Isn't there only the one?"

"Depends on who you ask."

"My mother would say that's blasphemy."

"Perhaps to her."

"But not to you?"

"Nor to you."

"Why not to me?"

He smiles again. He is rapidly becoming the most peculiar person I have ever had an opportunity to speak with, let alone share a meal with.

"A question for another time, I think," he replies instead of answering. He tilts his head at my hands that are still picking at my bread. "Eat, little bird."

I do. Then so does he.

# CHAPTER 6
## CORA

Sometime later when I come back out from cleaning up in the kitchen, our guest is no longer at the table, nor is the flower I left. However, it is impossible for me to wonder too long where either wandered off to with plenty of work to be done and a full belly to keep me moving.

For the most part.

After surviving on so little for so long, I feel incredibly lethargic as I change the severely rumpled bed sheets upstairs, wondering if he was honest about the quality of his sleeping arrangements based on the state of it. Surely the grand four-poster has to be better than sleeping on a bed that mainly consists of straw.

My knees nearly buckle as I linger too long near the side of the bed. Soft sheets and whispering scents of smoke and evergreen beckoning me closer like a lullaby before I manage to snap myself out of it. To avoid further temptation, I make myself busy the rest of the day with anything and everything in any other part of the house. Whatever I think might earn me Mrs. Jensen's good graces, and indeed, she does seem momentarily pleased when she comes back to find I already have a beef stew on for dinner.

"That'll do for the day," she says, herding me toward the back door. "I ran into the gentleman in the street on my way back, and he asked if I could bring his supper down to the saloon this evening. He has business there and won't be back until late, so you can go on home."

"I could take it to him for you," I offer, in no hurry to return to the hayloft but also more than a little interested to see him again.

"Absolutely not," she says, sounding cross now. "Girl like you will only find your way to ruin there. Go on with you. Besides, I have my own business to attend to." I know better than to ask what that might be, even if curiosity burns at me, but it's quickly forgotten when she says, "I'll see you back here tomorrow before breakfast."

"Really?" I beam. "You mean it?"

"Yes, I'm still needed at my daughter's. And the gentleman seems to think you did a fine job, so I suppose…" She gives me a sigh, but she also gives me my day's wages, and I am so overjoyed to have *any* kind of income that I don't even think to examine it until I am hidden away again in the hayloft.

She gave me a whole dollar. And yes, maybe it will take me weeks to scrape together enough for a bounty at this rate, but maybe everything will also turn out all right. Maybe Mrs. Jensen will come to find me so indispensable that she'll hire me on full time, pay part of my wages in room and board. Maybe she will help me find other work, too, so that I can leave here sooner. Find *someplace.*

There is a call from down below, and I go still, listening until I hear it again. As quietly as possible, I creep over to the hatch, lifting it just enough to allow me to peer into the stable.

A rugged face, half hidden beneath a beat-up hat, looks back up at me. "Thought I heard you up there. You move around like a flustered animal."

"I do not," I argue, glaring at him. "Besides, I was getting food for the horses."

"Mm-hmm," he mutters, and I am fairly certain he grumbles something else that sounds a lot like *a rotten liar, too,* before he switches to a different topic entirely. "You actually have a gun up there?"

"Yes."

"Then why didn't you use it?"

"When?"

"Just now."

"I guess I figured it was you."

He cocks an eyebrow at me. "And who do you figure I am?"

I'm not sure honestly, beyond that he's told me he isn't going to hurt me, and I still believe him. Even more so now since he's had the advantage twice and not chosen to take it.

"Grab your gun and come out back," he says in a tone that invites no argument before he disappears in the mentioned direction. Once again, and likely still against my better judgment, I climb down the ladder to follow him, but this time I do bring the sack with the gun.

Out behind the stable, he is already busy gathering a few of Elliot's whiskey bottles that have been abandoned on the ground, silent as he walks some paces away and places them in a line. When they are arranged to his liking, he strolls back to stand beside me, reminding me of the considerable difference in our stature. He tilts his head at the bag in my hand.

"What is that?"

"The gun."

"Why's it in a bag?"

I shrug. "That's where I keep it."

When he only stares at me, I shift on my feet, steeling myself to reach into the bag, which I finally do with an unsteady hand. I let the sack fall to the side once I have a grip on the cool handle, and he gives me a curt nod. "Shoot."

"What?" I blink at him, trying to make sense not only of this situation but also the day I've had up until this point. Three months exactly the same, and then—

"Shoot," he repeats. "Those targets."

I look at him and then at the gun in my hands, trying not to picture the last time I'd seen it before I'd stolen it. "I don't…I don't want to waste any bullets."

"I'll replace your bullets. Shoot."

I hesitate, close to breaking out into a cold sweat the longer I hold the weapon. I'd never actually watched my father use it. Not to hunt. Not to defend himself. He hadn't even had a chance to draw it that day.

"*Shoot,*" commands the voice to my left, startling me into raising the weapon with a trembling right hand.

"Christ." He snatches it away from me before I can even move my finger to the trigger. "Just as I thought."

My temper flares, and I make to grab it back, but he easily holds me off. "That's mine!"

"You don't hold it like it is." He bends his head as he examines the weapon. "Damn thing's not even loaded. And it's so dirty that it would have every right to backfire on you even if it was."

Without another word, he walks back down the barn aisle, and I'm left to storm after him until he sits on the old bench next to the stalls. As I watch, he takes the gun apart to clean it over his knee, and since I can't say I'd ever seen anyone undertake this task either, I decide to temporarily put my anger aside in favor of studiously overseeing each step he does

"I'm sorry," I say after a time, not really sure why I am apologizing but positive that I'd rather not have him cross with me.

He looks up, his expression relenting a bit as he sighs. "It's all right. You…you need to take care of this gun almost as well as you take care of that horse, you hear me? This weapon will help keep you alive."

He finishes what he's doing and sets about putting the gun back together before loading it with rounds from his belt, careful now to hold the chamber out so I can see.

"You keep this on you at *all* times. Not in some sack. *On* your body. At your waist where you can reach it quickly. And, when you have time, you practice with them bottles out there." He hands it back to me. "Now, let me see you hold it."

I start to lift it, but his hand snaps out quick as a rattlesnake to aim the barrel back toward the dirt.

"First lesson: don't point it at someone unless you intend to kill them. Yourself included, understand?"

"Sorry," I mumble again, raising it this time to point toward the open doors at the back. "Better?"

He nods, but then his head turns in the opposite direction toward the front entrance, and he stands, pulling a silver watch from his pocket to check the time. Like his weapon, this item also appears fancier than I would have expected of him, but then again, my father's had been, too. An heirloom handed down from his father when he was a boy. Now, it would get passed down in someone else's family.

My gun falls slowly back to my side as my eyes start to water, and I look at the floor, almost glad to hear him say he has to go so that he won't see. Almost. Brusque as he tends to be, I like having him here. I like *someone* being here.

He's moving fast now, swinging his pack over his shoulder and collecting that hot-headed mustang already saddled and ready in his stall. The black stallion, I notice, is gone already, which means Tess will be on her own tonight as much as I am. Judging by the way she's currently hanging her head over the door, she doesn't seem enthused by the idea either. I give her a consolatory pat as I join her in watching them leave.

"Do me a favor and keep to yourself for the next few days, okay?" my unlikely instructor requests before he goes, provoking my interest as he swings himself up into the saddle. "Don't go into town unless you need to."

"Why? Is something going to happen?"

"Not necessarily," he answers, dodging my question while calmly reining in his increasingly impatient horse. "But it's not safe for you to be wandering around here on your own until you know how to defend yourself properly."

"I know how to—" He looks me in the eyes as his brow lifts, and I look back with my hands on my hips for a few seconds before conceding.

"Fine. But what if I have somewhere to be?"

"Have it wait."

"I have a job." I think about the gentleman at the boarding house, about his business in town, and I suddenly feel concerned on his behalf despite being quite positive after only one conversation that he can handle himself. "Are you heading to the saloon?"

Dark eyes narrow in my direction. "Why do you ask?"

"I met someone earlier." I think about the black stallion again and decide he suits that man as much as the mustang in front of me does his own rider. "Maybe you've seen him in town?"

"I see a lot of people."

"This one would stand out," I say, still not completely sure why I'm asking except that there is something in the back of my mind insisting on it. "Dressed nice. Talks like he's high society, but there's something… *unusual* about him. You know how I mean?"

Rather than answer, he looks away and adjusts his reins, but it doesn't completely hide the way the corner of his mouth turns up. "You ask a lot of questions."

"You answer very few."

His head tilts as he considers me, then he points at the gun still clutched at my side. "Someone comes calling, you greet them with that pistol, clear?" I nod, and he returns the gesture before urging his horse forward. "Stay out of sight, Cora."

I don't turn away until he's gone, wandering back toward Tess's stall. That's when I see the parcel left behind on the bench, same as the one he'd given me the night before. I reach for it, opening it to find a similar offering. An apple, a few pieces of jerky, a few biscuits. My stomach grumbles appreciatively, and later as I stare up at the roof in my makeshift bed, I think about how much I would like to know his name. Along with how, exactly, he already knows mine.

# CHAPTER 7
## CORA

The next morning, I arrive at the boarding house so early that I sit for nearly an hour on the back steps before Mrs. Jensen lets me in, her dour face appearing at the glass as if I were the one keeping her waiting.

This time, she appears to have no reservations about leaving me on my own, staying only long enough to gather up some breakfast to take with her to her daughter's house. As well as to warn me once again that anything out of place will result in my immediate dismissal.

I don't mind her much. I am already too busy listening for the sounds of stirring upstairs, which come to pass around ten o'clock, with the exception of one loud thump from above about two hours earlier.

As soon as I finally hear him enter the dining room, I push my way through the kitchen door with his tray. My eyes searching until I find him, once again up and pacing, although this time he turns to give me his full attention without the need for any sort of prompting on my part.

"Cora." He greets me with that same grin, that same spark in his eyes as he stands in yet another all black suit. "Good morning."

"Good morning," I offer back, setting his tray once more at the head of the table. "Did you sleep well?"

"No, not especially."

I pause, his latest candid statement already throwing me, and my fingers knit together nervously. "Was your bed not made how you like it? Was the room too warm? Too cold? I could bring up some more blankets."

He shakes his head with a frown, coming closer so that we are standing only a few feet apart. "Nothing for you to mend, little bird. I'm afraid it's another personal failing of mine that I am often ill at ease in an environment that is not my own."

"I see." I open my mouth to ask where his *environment* is, but he draws me up short again when he shifts the tray in front of a side chair and gestures for me to sit.

"Oh, no, that's *your* breakfast," I tell him quickly, thinking again that he must believe I'm someone important.

"You take this one, and I'll get my own," he responds, inclining his head again in the direction of the vacant chair. "You can sit with me for a while?"

"But I'm not—I mean, I would really like to, but—"

"In that case…" He reaches out and gently grasps my hand, giving it a soft tug to get me moving until I am sitting as he asked. My skin tingles where he held my fingers, where I felt his breath fan against the back of my neck when he once again eased the chair up to the table.

"There," he says, satisfied. "Be back in a moment."

He walks around the table toward the kitchen with a level of comfort that seems to imply there is nothing at all shocking in what he is doing, which is probably why it takes several stunned moments for me to think enough to get up and follow him. By the time I do, he is already heading back. He sets his full plate in the spot across the dining table from mine, much closer now than when we had been at opposite ends yesterday.

"Looks wonderful," he says, watching me and waiting again for me to take a bite before he does the same. Thinking he must also be hungry this late in the day, I skip saying grace and go straight for the bacon, wondering if perhaps I could save half the plate and take it with me as Mrs. Jensen had done. Something about that feels like stealing, though, even if I can't be sure where the line of distinction is while I am currently eating at her table. It is being eaten either way, but here at least I can tell myself it is in service of her guest's overall wellbeing versus my own selfish desire not to starve.

My twisting thoughts must show on my face, because when I glance at my table companion between bites, he asks, "Everything all right?"

"Yes," I say, quickly putting a smile back in place before recollecting the line of questioning I had intended to ask when I first walked in here. "So, how have you found Preston?"

"Full of surprises," he says, still studying me. "Has that been your experience as well?"

"Not until recently." He grins, prompting me to continue. "I spoke with Mrs. Jensen yesterday, and she said you had business last night at the saloon?"

"That I did."

"And how did that go?" This really seemed less awkward last night when I had practiced in the hayloft. A lot more like casual conversation than an ill-conceived and intrusive interrogation. "Any, um, trouble?"

The corners of his eyes crease in consideration as he swallows his food. "I suppose it would depend on whom you asked."

"What if I asked you?"

"I thought it was great fun," he says with a smile and a note of mischief in his voice. "Hopefully my adversaries felt the same."

"Your *adversaries*?" I smile, too, his good humor infectious. "Can I ask what line of business you are in that you have *adversaries*?"

"These days? I gamble," he says with a small shrug. "Cards mainly."

"You play cards for your living?" Of all the answers I could have guessed, that one hadn't been on my list, and not only because my mother taught me to think of gambling as a sinful affliction rather than an occupation. But given his fine clothes and his ability to rent out an entire boarding house, I suppose, "You must be good."

"Very good," he replies with not an ounce of false humility, but then he turns more thoughtful. "Does it bother you? That I make money that way?"

"No," I reply, but then realize that I'm frowning again, although perhaps not for the reason I should be. Is it strange to be almost disappointed? That it's not something more…outlandish? More dangerous? "Why should it bother me?"

"Some people might consider it to be a dishonest line of work. Might believe that the type of person who does it is dishonest, too."

"Are you?"

"On the rare occasion." He clasps his hands over his chest and leans back in his chair, making himself at home in this conversation in a way that is admittedly mystifying. "It's not my preference, and fortunately, it's not often a necessity."

"Why's that?"

"People see what they want to see. Craft tall tales more convincingly than I ever could. Most often, all that is required of me is to reinforce that the lies they've told themselves are the truth. Not very difficult, especially in places like this. Hardly anything to do in a small town but lie. Fabrications are one of the few forms of entertainment."

I laugh, trying to think about what the people of Preston would have to lie about. "I suppose everyone has their secrets."

"Indeed they do." As if he knows I need the nudge to continue, he asks, "Would you like me to tell you one of mine?"

I nod, and he patiently waits for me to request the one I want rather than one of his choosing. "I met a man at the stable two nights ago. Saw him again last night…" I think of how to phrase my question for a moment before finally landing on, "Is he one of your adversaries?"

"Sometimes," he responds, seeming to know precisely who I mean. "Depends on the day."

"He knows my name."

"He does."

"Because you gave it to him."

"What makes you so sure?"

"It's simple." I shrug. "You're the only one in this town who's asked for it." His blue eyes never leave mine as I add softly, "See? Pretty simple."

He searches my face, and I wonder if he's trying to figure out how he could have mistaken me for someone important now that he knows I'm no one.

"I did give him your name," he admits, frowning and sounding tired. "I thought it might make things easier."

"Easier for him?"

"Easier for me. Harder for him."

"I don't understand."

"Today we are adversaries." His head falls back, eyes closing. "What else did he tell you? Apart from your name."

I let out a sigh, feeling that I have even more questions now than I did when I first walked into the dining room. "He told me to stay out of sight. And he told me to keep my gun on me."

"Neither of which you have done," he points out, the corner of his mouth ticking up before he makes a *tsk tsk* noise. "Shall we consider this the first of our secrets, little bird?"

"The first?"

He hums in confirmation, and maybe it's the thought that it could be both the first and the last secret I share with him that compels me to finally offer up a different one. "I'm not who you think. I'm… I ran away from home."

"So did I, little bird," he responds, cracking an eye open to look at me again. "And you are precisely who I think."

I sit with him a while longer, watching as his breathing slowly evens out. Rather than wake him, I tuck away my remaining questions the same way I tuck a spare blanket around him, resolving to ask more later today if the opportunity arises. Perhaps ask my other new acquaintance if it doesn't.

Standing this close to him and with the window lighting his features, I can see the scars on his face clearly now, my chest aching a little bit more at the sight of each. The one high on his left cheek, the one low on the right side of his chin, along his brow, beneath his jaw, the curve between his neck and shoulder. The few open buttons of his shirt give a glimpse of where that last one begins though not where it ends, and I find myself nearly reaching out to touch it before I jerk my hand back.

Why am I letting myself get so wrapped up in this? Why does it matter who he thinks I am? Who he is? Who either of them are? What does it matter if they know one another? By morning, they could both be gone, and I would still be here.

With renewed focus, I tidy up and take the dishes to the kitchen sink, scrubbing until every single pan is spotless. Every counter wiped down and every daydream I've started allowing myself about either of them firmly shut away.

Better to pull myself out of it now. Better to never know their names. Better to not ask any more questions. The answers won't change my outcome. The answers won't change that they'll leave.

I don't let myself walk back out into the dining room until much later, sure by that point that he'll be gone, and I tell myself it's a good thing when he is, even if my heart sinks and then immediately skips at the sound of a knock on the front door. I rush to open it, pinching my cheeks for color and already smiling before I see who is standing on the porch. Then I have to forcibly work to keep the expression in place.

"Deputy Mathews," I say, pausing in the middle of the doorway in front of the last person I would've expected to find waiting with his hat in his hands. "Sorry, I thought you might have been…never mind. I'm afraid Mrs. Jensen isn't home. You'll have to come back later. Unless you'd like me to give her a message?"

"That's no trouble." Zeke gives me a small smile that doesn't quite reach his eyes. "I'm actually here to see you."

"Really?" I ask, hoping he's not about to tell me that he's already found someone to take my bounty when I haven't even come close to matching the wages. All the more reason to remember my priorities. "How did you know I'd be here?"

"Overheard your employer giving her son-in-law an earful last night down at the saloon. Something about how she had to hire help since he wasn't taking care of things at home." Zeke laughs. "Practically dragged poor Jake out by his ear, but I have no doubt he'll still find his way back tonight." He pauses to wave cheerily at a passerby who calls out to him. "Had a chance to meet your guest last night, too. You had much chance to speak with him?"

"No," I say, not entirely sure why this seems like one of those occasions to lie that the guest in question had mentioned. "He keeps to himself."

"Does he? Seems an amiable sort, though perhaps not the brightest." I almost snort out a laugh, only to realize he's serious as he continues, "Dreadful card player, but then I suppose you can be when you come from his kind of money."

All I can think is that we have clearly met two very different versions of the same man, and I want so badly to believe that mine is the true one. That *mine* is…

Zeke clears his throat, and I can't help feeling as if I've been caught doing something I'm not supposed to before I step out onto the porch and close the door. "You, um… you said you had something to speak to me about?"

"I do," he says, looking serious now. "I've been thinking. And perhaps, I can see how things might be getting misinterpreted from your perspective."

"Misinterpreted from my perspective?" I repeat, smoothing out the wrinkles in my dress to compose myself. "Well, from my *perspective*, it seems that neither you or the sheriff believe that finding my father's killer is a priority. Does it look different from where you're standing?"

"Not in the way I'd hoped." He shakes his head. "I wish you would make an effort to see that I am trying to help you. I have been since the beginning."

The first day I met Zeke had been the same day I lost my father. As soon as the town doctor declared what I'd already known, I'd gone straight to the sheriff's office, drying blood already set into the fabric of this same dress while I gave them every detail I could think of. Every memory they could use.

Zeke had seemed equally as mystified by my presence then as he does today. As if he still can't believe I really intend to cause him so much inconvenience.

"I understand that you don't think you should give up on this, but you need to go home," he tells me again, taking out a small piece of paper from his pocket and offering it to me. "It's what's best for everyone."

On reflex, I take it, holding it up so that my eyes can quickly scan the print.

"It's a good stagecoach company. I know them well," he says reassuringly. "They'll get you back to Boston in no time. Under a month if they're really moving."

He winks at me and I stare at him in return, then at the ticket. "I don't want— Thank you, but no."

He lets out an aggrieved sigh. "Come now, I know you don't really have the money for a bounty hunter." He glances quickly over his shoulder, either to remind me or himself that there are people out on the street. "I know you know it, too."

"I'm not sure what you mean," I assure him, meeting the challenge in his tone even as my anxiety spikes. "I said I would get the money together, and I will. I have a job here and—"

"And you're sleeping in a stable."

"That's—" I start to say, reeling back and doing a poor job of concealing that he's surprised me. "What makes you—"

"You've been here months." Zeke gives me a look laced with pity. "You're not staying with anyone from town, so there's only so many other places you could be. People talk. They…" He sighs again. "I'm sorry about your father, I really am, but this has gone on long enough. I can't— Do you really think he would want you living like this?"

"I couldn't say, Deputy," I reply, shortly. "I'll be sure to ask him next time I visit his grave."

Zeke is the one to look surprised now. "You're still visiting the farm?"

Not feeling inclined to divulge more about my life than he already seems to know, I ignore his question as I hold out the ticket. "Thank you, Mr. Mathews. I appreciate your offer, but I have no intention of returning to Boston. Beyond you finding me a bounty hunter, I do not require your assistance. Or your charity."

He shakes his head again, but he doesn't take the ticket, only turns toward the stairs. "There's a coach that leaves tomorrow. You should be on it."

"I won't be."

He glances back, and gives me another long look before replacing his hat on his head. "I sincerely hope you change your mind. Before it's too late."

# CHAPTER 8
## CORA

My guest never reappears that day. Neither does Mrs. Jensen.

Hoping that at least one of them would, I had waited until well past nightfall before giving everything one last tidy and leaving, walking back to the stable as the dark took hold of the world around me.

Tonight, I don't mind. Feels easier to hide that way.

Ever since my earlier conversation with Zeke, I can't seem to settle myself, unable to sit still with the knowledge that the only one I have been deceiving in this town is myself.

It's not as if it should really be that astonishing. I already knew they believed me to be penniless and alone in this world, but I'd also taken comfort in the idea that they hadn't known the depths of it. That to an outside observer, I may not have been making it well, but I *was* making it. Now, it's hard not to realize they have known the truth all along. That they hadn't bothered asking my name simply because it's not a requirement for an unmarked grave.

When I arrive back at the stable, the black stallion and buckskin mustang are nowhere to be found, and my mood sinks further as I bring in Tess and move through my chores…right alongside my increasing unease. It only keeps building once I'm back up in the hayloft, and I hadn't fully realized how much I'd come to think of it as a small refuge until the curtain had been pulled back. Now, I find myself pacing over the hay-littered floorboards until midnight. Unable to stop moving, let alone to close my eyes to try and sleep.

I still have the ticket. I'd tucked it out of sight into the waistband of my dress when Zeke had refused to take it back, resisting the urge to cast it away when there was a chance I could exchange it for money, but now I can't help almost reaching for it over and over. *Before it's too late.*

Too late. It's the second time he's warned me. And what if it already is? Too late to go back to Boston even if I wished to. Too late to ever catch the man who killed my father. Too late for me to find a different life even if one was waiting for me.

For the first time since that day up on the hill, I can't stop the tears when they start to fall, my heart racing with the urge to run again. My throat aching with the urge to scream. Rather than give in to either, I grab my gun from its hiding place, and for once, holding it makes me feel a little less afraid. The weight of it in my hand very close to reassuring as I drop through the hatch and walk straight out the open back doors of the stable.

This late at night, the lanterns out here provide only enough light for me to see a few yards out into the endless desert, but I remember well enough where the bottle targets had been placed the day before. I walk up and down in a straight line, raising my weapon over and over, holding it out in front of me until my hand stops shaking so much.

Truthfully, I had only planned to use it as a means to distract myself, to get more familiar with handling it, or to even try to convince myself again that I am okay. That I can make it. That I'll *survive*.

What I hadn't planned to do was fire it.

"How about this?" a voice drawls from the darkness. "She came down all on her own."

As it was when Zeke appeared at the boarding house earlier, there's a fleeting moment where I hope it's someone else that's come for me, and I'm already looking for his quick sure steps and large frame before I see Elliot lurch into view.

"She's pretty, isn't she?" His speech is slightly slurred as he moves, a half-empty bottle in his hand. "She's quick though. Always ducking me."

A laugh breaks out from behind him, another figure emerging even as the shadows keep his features cloaked. "Everyone is quick when it comes to you, fuckin' dolt. But she is pretty enough, I'll grant you that."

I still haven't taken a step in retreat, my body seemingly locked in place, and all I can manage to get out is, "Don't—don't come closer." Even to my own ears, it doesn't sound nearly enough like a threat.

The second man laughs again. "Aw, you're not going to be like that, are you?" he calls as he draws nearer. "Wouldn't be smart after the night I've had. Would it, Elliot?"

"No." Elliot stumbles a bit. "Wouldn't. But 'member, Zeke said not to hurt her."

*Zeke.* My blood runs cold as my conversation with the deputy takes on an entirely new tilt. As I realize he might not have only been trying to save me from myself. Surely, if he'd known…

*People talk… I am trying to help you…* Had he known they were going to come here? Warned both me and them as a result?

"Won't need to hurt her as long as she does what she's told," says the second man. "You will, won't you?"

*Do something,* I keep thinking. *Do something.*

But I can't. I'm so afraid that I feel like I'm going to be sick, tunnel vision closing my world to nothing but the two figures before me. They can't be more than a few paces away now, and I can hear every step they take toward me as they try to box me in, can see the way they're thinking to reach for the gun still in my hand.

*You have to do something,* I think again, just before another calm, strong voice breaks through in my mind. The same one I'd wanted to hear before. *You fight or flee. Don't wait for someone to choose for you.*

I take one step back and then another before I turn and sprint inside the stable, heading for Tess's stall. Only, when I reach the center aisle, I quickly understand that even if I get to her, I won't make it much farther.

"Told you she was quick," I hear Elliot say to his companion as he comes up behind me where I've stopped dead. "That you, Jake? Thought you were going after the dandy."

"He'll keep until morning. Had someplace better to be."

There are two more men standing silhouetted in the dimly lit front entrance that was to serve as my escape route, one of them apparently Mrs. Jensen's son-in-law, who did indeed find his way back as Zeke said he would. The other one, much like Elliot's companion, I only vaguely recognize from town.

"He just doesn't want to break his neck riding in the dark." The man next to Jake chuckles at his own jab, and then receives a prompt shove.

"I said he'll keep," Jake snaps. "Will probably get lost in the desert anyway."

"Like how he was *probably* bluffing on that last hand? Should've seen the look on your face when he drew that ace."

"If you don't shut your fucking mouth," Jake warns, abruptly pulling his gun on his companion. "I swear to God, I'll shut it for you."

The other man puts up his hands, his laugh turning nervous. "Come on, Jake, I didn't mean anything by it. Was only having some fun."

"No, you're not, you fucking ass." Jake rolls his eyes, but reholsters his pistol as his focus turns back in my direction. "But we're about to."

I raise my gun, holding it out in front of me with my arm locked up from shoulder to barrel, and point it right at Jake. "I *will* shoot you."

"I'm not so sure you will," Jake goads, not bothering to step out of the direct path of my gun as the others move into a circle around me. "Besides, wouldn't do you much good if you did. You're outnumbered."

"I'm giving you a chance," I insist. "Leave and I'll let you live."

Jake chuckles. They all do.

"She's something," Elliot's friend says. "A bit mouthy for my taste."

"She is," Elliot agrees. "Bosses me about the horses."

"Sounds like Jake's mother-in-law," prods the one next to Jake, apparently feeling safe enough to do so again. "How mad do you think she's going to be when she finds out you roughed up her help?"

"Old hag needs to learn her place," Jake complains. "Keeps nagging at me that I ought to be home with her useless daughter. And what for? Been days since she had my son and all she's done is lie in bed."

"They get mighty lazy once you marry 'em," agrees his friend. "That's why a man has to find entertainment elsewhere." He looks me up and down. "Elliot has the right idea. Keeping something to play with right at work. Appreciate you cutting us in."

"I wasn't supposed to say," Elliot mumbles, looking worried. "Ain't supposed to touch her. Zeke said—"

"I don't give a damn what Zeke said," Jake cuts in. "I'm owed something after tonight, but she's going to be real nice and make it up to me. Aren't you, darlin'?"

They're laughing again as they successfully herd me into the corner of the barn, sidestepping into every one of my attempts to run. From too far away, Tess whinnies, sounding distressed in her stall.

"I'll shoot you," I say again, holding the gun tighter. "Get back."

They step closer.

My finger hovers over the trigger.

One of them makes a grab for me.

My eyes squeeze shut right as I squeeze the trigger, the booming sound and the recoil unexpectedly kicking me back into the wall. There's no time to try again or to even check if I hit my target before someone takes a fistful of my hair right at the crown of my head, pulling me toward the ground.

"Little bitch, didn't really think you had it in you," Jake says, unfortunately still breathing, though there's a red patch blooming on his upper arm now. He grabs my gun with his other hand and tosses it away. "You really had better start being nice now."

I kick out at him, but strike Elliot instead. He yowls in pain, gripping his shin before he retaliates against my ribs. I wince, the wind knocked out of me, but I still try going for my knife. That's when I'm thrown back, my head striking the nearby wall with a loud smack, and a sharp ache makes my vision blur.

"Someone grab her knife."

"We need to be quick. Zeke will—"

"I fucking told you—"

I keep struggling. They keep talking. Maybe Jake. Maybe Elliot. Maybe all of them. It doesn't matter. In my mind, they all have the same face. The same vacant soulless eyes. In my mind there's more than just the four that I'm fighting, and when the pain and the exhaustion start joining their side, I actually start to pray. So sure I'm about to meet death that I at least want him to know my name.

"Think she's giving up?"

"Probably realized she can't fight us all."

"*Gentlemen.*" I think I hear him. Voice like honey dripping on a knife's edge. "If it's an unfair fight you're after, I'm happy to provide."

Jake keeps his hold on me as he pivots toward the voice, and I feel a sense of hope at the realization he hears it, too. That it's not just in my head this time.

"The hell are you doing here?" Jake asks, the others taking a step back and clearing my view of the new arrival at the same time. "You're as stupid as she is if you thought it was a good idea to come back, Cypress."

*Cypress.* Somehow, the fact the name suits him so well makes me smile, as does the way he strolls into the line of fire with an unaffected air that contradicts the intense way his blue eyes are searching my face. He looks ominous, terrifying even.

But I am no longer afraid.

"I assure you that I am as eager to leave as you are to see me depart,"

Cypress says, looking back at Jake. "However, I cannot do so while I still have a debt to settle here."

"You're gonna give it back then?" my captor asks, sounding hopeful. "What you stole?"

"*Stole?*" Cypress clicks his tongue, coming to a stop only a few feet away with his hands set casually near the twin pistols at his waist. "Can you call it theft when you practically placed your money in my pocket? And, no, that is not the matter I am here to reconcile."

He settles his gaze on me again, and Elliot swears. The other men make similar sounds of disagreement.

"You must be joking," Jake says, disbelief and anger evident. "I'll fuckin' kill her before you take anything else from me." His free hand twitches in the direction of his gun, and the reactionary flurry of movement is so fast that it looks almost inhuman. One moment, Cypress is nonchalant. The next, he has a pistol in each hand, ready and aimed.

"She does not belong to you," he says, pointing a barrel at each man in turn. "Release her." When no one moves, Cypress sighs. "You know, I swore not to take a soul today, but as I have a somewhat obstinate nature and you seem determined to destruction, I suppose I'll simply have to ask for forgiveness instead." His head tilts, the corner of his mouth lifting and those blue eyes glinting as he draws the hammer back to cock each gun. "Perhaps you should do the same."

Seconds crawl by with no motion and no sound louder than my pounding heart. But finally, some sort of unspoken understanding must be reached, because Jake releases me. I fall forward, catching myself with my hands in the dirt right as a pair of shined black boots comes into view.

"Come on, little bird," Cypress says, extending his right hand to me. "Let's get you out of this cage."

I reach for him without ever questioning if I should, letting him secure me to his side with one arm while he keeps his gun raised with the other. My steps wobbly as we back away, he carries me more than guides me toward the rear doors, the scent of pine and mint flooding my senses as I cling to the possibility of sanctuary that he's offering.

"Tess," I mumble, hearing her cry out still, but he keeps moving. Under his breath, though, he assures me in soft murmurs, "It's all right now. We'll get her. We'll take care of it."

"We?" I realize that I'm shaking, violently trembling as he pulls me so close I almost don't see the shadowed figure that greets us as soon as we pass through the doors.

"Four of them," Cypress says quietly. "They'll be running, Aiden."

There's a gruff reply, the soft scent of smoke and leather, and then a calloused hand brushes the side of my face before I see brown eyes seeking mine. His brown eyes. *Aiden.*

"I tried," I tell him. "I did what you said."

"What I said?"

"Fight…or flee." If I could only shut my eyes for a minute, I think I could get the words out better. I could tell him so he won't be disappointed. "I tried."

His jaw tightens, his eyes flicking toward the barn. "I know you did, sweetheart." He starts to walk away before biting out a quick, "Don't let her see."

I try to turn my head to follow him, but the resulting throb at the back of my skull makes me sway before I suddenly feel weightless.

Caught in the sensation of falling until I find my head resting against Cypress's shoulder, my gaze landing on that same scar I'd wanted to trace this morning.

My eyes close before the gunshots ring out. And all I see is black.

# CHAPTER 9
## AIDEN

They actually beg. As if me taking them from this earth isn't the true mercy. As if I would offer them any when they had offered her none.

Four shots, and they're silent. Four bullets, plus a few extra, removed from their guns, and I look into the shadows to wait for the answering sound of someone coming to the rescue, albeit too late, but no one does. Everyone in this town knows better than to go looking for trouble that isn't already theirs.

Truth is, I already wanted to kill them before they ever laid a hand on Cora. A few days of watching them paw at the girls at the saloon and listening to the way they talk about their wives had been enough to make me think about it more than once. Not necessarily unusual for the men that Cypress tends to sit down to cards with, but even so…

Some are easier than others to leave breathing.

I left Jake for last. Mainly because I disliked him most and wanted him to know the end was coming as I followed him outside the stable to a graveyard of old wagons and barrels. Wasn't hard from there to make the gruesome scene look like an argument between them that had gotten out of hand, would have believed it myself had I not been the one to arrange the bodies and the few remaining dollars between them that would have added up to the cost of their lives.

I'd seen men die for less.

When I get back inside, I see Cora's gun and knife on the ground and pick them up, disturbing the clear signs of struggle in the dirt until I find a small piece of paper, too. It's a stagecoach ticket, and I feel a strange mixture of relief and guilt at the thought that Cora must have already been planning to leave before it became a necessity. I tuck the ticket and knife inside my pocket and the gun inside my belt for safekeeping before I'm moving again. Before I'm trying not to think about what she said.

*I tried.*

If I'd had more time, I would've made them suffer longer. But as it is, I'm acutely aware while I climb up into the hayloft that we're long past our time to be gone.

I already know there won't be much up here to speak of. A bag of clothes and a Bible hidden away behind a loose board, a thin bedroll from the floor, a tin with a few dollars inside, but… Can this really be all she had? I search the loft again quickly to make sure I don't leave anything behind, especially something she may be sentimental over. When I come up empty, I head back down the hatch.

Her mare is anxious in her stall when I approach, ears pinned back and eyes wild. I don't blame her after what she witnessed, but I also need her to realize I'm not a threat to her and quickly.

"Easy, girl." I slip an apple from my pocket and give her a few pats once she takes it. "I'll take you to Cora, all right?"

She eyes me warily as she chews, but we have enough of an understanding at least that she doesn't also try to take a bite out of my arm when I put her saddle and bridle on and lead her out back to where Cypress is waiting.

When I find him, he's pacing, Cora in his arms. He switches between looking at her and the night sky, talking a mile a minute. My gut sinks.

"Cypress," I call out, and he stops to look at me. The mare behind me gives a soft whicker of recognition. "Is she…?"

"She's alive." He readjusts her limp body in his grip, situating her so that her head is cradled in the crook of his neck, and God, she looks so small. So defenseless when she isn't staring up at me with all that fire in her eyes. "The way that one was holding onto her…I think they hurt her. Before I got there, I think they really hurt her."

"They won't get a chance again."

"What about you? Are you—"

"I'm fine," I answer as I draw closer to him and take a chance to look Cora over for myself. "She doesn't seem to be bleeding."

He shakes his head, but I can see the anxiety in his eyes that he's trying to keep at bay. "Cy…" I start.

"I said we should have come here first," he snaps, angry with me now, though not in any way I don't expect. Or deserve. "We should have kept her with us."

"How, exactly?" I shoot back, hoping to make him see reason for once. "How would you have explained it to her?"

His eyes narrow before he looks away, one of the few tells he has that he allows only me to see. "She belongs with us."

"She belongs somewhere *safe*. We aren't that," I counter, kicking up the same argument we've had countless times over the last couple days. "We got lucky tonight, but we might not next time."

There's a beat of silence, and then he looks at me again. "All right." He shifts as if he's going to hand her over to me. "Put her back inside then. Leave her here. If you're so certain that she would be better off."

I've watched Cypress play cards enough that I know exactly what he's doing. He's calling my bluff, and as I stand here holding all of her belongings, I'm not sure I can effectively pretend that I don't have the weaker hand.

"She has no one," Cypress continues. "Nothing to hold her here."

"She has a job."

"Not anymore."

"Why not?"

"I heard that woman tell her if even one thing was out of place, she'd be gone."

"And?"

"And seeing as how you just displaced her son-in-law from this world…"

"There's no witnesses. She'll have no reason to think Cora was involved in any way."

"She'll also have no reason not to. Cora is an outsider. You know what that means. Especially since this town lost four sons tonight."

"They should have had better sons."

"So they should have. But what they'll do is look for someone to blame. Are you really suggesting that we leave her to take her chances with the consequences of that?"

My jaw works side to side as I lift my hat and run my fingers through my hair before giving the ends a firm tug, and I see him see it. See the satisfaction on his face as I show him one of my own tells.

"Fine," I spit. "We take her with us."

Seemingly satisfied, he turns and starts toward his horse without looking back, which is why I say before he can get too far ahead, "This is temporary, Cy."

He doesn't slow, doesn't even hesitate as he replies, "Everything is, wolf."

# CHAPTER 10
## CORA

I wake in a grave. Dark and quiet. Suffocating and still.

I thought death was supposed to be peaceful, but it isn't. I can't find my way, can't feel anything but rough walls surrounding me, can't suppress the urge to scream just in case I can still be saved.

"Cora." Someone murmurs my name and places a hand on my arm. *"Cora, you're all right."*

I try to move toward him, but I can't assign a meaning to the words. I see nothing but concealed faces. The sound of laughter and gunshots. Blood pooling in the street. On my dress. Everywhere.

"No, please, I don't—" I still can't find my way. *"Please—"*

Iron arms grab me, lifting me effortlessly even as I thrash. Carrying me, carrying me, carrying me until…everything falls away. Everything but him.

"You're all right, Cora," soothes a deep voice in my ear as its owner continues to hold me tight. "That's it. Just breathe. Just breathe for me, sweetheart."

I feel myself start to calm, counting lungfuls of brisk air along with the stars now visible in the sky above me. I'm not dead. Although the embarrassment I feel as soon as I finally do get my bearings makes me wish I was.

Rather than a tomb, there is a covered wagon visible in front of me, several quilts half hanging out of the back after the war I'd waged. And behind me, still keeping me flush against him so that I don't accidentally injure myself or, more likely, him… "Aiden."

"Mm-hmm," he murmurs in confirmation, holding me a few heartbeats more before he lets me go and steps away. I turn slowly to face him, though my eyes stay resolutely on the ground.

"Sorry," I mutter. "I thought for a minute… I didn't know where I was."

"Still don't, I'd bet," he points out, and I do look up then to take in his crossed arms and his furrowed brow. He looks as rough as I feel, his facial hair scruffy, his burgundy shirt rumpled, and his brown eyes more tired than I'm used to seeing, though I have to remind myself that I'm not really *used* to seeing them at all.

"We're about fifty miles east of Preston. Give or take a few," he supplies, quickly sweeping his hair back beneath his hat. "You've been out a few days. We were startin' to wonder…"

The longer I look at him, the more things come back in fragments. The conversation with Zeke on the porch of the boarding house. The men at the barn. My hand lifts to gingerly touch the back of my head.

"Does it hurt?" Aiden asks, tracking the movement. "Maybe you should sit?"

"No," I say, letting my hand fall to my side. I take stock of myself at the same time he does, noting that my ribs, too, are still a bit sore. "I'm all right, I think. My head… I hit it when Jake threw me backward. He was the one who—"

"I know which one he was," Aiden says, tone agitated, but his voice softens the smallest amount as he adds, "You won't have to worry about him anymore."

It's not hard to guess his meaning, not when one of my last memories is Aiden striding toward the stable like an oncoming storm while Cypress and I…

"Cypress," I murmur, and the sudden worry already has me searching before Aiden can draw my gaze to a campfire simmering a few feet away. Standing near it, a tall, familiar figure dressed in black bows his head and offers me a smile.

"Hello, little bird."

Much like Aiden, he doesn't look entirely himself, his appearance far less pristine and his presence far less commanding than that of the person who had strolled up to four armed men. Four men who, based on the considerable distance we've rapidly put between us and Preston, likely all met a similar fate.

"They're dead?" I ask, looking to confirm my suspicions as my gaze flips back to Aiden. "You killed them?"

"Yes." He keeps his eyes on mine as he waits for my reaction, and I suppose I'm waiting for it, too. Still too busy trying to piece things together to try to figure out where I fit.

"Did you know?" is the first thing I manage to ask.

"Did I know what?"

"Is that why you came? You heard people talking? About me?"

"No, I came because…" His eyes narrow. "Why are you asking me that?"

"Because Zeke said…"

I can still hear them talking to each other in the stable. *Zeke said. Zeke said. Zeke—*

"Zeke said *what*?" Aiden asks, but I'm already shaking my head to try to get rid of the sound of their voices.

"You told me to stay out of sight."

"It was the safest thing for you to do."

"Why? Because—"

"Because you don't know how to defend yourself."

"And because you heard them talking about me. You knew they were going to—"

"*No*, if I'd known— Cora, I didn't *need* to know what they were going to do. I already know what this world is."

*And you don't* is the implied end of that sentence, and it stings more than it should, realizing he's yet another person who doesn't think I'm capable. That he has the evidence for it, too, considering he had to step in and save me. They both did.

"I tried," I say pathetically, watching the crease in Aiden's brow deepen as I press my hands tighter together in front of me. "I tried to fight back. I know I should've—"

"There's nothing you *should've* done," Cypress says, coming closer to where Aiden and I stand by the wagon. "You're not to blame for anything. It was—"

"It was our fault," Aiden interrupts, looking from me to Cypress pointedly. "We're to blame for what happened."

"But I thought you said..." More of Jake's words resurface from the darkness, and I, too, turn my gaze to Cypress. "You stole money from them."

"You wound me, little bird," Cypress replies, not sounding at all hurt as he places a hand over his heart. "I am a law-abiding citizen."

Aiden barks out a laugh. "The letter of the law, maybe, but not the spirit of it. And I would say both are currently shot to hell by the four bodies we left behind."

Cypress shrugs, staring at Aiden as he replies, "A man has a right to defend what's his."

"What's yours?" I repeat.

"The horses." Aiden's jaw ticks to the side, the corner of his boot digging into the dirt. "We had to come back to get our horses."

"Oh." I flush, feeling embarrassed again for not immediately realizing. Because what else would there have been to make them... "*Wait*, I have to go back," I blurt out. "Tess is..."

Aiden pivots his body slightly, now giving me a clear view of three horses standing underneath a nearby tree. Not one of them is tied up, though judging by the way Tess is currently dozing snugly between the two others, I don't think she's in a hurry to run off.

"We have your things from the hayloft, too," Aiden says, reclaiming my attention. "You shouldn't go back to Preston, but we'll take you anywhere else you want to go. Won't we, Cy?"

Cypress nods, his fingers starting to tap against his leg as he says, "Of course."

"I don't..." *I don't have anywhere else to go* is what I was about to say, but instead, I opt for something that hopefully sounds far less pathetic. "I had things to take care of there. Zeke was supposed to find me a bounty hunter."

I leave out the part about how he told me that he knew I couldn't afford it, about how he was trying to convince me to leave instead. How he had also given me a warning and I'd been stupid enough to think that the greatest wound was to my pride.

"Zeke?" Aiden repeats. "The deputy?"

I nod, and they exchange a look before Cypress asks, "Why do you need a bounty hunter, Cora?"

"My father was killed a few months back. Someone shot him down while we were in Preston as he was walking right outside the sheriff's office, but a bounty hunter was the only way to get them to do something about it. The law wouldn't really help otherwise."

Aiden makes a noise that's caught somewhere between a laugh and a grunt of frustration. "I'll bet not."

"Do you know what he looked like?" Cypress asks next. "The man who killed him?"

"Tan hair. Short beard. Light eyes. A powder burn on his left arm," I recite for what feels like the hundredth time, only Cypress is the first person who actually appears to be listening. "He took off headed northwest."

Cypress nods, then claps his hand together. "Well, that's settled then."

"What is?"

"We will help you find him."

"*What?*" both Aiden and I say at the same time.

"We will help you find the man who killed your father," Cypress repeats, as if it's the simplest thing in the world. "Least we can do considering the trouble we've caused. Isn't that right, Aiden? You said yourself that we hold responsibility here, and it would be *unforgivable* if we didn't try to make amends."

Aiden stares him down in such a way that I'm certain if I was on the receiving end of it, I would be shrinking back to avoid the impact. Cypress, however, seems perfectly relaxed as he stands as one of three points on a triangle, apparently having no intention of being the first to fall in line.

"You don't have to help me," I say, refusing to invest any real hope in something that sounds far too good to be true. "You've already done enough. And you both must have better things to occupy your time."

"Not a thing that I can think of," Cypress attests. "And even if we did—"

"*You* should," Aiden says, blocking off whatever Cypress was about to say as he steps in front of me again. "Cora, I would think carefully on if this is what you really want."

"It is," I say, sure of that at least after being asked so many times by the sheriff and his son. "I *want* to find my father's killer. I owe him that much."

"It won't give him his life back."

"I know."

"And it might take yours."

"Aiden," Cypress interjects, "we—"

"*Don't*. Don't make her promises we might not be able to keep," Aiden fires in his direction. "She deserves to know what she's getting into. To know the type of *law-abiding citizens* she's getting into it with."

He sighs and looks at me again. "If you have something else, something you can go back to… What about your family?"

"They're all gone," I tell him, hoping he'll assume the worst because, somehow, that's better. "Finding this man *is* what I have."

Aiden stares at his partner, the accusation that he's insane for offering heavy in his gaze, and maybe I'm just as insane for even considering taking him up on it, but my choice is already made. Not only because I have no other options, but because, despite the fact that they're self-confessed killers, they're also the reason I'm alive. They've had multiple chances to hurt me and haven't, which is more than I can say for anyone else.

I also just don't want to be alone anymore.

I wait, seeing the moment that the silent communication passing between them ends in acceptance, though not in agreement. In Aiden staring at the ground as he mutters, "Fine, we'll set out in the morning."

He leaves then, walking away to tend to the horses as if he can't stand to spend one more moment in the present company.

"Have patience with him, little bird," Cypress says, watching him go. "Not all of us change direction easily."

I peer up at him, those light blue eyes of his immediately on mine. "Why do you call me that?"

"Hm?"

"Little bird. Why do you keep calling me little bird?"

"Suits you." He removes his coat and wraps it around my shoulders before I even realize I'm shivering. "Puts me in mind of a songbird I used to see."

"I'll bet she could actually sing," I mutter, trying not to be too conspicuous as I tuck my nose into the collar and take a deep breath in. "Fly, too."

"Indeed she could. Once she learned how," he replies, smiling softly, and my chest warms in a way that has nothing to do with the added layer of clothing. However, when I catch sight of Aiden's turned back again, the sensation wanes.

"It seems that you are still adversaries," I say to Cypress, nodding in the direction of his partner. "Because of me."

"Because of *us*," Cypress corrects. "He thinks you will come to harm traveling with us."

"Will I?"

"I don't know," he says truthfully. "Perhaps. But then, you could just as easily come to harm without us, and I've always been inclined to believe that certain paths cross for a reason."

I wrap myself up tighter, simultaneously finding comfort in the impossible idea that I'm not really as lost as I feel. "Is that your god then?" I ask him eventually. "Fate?"

"One of them." He sighs, then gestures back toward the fire. "Come on, you'll feel better after you've had something in your stomach."

I laugh, following his lead. "Seems like every time I see you, you're trying to get me to eat."

"I am," he says simply, no pity in his tone. Only understanding. "I know what it feels like to be starving, Cora. To be so hungry that you stop fearing death because the hunger itself has become a vicious, living thing."

There's truth in what he's saying, but so is there in the fact that I *do* still fear dying. That, even more so, I fear never getting to live. That I

am *terrified* I might never get the chance, and I want to tell him that…
but I don't.

Somehow, I think he already knows.

# CHAPTER 11
## CORA

This time when I wake, I know precisely where I am.

Outside the wagon, I can hear the unmistakable sounds of morning activity. Horses, people, and things all moving about as their outlines pass by on the canvas walls. Inside the wagon, everything is still and sweltering, tinged with the scent of last night's campfire until I push off the blankets and move toward the promise of fresh air. I take a deep pull of it before I'm even fully outside, then another as I look around.

Aiden is once more over by the horses, busy tacking up his own when he glances over his shoulder in my direction. His eyes sweep up and down when they land on me, his jaw tight, and then he turns back to his task. As soon as he's finished, he hoists himself up into his saddle and is gone, disappearing into a cloud of dust without so much as a word or a backward glance as I'm beginning to believe is his habit.

I press my lips tightly together, wondering how, precisely, to go about returning to his good graces. If I ever held a spot there to begin with.

"Good morning, Cora," Cypress calls from behind me and I turn to see him, crouched near the ground as he rolls up what appears to be the second of two sleeping mats that had been situated near the fire. "Did you get some more rest?"

*Oh, God.* I had been so tired last night that I hadn't even given thought to where they would sleep with me being in the wagon. No wonder Aiden is upset with me staying longer.

"I'm so sorry," I say quickly, and Cypress immediately looks concerned. "Why?"

"I slept in the wagon."

He stares at me. "Yes."

"I took your beds."

Cypress chuckles. "You did no such thing, although you are welcome to." He must see the need for clarity still on my face because he quickly explains, "I don't sleep in the wagon unless it's a necessity. Neither does Aiden."

"You don't?" In all the months we'd spent on the wagon train, my family and I had always slept inside, no matter how tight the quarters. "Why not?"

He stands, brushing the dirt off his pants before straightening. "Can't see the sky."

"But you're sleeping. You wouldn't see it anyway."

"I've told myself the same, but I cannot be convinced," he says then shrugs. "How about some breakfast?"

I laugh, remembering last night's conversation about how he's always trying to feed me. In truth, I'd eaten so much deer meat and so many potatoes before falling asleep that I'm not nearly as hungry as I normally am. A good thing, because when I see myself in a small mirror hung on the side of the wagon, I determine there is only one need that can take priority.

"Is there a place I could wash up?" I ask Cypress, taking a step back as if that will keep him from seeing the sheen of sweat near my collar or the decidedly wild tilt of my curls. "Before we eat?"

He nods, gesturing off to his left in the opposite direction of wherever Aiden had taken off to. "There's a stream not too far that way. Wasn't too cold when I was there earlier this morning, and it's fairly deep."

"Thank you," I say, feeling almost excited by the prospect as I look around for my things. "Do you know where…"

"Aiden put your bag in the wagon," Cypress says, making a point to add, "He's the one who made sure to collect everything for you."

I'm touched by the gesture, even if he now seems completely uninterested in being near either me or my belongings. "That was kind of him."

"Indeed it was," Cypress agrees, his expression amused, and I'm about to ask him what is so funny before I catch sight of myself again and decide that bathing is not something that can wait.

A few minutes later, I'm heading in the direction of the stream with Tess ambling along happily enough by my side, even if it had taken a bit of convincing to get her to leave Cypress's horse behind. I can't really blame her, since she's been sorely lacking in consistent company as much as I have been.

"Doesn't hurt that he's very handsome, too, I suppose," I say to her, not entirely sure I'm still talking about the horses when I add, "They both are."

Up ahead, a small grove of trees comes into view before the sound of the stream greets my ears, growing loud enough by the time I reach the bank that it almost drowns out my happy sigh. I can hardly wait until I'm able to get off this dress, but I still am nervous stripping out in the open air. I look around more than once before finally ducking behind a tree, leaving my clothes in a rumpled heap, and making a dash for the water. I gasp as I wade in, the chill seeping into my bones, but I don't care enough to stop until I sink up to my neck in the center of the stream.

It feels heavenly to drift here for a while, weightless as the lazy current washes away days of dirt and as the cool water soothes lingering bruises. I carefully touch each one before I finally feel up to the task of lathering myself with the bar of soap from my bag, taking extra care to work through the tangles in my hair where the strike to my head still stings.

*I'm glad they're dead,* I think as I wince at how tender it is. *They were bad people. I'm glad they're dead.* I close my eyes and put my head beneath the water, everything going quiet but my thoughts. *Does that make me bad, too?*

Surely a godly person would pray for their souls. Would mourn the loss of life. Would try to find a way to forgive. Although, my mother was the most pious person I knew, and she had done none of those things for my father.

I doubt she had done them for me either.

The sound of rapid hoofbeats when I resurface pulls me back into my surroundings, and at first, I worry Tess has run off until I look over to see her napping in the shade a ways off from the bank. Which can only mean… I quickly slink behind a rocky outcrop, dipping down into the water until only my eyes and nose are above the surface right as a highly recognizable rider comes into view.

*Aiden.*

He dismounts before his horse even comes to a full stop, but he's steady on his feet when he hits the ground, no more than twenty paces from where I'm hiding.

He heads for the edge of the water, crouching once he reaches it and dipping a hand into the stream before bringing it to the back of his neck. As he does, he seems to be breathing heavy, winded like he's been running, too.

"Fuck," I hear him say, then a more decisive, "*Fuck.*"

He stands again along the water's edge, facing away from me with one of his hands dragging at his hair beneath his hat, and I use the opportunity to move just enough to try to warm up my limbs now that I'm stuck stationary. The water feels like it's growing colder with every passing moment.

What if this is actually how I die? What if I freeze to death because I am too cowardly to tell him that I'm here? *Naked*, I tack on as a silent excuse. *You are here naked.*

I try to make myself harder to spot, huddling behind my rock until I can barely see him when he turns back around. But it's still enough that my breath catches in my lungs when he abruptly tosses his hat to the ground, takes off his jacket, and starts to make quick work of the buttons on his shirt.

I shut my eyes out of respect for his privacy, but quickly rationalize that if I can't see him, then I also won't know if he sees *me*. Cautiously, I open my eyes again, but now, his shirt is fully unbuttoned, exposing a broad, muscled chest and a tapered waist. A line of dark hair that dusts his tan skin draws my gaze down his abdomen, and my own stomach swoops.

*Handsome*, I think again as I stare at him. A man fully grown and nothing like the boys in their fine church clothes that I used to have crushes on back in Boston. No, Aiden is handsome in a way that sends a thrill up my spine, in a way that feels as dangerous as the shining silver pistol that sits at his belt.

Well, *had been* sitting at his belt.

Noticing that her new friend is nearby, Tess chooses this moment to announce herself, calling out in a loud whinny that Aiden's horse returns while his rider pulls his pistol and points it in her direction. I'm about to call out, too, to stop him when Aiden sees that it's Tess and his arm immediately drops.

"Christ." He looks down at the dirt, muttering, before his head whips back up. "*Cora*, you here?"

I seriously consider not answering. Thinking it might be better to let him believe that Tess simply got loose rather than that I've been hiding behind a rock watching him take his clothes off.

"*Cora*," he shouts, and I press my lips together to hold my silence until he starts, seemingly on instinct, to move in my direction. "Cora, are you—"

"*Yes*," I shout quickly. "*Yes*, I'm here."

My words have the desired effect of getting him to stop in his tracks, although now he knows precisely where to look when he says, "Are you all right? What in God's name are you doing?"

"What do you *think* I'm doing?" I snap back, irritated now as well as freezing. "I was washing up. Just as you were apparently about to do."

He looks down at his open shirt and hastily shoves the loose ends into his trousers instead of taking the time to button it back up. "Dammit, Cora, you shouldn't be out here on your own. You're still hurt."

"I'm fine."

"That so? You have your gun? Your knife?"

I don't respond, my gaze shooting to my bag where it lies next to my dirty clothes.

"I'll take that silence as a no."

I bristle. "Can you leave? I was here first."

"Cora—"

"*Aiden*," I interrupt, the impact of my retort likely lessened a bit by the fact that I can't stop my teeth from chattering. "I said I was fine. Now, unless you would like to stand there and watch me bathe…" He shifts his weight, his eyes closing briefly at the undeniable rudeness of the suggestion. "I will see you back at the wagon."

I close my own eyes and listen for him to go, about to yell at him again when I at last hear his receding footsteps and then hoofbeats. Tess whickers sadly as she's left behind.

"Traitor," I mumble to her once I'm sure that he's gone, not lingering another minute before climbing out of the water and going straight for my clean clothes. My skin is still wet as I pull on my undergarments and hurriedly pin up my hair to dry in the heat, not even close to relaxed again even once I pull on my old brown dress for chores. My *only* other dress, I remind myself, as I stare at the remaining pile of my discarded clothes and wish I could leave them where they lie. Right alongside every awkward memory of that interaction with Aiden.

Instead, I take them to the water and try once more to remove marks that will never fade.

# CHAPTER 12
## CYPRESS

It feels so good to be home. To lie sprawled out up on the wagon bench, drifting off with a book in my hand, a small white flower pressed between its pages, and the lullaby of the fading summer wind in my ears. Ah, and one particularly surly cowboy who is currently blocking out the harshest of the sun's rays. *Perfect.*

"Hello, wolf," I greet him. "How was your ride?"

Aiden lets out an annoyed huff in response, staring down at me with an expression that is even more grim than usual. "I hope you're real fuckin' pleased with yourself."

"Generally, yes." His glare intensifies. "Not a question. I see."

"You know, more than once," he continues, folding his arms against his chest, "I have found myself asking God what particular penance it is that I'm serving."

"And what has been his reply?"

"He's kept his own council on the subject."

"How typical." I shift to sitting, leaning my back against the canvas and enjoying the fact that Aiden now has to be the one to look up. "Perhaps if you were to ask while on your knees."

The corner of Aiden's mouth twitches, but he refuses to smile. Also typical, even if the duration of our discord is not. Usually, we are able to come to some sort of truce, through some means or another. But on this matter, neither of us appears willing to give ground.

"She doesn't know how to protect herself out here."

"We'll teach her."

"She's too headstrong to listen."

"Sounds familiar…"

"*Cypress*," Aiden barks. "This isn't a game. Has it ever occurred to you that you could be wrong?"

"No."

"Why?"

"I wasn't the last time."

Aiden looks away, transported momentarily somewhere else before coming back to argue. "She could get killed," he says, one of his hands in his jacket pocket. "*We* could get her killed. If she has a chance at something different…"

"Then she can decide whether or not she wants to take it," I reply, and since it looks like maybe he's thinking about talking to God again, I continue on. "You know, wolf, as it happens, I have also done a fair share of reflection recently."

Aiden rolls his eyes. "This ought to be good."

"And do you know what I've determined?"

He waits for me to say more, but knowing I have a captive audience, I draw it out for the length of time it takes for me to note the agitated way that he fidgets, his blown black pupils, and the exact number of buttons undone on his shirt. I sacrifice the urge to smirk so that I might instead keep my expression pious.

"I have come to the conclusion that, while your God would have you believe there can be no salvation without penance, more often than not, they are quite indistinguishable from one another."

He stares at me, likely wondering if he should take me by the neck. "You're saying I should try to enjoy my suffering?"

"I know I certainly am."

Under his breath, I think Aiden mutters *I'll bet you are, you fucking sadist,* but it's hard to be certain when he is already walking off.

"If you're planning to go clean up, you'll want to wait. Cora went down to the stream a while ago." Aiden stops but keeps his back to me as I add, "Perhaps you already know that."

This time, when he curses me to hell, he makes sure I hear every word.

# CHAPTER 13
## CORA

We set off not long after breakfast, Cypress and I riding in the wagon, Aiden riding alongside as he constantly moves from side to side with his eyes on every horizon.

According to Cypress, we are planning to make our way to a frequently visited town that lies far northwest of Preston, doubling back somewhat on our initial path so that we can make inquiries with the description of my father's murderer in the same direction that I saw him escape.

According to Aiden…well, nothing.

He hasn't said so much as a word to me since I returned from the water. A blessing, since I still feel too tongue-tied by shame to say anything back. I cannot believe I had really suggested that he watch me *bathe*.

He must think I'm so incredibly *sinful*. The charge only more damning when you consider I had been about to watch *him* bathe had

Tess not interrupted. Well, I wouldn't have *really*. I absolutely would have shut my eyes. I had been about to…

"Everything all right, little bird?"

I startle, clearing the vision of Aiden by the water from my mind as I turn my head to Cypress, worried that somehow he'll know the direction my thoughts had wandered as I watched his partner's movements on horseback just now.

Would Aiden have told him about what happened? *Probably*… I flush scarlet, and it's only when I unclench one of my hands to fan myself and pretend it's the midday heat that I realize I've been fisting the skirts in my lap to the point of causing deep wrinkles.

I clear my throat and smooth out my dress, mumbling, "I was only thinking."

"Oh?" His face is the picture of innocence but his eyes are sparkling with poorly contained amusement as they flick from me to Aiden. "What about?"

I wonder, if I throw myself from this wagon, would it be enough to knock me unconscious for a few days again? Likely not. Likely would only be enough to injure myself. Both physically and emotionally when the humiliation proves not to be fatal.

I opt instead for a change of topic. "I was only thinking…is it wise for us to go this way? To go into any town for that matter? What if someone comes looking for us after what happened in Preston?"

"Always a possibility, but people *usually* don't have much desire to see me again after we part ways. Don't like to be reminded of their missteps," he says, grinning. "And Aiden made sure that no one could easily connect us to the other matter."

I note the way Cypress holds the wagon reins loosely in his hands as he sits at my side and casually mentions the four men his partner killed as "the other matter." All the while, his horse—who I have now come to understand has the very dignified name of *Cerberus*—needs little encouragement to follow where Aiden and his own horse *Helios* are leading us. I don't need to ask to be positive that Cypress had a hand in naming both of them.

That, along with the other clear shows of blind faith, makes me wonder even more how long they have been traveling together. How long it took for them to develop the sometimes silent way they communicate, the effortless way they pass off tasks and belongings while knowing exactly where the other will be. What the other will need.

Watching them efficiently pack up camp and hunch over spread-out maps to settle on a path of travel this morning had been strangely fascinating to me, the trust between them something I had never come close to encountering within my own family.

Must be freeing…to have someone to depend on in that way.

"How did he make sure?" I ask Cypress. "Won't people realize that you and Aiden left town the same night those men were killed?" I suppose I should ask the same about myself. Although, I can't really picture anyone being terribly concerned about my absence. The sheriff and Zeke are probably relieved I'm no longer around to pester them, and Mrs. Jensen will likely be busy with her daughter after what happened to Jake.

"Lots of people passing through Preston on any given night," Cypress says. "Many of whom saw me leave without looking back. All of whom likely never noticed Aiden. I'm not concerned."

*How could no one notice Aiden?* is what I want to ask, but given it might draw attention to how much *I* notice him, I instead reply, "Then why put so much immediate distance between us and Preston?"

"An abundance of caution," Cypress replies, posture still relaxed despite my questions. "Aiden tends to be somewhat of a worrier."

The warning look Aiden sends Cypress over his shoulder tells me that he is listening even from a few paces ahead, as does his grumbled reply. "Someone has to be. Usually it's the only thing keeping you alive."

Cypress frowns, confused. "I thought it was my personality."

Aiden barks out a laugh. "No, that's what usually almost gets you killed."

I look at Cypress, half expecting him to appear upset, but he only grins as he turns to me. "What is your opinion, Cora, since you've been sat beside me all day? Are you currently thinking of how to kill me?"

"*No*," I answer a little too loudly. My cheeks redden again. "I like your personality."

His smile widens further as Aiden shakes his head and cues Helios to a brisk trot a few paces ahead. Cerberus, likewise, picks up the pace, and I turn back to check that Tess is still cheerily following the wagon. These last several days have given her more exercise than she's had in months, though she seems delighted rather than fatigued.

The longest journeys I had been taking her on recently were back to the farm to visit my father's grave, and I feel a pang of regret thinking I may never have the opportunity again. If I'd known, I would have brought him something, not that I really have anything to give.

Maybe someday, after we find the man responsible, I will be able to pay him a visit. If only to tell him that it's over, to say how sorry I am one more time. Maybe I could check in on Mrs. Jensen, too. The chilliness of her reception aside, she had given me more of an opportunity than anyone else, and I'd thanked her by leaving her with a mess despite my word. As well as without a son-in-law. Poor of an excuse as Jake had been for one, I can't help feeling I owe her something for the trouble, especially since I never would have met Cypress if she hadn't given me the job in the first place.

I frown, remembering a question I'd had once before, but it puzzles me even more now that I've had an opportunity to witness Cypress and Aiden together.

"Cypress?" I start, keeping my voice low, and he bends his head to show he's listening. "Why didn't Aiden stay at the boarding house, too?"

The corner of his mouth lifts. "Did he not?"

"Mrs. Jensen said you were the only guest."

"Perhaps she miscounted."

"He wasn't at breakfast."

"He could've slept late."

I arch an eyebrow at him. "There was only one bed slept in."

"Ah, of course."

"So why didn't he stay there, too?"

Cypress looks at me, frowns slightly, then looks to Aiden who is still ahead. "We make it a habit not to be seen together in the towns we visit."

"Why?"

"Another precaution," Cypress replies, his partner keeping his eyes forward this time while he continues. "Another worry, that Aiden's presence will be a hazard rather than a help."

I consider that, trying to imagine how Aiden's sometimes intimidating appearance could be anything *but* a help in these types of situations.

"Wouldn't it be safer, if people knew you weren't alone?"

"You would think." Cypress rotates his right shoulder, grimacing slightly as if pained by it, and I remember the long scar I'd glimpsed there. "I suppose an advantage is that if I look to be on my own, then others are more likely to try to make themselves my company. Do you remember what I told you? About how people see what they want to see?"

"Yes."

"So say a man comes to your town. He arrives alone and stays alone. Overspends on his accommodations, stumbles his way through hand after hand of cards, but seems not to care a bit about the impact to the sizable pocketbook he tucks back into his coat. What would you see? If you were a person inclined to place a wager?"

I mull it over, remembering the way Zeke had inexplicably described him as foolish. "You want them to see someone rich. Who can be taken advantage of," I say slowly. "Because then they'll bet more money…if they think it's a sure thing."

Cypress beams. "Exactly right, little bird."

"Is that not cheating?" I suggest. "Since you're purposefully deceiving them?"

He shrugs. "Not in the way I see it. A good bluff is one of the most essential parts of poker. Is it my fault they fail to realize the game is being played before they even sit down at the table?"

I shake my head at him, but I'm smiling. "I see now why Aiden thinks your personality will get you killed."

Cypress grins again as if I've paid him a compliment, and I think I hear Aiden chuckle up ahead, too, even over the sound of the wagon and the horses.

"They do get a bit…upset," Cypress admits with a dramatic sigh. "Unfortunate, because then I have no choice but to cut my stay short."

"Very unfortunate," I agree, though something tells me he's never all that sad to go. "You said they don't usually come after you. But they do sometimes?"

"Yes."

"Doesn't that scare you?"

"No."

"Why not?"

"Because mighty Cerberus has yet to be caught," Cypress says with obvious pride. "And if he ever were, Aiden would be there."

My chest pangs with that same longing curiosity over the trust he has in his partner. "I thought you said you weren't together in town."

"I said we weren't *seen* together," he counters. "Doesn't mean he isn't nearby. Waiting in the wings for calamity. Like an avenging angel."

Up ahead, Aiden shakes his head again as I think through the explanation with the evidence I've seen with my own eyes. And at the end of it, I am certain I understand. Cypress's job is to win. Aiden's job is to make sure they don't lose.

# CHAPTER 14
## AIDEN

I must have been a real bastard in a past life. Not that I'm not in this one.

"All right, focus on breathing for me," I hear Cypress murmur, lingering over Cora's shoulder as she stands with a gun pointed at an old can set up about ten paces away. "Steady. In and out. In and out."

She had been insulted at first by how close I'd placed the target, then she'd failed to mark it…not once, but *four* times. Growing more and more frustrated each time until I thought she might turn the pistol and its only remaining bullet on me just so she could hit something. Honestly, part of me wishes she would have. It might have been kinder.

"Shoot again, Cora," I'd told her when she attempted to shove the gun in my direction. "You're not done."

"*Yes*, I am," she snapped back. "I can't do it. I tried."

*I tried.* God, I can still hear the way she sounded that night when we found her, two weeks ago now, and it still nearly breaks me every time I think of it. *I did what you said. I tried.*

Cypress is right. We should have found a way to protect her better. And while I'm damn certain I'll never allow something like that to happen again, I'll also be damned if I leave her any longer in this world without knowing how to defend herself.

"Ease up," Cypress is telling her now. "Unlock your elbows a fraction, put both hands securely on the grip. Let the weapon be an extension of you, not something to fear."

I feel a spike of frustration as I keep my place near the wagon, wondering why I hadn't seen it sooner, or recognized the signs after so many years of knowing exactly what they look like. Of course, Cypress hadn't missed it.

"Here, little bird," he'd said as he stepped in, taking the old pistol in her trembling hands and neatly exchanging it for one of the gleaming twin Colts he keeps at his waist. "Try this one instead. You might like the feel of it better."

She eyed him warily, the recoil of her agitation with me catching Cypress, too. "Why?"

"It's lighter," he said easily, even knowing as well as I do that the gun he'd placed in her hands was larger than her own. "Can I show you?"

She hesitated, her breaths coming in shallow doses as she looked at him, and only then did I notice she was trying not to cry. *Dammit.*

"Cora…" I started to say, but she was already turning on her heel to return to the line I'd drawn in the sand. Cypress clapped a consolatory hand on my shoulder and squeezed before following.

"All right, now keep both your eyes open and fixed on your target, understand?" Cypress is saying. "Wily bastard could take off on you at any moment."

She laughs, soft and still a little unsure, and it soothes the ache in my chest when I hear her say back, "I don't think the can has plans for escape."

"That's what he wants you to think. Remember, both eyes open," Cypress murmurs, the tip of his boot gently nudging the inside of her foot. "Spread your legs a bit wider. That's it." She shifts, accidentally leaning back into him in the process, and when she stays like that rather than pulling away, Cypress's eyes close for a moment before he regains his composure. "Good. That's good, Cora."

*Christ*, I think, feeling a spike of something else now pooling low in my gut as I watch them and try not to let my mind race back to that morning at the stream.

*Unless you would like to stand there and watch…* If she only knew how much that single sentence has taunted me, if she had any idea how it had turned something already simmering in the back of my head into a snarling inferno with sharpened teeth.

I wish I could even explain why. I shouldn't want her. She's too naive, too damn innocent to even realize the effect she has. On either of us.

I keep watching as she tries to follow Cypress's instruction, and when she tips her head back to glance up at him, I can see the growing adoration in his eyes while he reaches forward to gently correct her hold.

"Use your thumb to pull back the hammer. Hover your finger beside the trigger until you're ready to fire. Then *squeeze*." His finger presses into the back of her hand in an imitation of the movement. "Do not pull. Some make the mistake of thinking you need a lot of pressure but you do not. You only need the right technique."

She nods, and Cypress's hand drops from hers. She takes one more deep breath. I do the same.

Why do I want her? Why *her*? Cypress has his reasons, and regardless of whether or not I believe in them, I envy the resoluteness of his conviction. Always have.

Without any more hesitation, Cora squeezes the trigger, both eyes open to see the way the can goes flying into the air on impact. I grin as she practically leaps out of her skin in celebration, turning and throwing her arms around Cypress in her excitement, laughing as he spins her in a big circle with her long hair and her skirts flying out behind her.

By the time he sets her back down, she's winded, but she's still beaming. Still so achingly beautiful with those sharp green eyes creasing in the corners, those freckles across her nose scrunching, that hair windswept around her face… I can't make myself look away, not when I can see that light shining out of her, only a flicker at first but growing brighter by the day. And here I am, drawn to it, as if me getting closer isn't the very thing that could extinguish it.

With a whispered thank you, she holds the pistol out for Cypress to take back but he only shakes his head. "You hold onto that one for a while, little bird. To practice with."

"But…" I can see her working herself up to protest, already thinking through all the reasons why she shouldn't accept it, and I know that feeling well. When you've lost as much as she has, you don't trust anyone to give you something. You only trust them to take.

"Just for a while," he assures her, then nods at the can where it landed. "Better hit him again. Looks to still have some life in him."

She smiles hesitantly, but sure enough, she walks back to the line, this time without Cypress and with less time passing before she fires. The can goes airborne with a loud metallic *ding,* and she dances a bit in her place before she does it all over again.

I chuckle, still observing her as Cypress comes to stand beside me. "That was good instinct," I tell him quietly. "Switching out the guns."

"I figured that since it had already failed her twice…" he says back. "Some things start to carry a weight all their own."

I frown, disturbing the dirt with the toe of my boot as I drop my gaze. "Yeah, suppose they do."

"I know it's important to you that she learn these things, wolf, but if it's too hard for you to—"

"I'm fine," I tell him, straightening back up in time to see her hit the target again. "I'll *be* fine. I should've realized with the gun. I should've been…" I lift my hat and drag a hand through my hair. "I'm fine," I say once more. "Won't happen again."

# CHAPTER 15
## CORA

"I already *know* how to ride."

Aiden looks at me from under his hat, the wide brim tilting up enough that I can see both the warmth in his brown eyes and the contradictory set of his mouth. "Then you won't mind a demonstration."

"I do, actually," I say, standing next to Tess with reins in hand. Not at all happy about being pulled into another one of Aiden's *lessons* when I had been perfectly content listening to Cypress read by the fire until a few moments ago. "I really do mind."

His jaw works to the side as we square off, this little evening showdown that we do an apparently integral part of the new routine we've developed over the last several weeks of travel. The rest of it goes something like this: I get up in the mornings to find Aiden is already gone. I have breakfast with Cypress. Aiden returns and silently packs up camp. We set off. I ride in the wagon with Cypress and Aiden rides alongside. When we stop to rest, Cypress helps me practice my shooting. Aiden silently watches from nearby. We find a place to stop for the night. Aiden silently sets up camp. I help Cypress make dinner. Aiden finally decides to speak to me. We argue. We eat. We go to bed. We start again.

"I know how to ride," I repeat.

As if he's actually giving up, Aiden steps toward Tess's left side and loosens the cinch, pulling both the saddle and blanket free. Then, with a level of ease that only makes me more irritated with him, he carries them over and hoists both of them into the wagon. He also says, "You don't know how to ride, Cora. You know how to hang on."

I glare at him as he returns and loops a piece of rope around Tess's neck, tying it off loosely but securely before removing her bridle. Finished, he tugs the now useless reins from my hand and places them with the rest of her tack before looking at me expectantly.

"What?" I ask, right at the same time he says, "Get on."

I look between him and Tess, sure that his damn hat must be on too tight to allow him to think clearly. "I can't get up there without stirrups."

"You can."

"No."

He runs a hand over his face, then plants his hands on his hips before actually conceding, "Fine, we'll practice that later." Then he steps forward, and my eyes widen as he takes a knee in front of me and cups his hands together. "All right, *now* get on."

I only stare at him, and with his eyes also on my face, I suddenly feel a lot less angry with him and a lot more like I want to run my fingers through his hair in the same way he's so fond of doing. I shake my head. "You must be joking."

He says nothing, only waits until eventually his head tilts, his tongue peeking out over his plush bottom lip, and I tell myself it's still my lingering annoyance that has me thinking of sinking my teeth into that same spot.

"Fine," I say, sounding a bit too breathy as I place my foot in his waiting palm and allow myself to be hoisted up onto Tess's bare back, relenting if for no other reason than to create some distance between us. "Happy?"

"Overjoyed," he bites out, before he gets to his feet and steps back. "How ya feel?"

"Honestly?"

"Yes."

"As if I'm about to fall off?"

"Thought you knew how to ride?"

"Oh, don't worry, I'm sure I will be able to *hang on* long enough to have Tess trample you." Tess snorts as if she understands the threat I've just made, and I'm not sure who appears more offended: her or Aiden.

"She would never, would you, Tess?" he replies, patting her neck affectionately as his voice drops into a softer, lower register. "She's too good a girl for that."

His eyes flick back up to hold mine, and my stomach flips, my skin heating as I shift in the saddle. Well, where there *should* be a saddle. Instead, there's only Tess's wide, smooth back and hardly anything to use to get a solid grip. "I really don't think this is a good idea."

"We'll take it slow," he says, sounding very close to patient, although I suspect that it will be short-lived when *slow* proves to be all I *can* go. A walk I can hardly handle. Anything faster than that has me quickly careening to the side. Before a half hour passes, I fall off about half a dozen times, and even with Aiden there to catch me, I'm still getting sore.

"Perhaps a more hands-on approach might help?" Cypress calls out from his spectator's seat by the fire. An interesting statement to make considering Aiden already has his hands on me, fingers at my waist to hold and steady me before setting me back on my feet.

"She's fine," Aiden barks over his shoulder as he kneels once more to lift me.

"You're the instructor," Cypress continues, holding up his hands. "Only trying to be of service." When I go sliding off again a few minutes later, he adds, "Maybe you should get the guns out again."

Aiden rounds on him, still holding me as he yells, "Would you butt out? She needs to learn this."

"Why?" I snap, shoving him away before massaging my lower back. "I have a saddle. I have reins. This isn't—"

"You should know how to ride without them."

"Why?"

"Because it's better that way. Get on the horse."

"*No.*"

He's still standing inches from me, his eyes dark and his mouth opening as if to shout, to say *something* else at least. Instead, he starts to turn his back.

"Wait," I say, because as good as it feels to push back, him pulling away feels worse. "Can you just tell me why?"

He stops, his jaw tense as he stares at the ground and crosses his arms over his chest. "Because it will teach you to be a better rider. I've seen you, Cora. You always hang on to the saddle horn when you ride.

You rely too much on giving direction with your reins. You need to be less dependent on them. That way if you ever need to—"

"Need to what? Try out for Buffalo Bill? This is ridicu—"

"If you ever need to get *away*," he snaps, his eyes finding mine again. "If you ever need to ride like your life depends on it, actually knowing how to ride *well* could be the thing that means you survive."

"Oh." I remember running toward Tess's stall with Elliot and his friend on my heels. Even if I'd made it, I wouldn't have had time to tack her up. I wouldn't have been able to get away. Which is exactly what Aiden is trying to prevent.

And I'm fighting him every step of the way.

"I'm sorry," I say, my shoulders sagging as my anger fades. "I didn't—"

He shakes his head. "I should've explained from the start. I'm not very good at this…" He sighs and glances back at Cypress, who is watching intently. "Maybe you'd rather have Cy teach you this, too."

"No, it's okay," I tell him, a little surprised that I mean it when I say it. "I'd like you to teach me. But I would also like not to fall off." I rub my right arm and wince when I feel a bruise that is beginning to form. "It hurts."

He nods, even almost smiles. "Okay, no more falling off. For today."

I consider that about as good as I'm going to get, so when he kneels again, I place my foot and let him swing me back up without argument, although I don't hide my surprise at all when Aiden stands and swings himself up, too. As soon as he settles behind me, I feel somehow both more secure and more off-balance than on any previous attempt.

To get us moving, he squeezes his thighs against Tess's sides and clicks his tongue, the sound so close to my ear that it has a similar effect on me.

"You're all right," he murmurs, mistaking the source of my nerves when I jump. "I meant what I said. No more falling off today."

"Okay. Is this…is this okay?"

"Mm-hmm. Keep your back straight," he encourages, and I feel his broad chest against my spine, the heat of him carrying through the thin material of my dress. "You feel how my legs are at the sides? See the angle? Right, that's perfect. Keep your heels down."

I'm not sure I'm breathing. Not with him so near, stealing all my air. So different from the way I feel when Cypress teaches me, his calm, relaxed presence putting me at ease. Right now, I am a lot of things. But not one of them is *at ease*.

"Grip with your thighs. Roll into the movement with your hips." He shifts nearer, showing me by example, and my body responds with far less reluctance than I had shown him earlier. "Yes, good. That's good."

We make circle after circle as he offers quiet corrections to my posture and cues, but it becomes increasingly harder to focus with each pass. I am so *aware* of him. How close he is. How strong. How surprisingly sweet.

I don't even realize we've stopped until he shifts away, drops back down to the ground, and then turns to lift me from Tess's back. He sets me down slowly, still *so* close to him.

"Think that's enough for today," he says, voice husky, his hands lingering on my waist. "You go on. I'll take care of Tess."

I nod, still half in a daze as I walk around him, feeling his fingertips fall away as I pause at his side to look up at him. "Aiden?"

"Hm?"

"Thank you."

He dips his head. "You're welcome, Cora."

I smile, feeling hopeful that maybe we've altered our routine as I head toward Cypress, who stands waiting. But once I make it to the halfway point and see his expression shift, I don't even have to turn around to know nothing has really changed.

Aiden is already gone.

# CHAPTER 16
## CYPRESS

"Little bird?"

"Hm?" Cora is frowning as she turns to where I stand by the nearly loaded wagon with my hand outstretched. Getting us ready to go, although her mind is clearly already elsewhere. I glance meaningfully at my bedroll and coffee pot in her arms, and her eyes follow my gaze before she blushes. "Oh, sorry."

"It's all right," I reassure her as she passes them over. "Something you want to talk about?"

She shakes her head, but I keep an eye on her as I place the last few items in the wagon, watching the way she scans the distance for an approaching rider, and I'd have to be a half-wit not to realize what's bothering her.

As well as a liar to pretend it's not bothering me, too.

"He'll be back before we leave," I say gently, and the effect is immediate. Her spine straightening and her chin jutting up as she crosses her arms.

"I know," she says.

"Of course," I reply with a nod, but given the way her teeth are digging into her poor bottom lip, I still explain, "He's scouting ahead. Making sure the coast is clear for us to come into town."

"Right," she replies, continuing to sound a bit worried when she asks, "Do you think it might not be?"

I shrug, reaching for a rope in the wagon to tie a few items down more securely. "Aiden has a keen nose for trouble. If something is amiss, he'll know."

"You put a lot of faith in him."

"I put *all* my faith in him. Well, half of it at least." I look over my shoulder again to see her brow crease a little in confusion, though she makes an attempt at humor to dispel it.

"Is Aiden another of your gods?" she asks.

I let my grin turn mischevious as my hands easily tie one sturdy knot and then another. "There are certainly times he'd like to think so."

She chuckles, but the pretty flush on her cheeks remains. "He's so…"

"He is," I agree.

Her eyebrows rise. "How do you even know what I was going to say?"

"Because I would have said much the same when I first met him."

"How *did* you meet him?" she asks, her curiosity piqued.

"Oh, you know what they say, little bird, adversity makes for strange bedfellows." I finish strapping down our belongings, turning back to her fully as I say, "He chose to intervene at a very opportune moment."

Her eyes narrow, her mind thinking through what I've said for a while before guessing, "He saved your life?"

"He did. It was some years ago now. I haven't always been so... *discerning* with whom I choose to sit down with at a card table. If I'm being honest, I once had a tendency to pick more out of boredom than design, and I usually felt all the better if the hands ended up as fists aimed at my face when the evening was done."

"And now?" she asks, the corner of her mouth curving.

"Now, I'm old enough and wise enough to try to dodge at least a few. Not to mention pretty enough."

She rolls her eyes, shaking her head again slightly, and the expression reminds me so much of Aiden that I have to press my lips tight together to conceal my smirk as she asks, "Why would you have *wanted* to get in fights?"

"I wanted to get hurt," I admit, and her expression falls, that delicate line back in her brow.

"Why would you want that?"

"So that I could hurt them back." She doesn't ask why again, and I know this is another case of our three circles intersecting, of there being things in her that remind me of myself just as much as they do of Aiden. I meet her gaze, refusing to let either of us hide as I confirm for her, "Some people don't deserve forgiveness."

Her eyes widen a fraction as she studies me, but instead of shying away from what she finds, she takes a step toward it. "And you can decide that over a game of cards? Whether they deserve forgiveness?"

"Not entirely."

"Then how?"

"I told you, Cora, the game starts long before they take their chair."

She doesn't doubt herself before she guesses this time. "You watch them before you play them."

"Why shouldn't I? They watch me."

"*Discerning*, indeed." Her head tilts. "Sounds a little like hunting."

"Only a little?"

She laughs, and I find I love that sound. Love the way it makes her eyes dance, the way it brightens her smile. There's so much *life* to her that the world has been unable to snuff out… I'll probably kill anyone else who tries. If Aiden doesn't first.

"If you were hunting, how did you become the one that needed saving?" she asks, lightly teasing now. "How did you become prey?"

I look over her shoulder, catching the sight of a far-off rider flying closer. "I forgot who I was supposed to be hunting."

# CHAPTER 17
## CORA

"Its name is actually *Last Chance*? I thought you were joking."

Cypress and I are stopped right outside the beginning of the town's main street, both of us on horseback since we left the wagon in what Aiden declared to be a safe location a ways back. He took off again almost as soon as we'd stashed it, riding ahead to town so that he could make inquiries and so that no one would see all three of us arrive together. And so that Cypress would be the one stuck nannying me, since that's apparently what Aiden thinks I need.

"I believe the name was given because this is one of the last places to supply before people travel farther north," Cypress says before his brow furrows. "Although they might also simply be trying to set expectations."

He clicks his tongue at Cerberus, urging him forward into the sparse throng of people on the street, the number growing as we make our way into town, and I immediately understand why people *watch* him when he appears. I'm having trouble not doing the same.

While Aiden tends to ride with an air of comfort that speaks to countless hours in the saddle, Cypress rides like a conquering king returning from a successful campaign. His black clothing catching in the sun, his back straight, and his head held high as Cerberus struts beneath him. He's gorgeous, so much so that I don't blame a single person who turns to look in his direction with obvious awe.

But then their eyes land on me, and based on their frowns, I realize how we must look together. Slowly, I hold Tess farther and farther back until Cypress notices and draws up to wait for me.

"Maybe I should have stayed with the wagon," I tell him when we come even again. "Might have been better."

"In what way?" he asks, appearing genuinely unsure. "Are you nervous to be in town? We can go back. Wait for Aiden to tell us if his contacts have any news."

"No, no," I reassure him, following him when he starts to lead us toward a nearby hitching post. He gets down first, secures both horses, and I glance around to see who is still looking when he reaches up to help me down as well.

"I only remember you saying you usually come into town alone," I reply as he gently takes my waist, and I can feel the rapidly blooming color in my face telling my secrets. "That it helps with your, um…*hunting.*"

He settles me on the ground, only to guide my arm through his as we step up onto the sidewalk planks. "Don't concern yourself about that."

"Why not?"

"I'm a very versatile hunter, little bird," he says, nodding politely at someone who walks by in the opposite direction before he grins. "Besides, having you here will likely bring others closer to my trap."

"Only so they can try to work it out for themselves," I mutter before I can stop myself.

"Cora?" Cypress asks, noticing my growing unease. "What's upsetting you?"

I sigh, frustrated with myself for not holding my tongue while also wishing I could avoid this topic all together. Suddenly running away as Aiden does seems mighty tempting, but since his partner still has my arm captive in his, I'm not sure that's an option.

"People are staring at us," I point out to Cypress, not able to meet his eyes. "With you looking like you do, and me looking like…"

His steps start to slow slightly, until he stops entirely. "Does it bother you how I look?"

My head whips his direction so fast that I nearly injure myself. "How *you* look?"

"I know the scars…"

*The scars.* It had never occurred to me that he might think I see them in a negative light. Not when they are a feature on a face I so like to admire. The same as his clever eyes and his mischievous smile, they are simply…him.

"No, I didn't mean—I think you're beautiful, Cy. I meant *me*."

The temporary concern in his eyes vanishes, giving way to that very smile. "You think I'm beautiful?"

"*No*," I blurt, my face undoubtedly turning a violent shade of crimson right up to the tips of my ears. "I mean, well, yes, I do, but…"

He brings the hand that I have resting on his arm up to his mouth and brushes his lips across my knuckles. In response, my stomach tightens. "Thank you, little bird. I think you're beautiful, too. And I think I like when you call me Cy."

I hadn't even realized I had, but more to the point, I also hadn't intended to pressure him into saying something that isn't true. "You don't have to say that," I tell him quickly, glancing down at my worn dress as we start to walk again. "That I'm beautiful, I mean."

"Why shouldn't I?"

"Because…you know why. Just look at me."

"I do, Cora. To an extent that some might argue borders on unhealthy—"

"I know that we're together a lot—"

"—or even obsessive."

"—but I am very aware of how I appear in comparison, and you don't need to pretend."

"To pretend?"

"Because I don't belong—"

He halts us once more, turning to face me, right in the middle of the sidewalk, so that several people clear their throats in annoyance at having to move around us. Cypress doesn't seem to notice or care, the intensity in his gaze finally putting an end to my rambling before he murmurs softly, "You do belong. You're right where you're meant to be. Now, tell me what is making you think that you aren't."

"You look so nice," I say, gesturing at the neat lapels of his long black coat before moving to the frayed skirt of my dress. "And I look…"

"Clothes?" he asks, my point setting in at long last. "You're worried about your clothes? What people think of them?"

I give him a look of exasperation. "*You* of all people—"

"Ah," he starts, knowing where I'm headed. "But I wear these clothes because *I* like them. Yes, they do also help with certain aspects of my profession, but the main reason is that I, as Aiden so nicely puts it, prefer to dress as a well-moneyed undertaker."

I burst out laughing. "You do *not* look like a—" I take in his usual all-black ensemble, and I do have to agree, there is a certain element that makes him look like he's headed for a funeral. "Well…"

"Don't feel that you must protect my vanity," he says, smiling himself. "I enjoy looking like I shepherd souls as much as Aiden enjoys looking like he shepherds cattle. The point is that if *you* like your clothes, that's all that matters."

"*But*," I argue, "aren't you concerned that no one in this town is going to think you're rich if they're looking down their noses at—"

He pulls me closer with a hand on my waist, and suddenly I'm far less focused on my dress and far more on his proximity. "First of all, certain people will always find a reason to look down on you. Only you can decide if you'll bend low enough to let them." He places his fingers under my chin, tilting my face up as he murmurs close to my ear, "Second, I couldn't care less what you wear, Cora. If it were up to me…well, we will leave that confession for another time, but suffice it to say, when it comes to your clothing, my only *concern* is if *you* like them. Do you?"

"No," I say quietly.

"Then why are you wearing them?"

"They're all I have."

"Mm," he hums. "Well then, let's change that."

Before I have a chance to get my wits about me again, we're moving, walking halfway down the street until Cypress unhooks his arm from mine to instead place a hand at my lower back and steer me into a nearby shop. As the tinkling bell overhead announces our arrival, a pretty, middle-aged woman behind the counter looks up. "Can I assist you?"

"No," I say as Cypress replies, "Yes."

"Perhaps you need a moment?" the shopkeeper asks, unconsciously straightening her white blonde hair and her blue blouse as she looks at Cypress. Then she glances between the two of us in obvious interest. "Or perhaps you're looking for something in particular?"

I shake my head, knowing there cannot be a thing in this boutique that is realistically within my reach. "Cypress, I don't…" I spy a gorgeous, dark green dress in the window, and I nearly bite my lip to keep a sigh from escaping. "I don't have money for new clothes."

"I do," he says easily. "Whatever you want. It's yours."

"I can't ask you to do that," I argue.

"You're not. I'm offering."

"But I don't know when I'd be able to pay you back. And you're already helping me. That's bad enough."

"There is nothing owed to us for helping you find your fugitive. Especially not after what happened…" he responds, shifting his body so that he's shielding me from the shopkeeper's nosey looks. "Cora, I can't help but notice you seem to be under the impression that there is shame in needing help. The only true shame comes in not offering it when you have the means. And I do. Buying you some clothes comes as no burden to me, although you catching your death from chill now that we are this far north certainly would. We're nearly to the mountains."

"The *mountains*?" Admittedly, I'd had to reach for a few extra blankets while sleeping in the wagon over the last week but I simply dismissed it as the changing of the seasons. Apparently too busy watching my travel companions to also watch the evolving scenery. What is *wrong* with me?

"I'll be fine," I mutter. "I'll manage."

"You'll freeze if you have nothing warmer," he says matter-of-factly. "Unless you're planning to borrow clothes from me or Aiden."

"Aiden is *huge*," I say, immediately balking.

"He is indeed," he replies, the corner of his mouth twitching. "Although, I'm confident we could make it fit."

"*How?*" Cypress's eyes look up toward the ceiling as if he's praying for help, and I move quickly to change the subject. "He wouldn't want me wearing his clothes anyway."

"Oh, I'm not so…"

"*Cypress*, really, I'll be fine." I cross my arms against my chest, and he returns the gesture.

"All right, then, little bird, can I convince you if it's an exchange?"

"An exchange?"

"For the help you have given me, you'll let me buy you some clothes."

"For the help I've given you?" I question, struggling to figure out how I've contributed in any remarkable way thus far. "How have I helped?"

He opens his mouth to respond, but then his eyes flick in the direction of the shopkeeper again, apparently debating what to say with an audience so close. I'm reminded of our prior conversation out on the sidewalk.

"You mean with your *hunting*?" I suggest quietly, already somewhat enticed by the idea even though he has yet to actually suggest it. "I can help?"

His eyebrows rise, his expression quickly shifting back to his usual smile. "If you'd like."

"I would," I say, even as my eyes fall to the floor, half nerves and half anticipation as I ask, "You really think I could?"

Cypress holds my chin between his forefinger and thumb again, bringing me back to him. "Oh, little bird, I can speak from personal experience that you're a very effective siren's call."

"Cy…" I want to believe what he's saying. Want to believe that someone like him could see something of value in me.

"I will gladly take your help, Cora, if it will make you feel more comfortable accepting it in return," he says, bending his head close to my ear. "But to be *crystal* clear, it is not a requirement for me to do this for you. And not only because your side of the exchange was already fulfilled long ago." His attention drifts back to the woman at the counter before I can ask what he means. "Ma'am, would you please assist my lovely bride in picking out whatever it is that she wants? No exceptions."

*Bride?* He tucks my hand back into the crook of his arm and walks me closer as I gape up at him. *Did he call me his…?*

"She lost most of her belongings on our journey, so I think a full new wardrobe is in order." He leans down and brushes a kiss against my forehead once we come to a stop at the counter, and I am incapable of speech as he then reaches into his pocketbook and drops multiple large bills on the counter as if they really are of no consequence. "I trust you'll help me make sure she gets everything her heart desires? I don't wish to receive back a dime. Perhaps you could start with that dress in the window?"

"Oh, of course, sir, that won't be a problem *at all*." The shopkeeper is now practically leaping for me along with a selection of fabrics. "I will see to it personally."

"Wait." I try to hold onto Cypress's arm when I feel myself being tugged away. "This is too much. I can't—"

"It's not nearly enough, Cora, I promise you." The very insistent shopkeeper is now looping her arm through mine on my other side, and he only smiles when I look up at him with something close to panic. "I'll be at the cafe across the street when you're done. Try to have some fun."

# CHAPTER 18
## CORA

Although it takes me a minute to latch on to precisely what that word means, in the end, I decide that pretending to be someone else actually is *fun*. Whether that identity be Cypress's *wife* or simply the woman staring back at me from the long mirror, both feel a lot more fun than the person I'm sure I really am.

Because this woman, this one standing in the boutique in a long and elegant dark green dress, with matching ribbons in her shining hair and a happy smile on her face, surely can't be me…right?

Where once gaunt and sallow features marked my face, there is now a softness that hadn't been there before. The rest of my figure, too, has changed to be fuller, stronger, curving in and out from the slope of my neck and chest to my stomach and my hips. I hadn't noticed with how shapeless my clothing had become but now, standing in a new dress with a bodice that hugs me neatly and nips in at the waist before flaring outward into long full skirts, I look, well, I do look…beautiful, as Cypress said.

"Will there be *anything* else?" the shopkeeper, Cynthia, asks beside me. Even as she does, her fingers are still busy, adjusting hems here and there as she turns me in the mirror. "You look wonderful in this dress. I knew you would."

"Thank you," I say, shocked to find myself not wanting to disagree. "You think the color is flattering?"

"It's made for you, although with a husband that has that kind of money, anything can be made for you," she says with a laugh. "Especially when he looks at you like you hung the moon."

I frown. "Why do you say that?"

"The way he looks at you?" she says again. "I know a man who is smitten with his wife when I come across one and that one…" She smiles. "Wait until he sees you."

"You think he'll like it?"

"Oh, bless your heart, you are sweet, aren't you?" she says, patting me gently on the arm. "Yes, he will. Although…if you really want him wrapped around your little finger…"

She disappears and then comes back with a small shining gold pot and a delicate matching brush. "You can have this rouge. I haven't even opened it yet." She twists the top off to reveal a rich red cream. "Here." Cynthia runs the brush through the red and reaches up to carefully paint my lips with it, turning them a vibrant scarlet.

I step closer to the mirror to get a better look, my eyes widening. "You're sure he will like this?"

"For sure and for certain. Men can be very simple creatures." She laughs again. "Little smile, little flutter of your eyelashes, and you'll be their queen."

She steps back, clearly admiring her work. "I can't get you anything else? I think there's still some money left over even after the dresses, the riding clothes, the undergarments, the coat, the boots…" She comes back to me and uses her fingers to curl a few pieces of hair away from my face, and I try to memorize what she's doing, storing it away for the future. She must see me watching, because she asks, "Didn't your mother teach you any of these things?"

"No," I admit. "She wasn't really one to…"

She nods and gently pats my cheek. "Some mothers are like that. Unfortunately, the family we need isn't always the one we're born into." She turns and starts gathering the large amount of bags and totes and hat boxes. "I'd say you've found your way into a good one, though."

"You think?" I ask, beginning to feel badly that she's been given the wrong impression when she's been so kind. And that's even before she says, "I do. Not only men that I can tell when they're in love."

She smiles at me, but my mind is already spinning. Am I in love with Cypress? What about with—

"You come back and visit me again, Cora. You hear?"

"I will," I say, finally returning her smile and hoping I get to mean it. When she offers me back the remaining money, I wave her off. "You keep it."

"Thank you. Maybe next time we can get your husband some new things as well," she says, helping me to the door since I'm comically weighted down with purchases. "Never seen a man wear so much black."

I bite the inside of my cheek, still thinking of the way Cypress said Aiden describes his clothes, but it's a losing battle as I step out into the street and the first laugh breaks free. The rest unable to be contained until I'm fighting my way inside the cafe with my purchases. Well, really *Cypress's* purchases.

"There you are, little bird," I hear him say as soon as I'm inside, already lifting bags from my arms so that I can breathe while the sounds of conversation and busy plates and utensils fill my ears. "I'm delighted to see you actually followed my advice."

"I did," I say, still smiling as I straighten and turn toward him. Not exactly a grand entrance, but at least he had no trouble knowing it was me. "Thank you again. I don't know how I'll…"

For the first time since I've met him, Cypress appears to be speechless. His eyes growing dark as they travel over every detail of my face then down my dress and back up before hanging for several long moments on my lips. Remembering the red, I clap my hand over my mouth before muttering, "Sorry, is it too much? Cynthia suggested it."

He clears his throat and gently pries my hand away so he can see again. "Cynthia is the shopkeeper?"

"Yes."

"And the rouge was her idea?"

"Yes. She said…she said you might like it."

"Did she? I'm not sure I paid Cynthia enough."

"Oh, no, there was money left over. But I let her keep it, since you said you didn't want it back…" I start to grow restless under his gaze. "Do you not like it? You look…angry."

He shakes his head. "Wrong emotion, little bird." He swallows, dragging a hand over his face. "You didn't happen to run into Aiden on the street?"

"No, why?"

"I would hate to have missed it." He guides us to a table near the door. "Here, let's sit down."

I walk beside him, watching him closely as he sets down the bags and pulls out a chair for me to sit. Once I'm settled, he does the same, his hand automatically claiming mine where it rests on the table, in full view of everyone. His thumb rubs soothingly over the back of my hand, my wrist, although I'm not sure if it's for my benefit or for his.

"Cypress…are you upset? Do you not like the clothes?"

"No, no," he says, moving his chair even closer and tucking a stray ringlet behind my ear. "No, I'm not upset. I apologize." He lets out a low chuckle. "I think I simply…underestimated."

"I told you it was too much. I can take the things back."

"They are *lovely*. And they are lovely *on* you," he says, though the words might be more reassuring if it weren't for the way his free hand is gripping his thigh beneath the table. "And you're sure Aiden hasn't seen you?"

"No, I don't even know where he is. Why are you asking? Will *he* be upset?"

"Not at you," Cypress says quickly and then, sensing my distress, he smiles. "You look stunning, Cora. Not that you didn't before, but now…" He studies my face again, my dress, before bringing my hand to his lips and pressing a kiss to the back. The second time he's done that today, and I think I like it more each time. "Do *you* like the clothes? You look like you do."

"I do," I say, still unsure about his reaction. "I think they're pretty."

"Very pretty," he agrees.

"So I can still help?" I ask, trying to get back on solid footing. "I'll make a good, um, siren?"

He grins. "An irresistible one. Look." He inclines his head toward the rest of the room, and as I let my eyes sweep the other customers, I do indeed see quite a few heads turned our direction.

"They're probably wondering how one person could have so many packages," I say, squirming a bit under the attention.

"They're wondering about *you*, Cora," he replies swiftly. "I can assure you, I did not have nearly as much interest before you arrived." He leans in as if to whisper in my ear, but instead, he takes a deep inhale, his nose brushing against the curve of my neck. "As I said, irresistible."

I turn my head toward him, my mouth stopping a hair's breadth away from his, and I can't help but let my eyes fall there as his had with mine. "Cy?"

"Yes?"

"Just now, when I asked if you were angry, you said I had the wrong emotion," I say, my voice barely above a whisper. "What's the right one?"

He hums, the hand that had been on his thigh coming up to cup my jaw, his fingers skimming into the hair at the back of my neck, tangling in the strands so that my head is gently tugged back. And suddenly, all my lovely new clothes feel too tight, too constricting, and all I want to do is dissolve into the way it feels when he touches me.

"Oh, little bird," he murmurs, my breath catching in my throat when he traces his thumb down the side of it. "I think you already know."

# CHAPTER 19
## CORA

Aiden is already back at the wagon when Cypress and I arrive, busy putting away a few supplies that he'd restocked while in town. He looks up when he hears us coming, glancing first at Cypress and then at me. He goes still.

"Cora," he says once I'm within earshot, standing there with his arms crossed until I'm close enough for him to take my reins. "You look…" His eyes shoot back to Cypress. "Do some shopping while in town?"

Cypress shrugs. "She did not have a coat."

Aiden's gaze sweeps up and down my dress, catching at the way it's ridden up slightly on either side while I'm on horseback to expose tall, laced black boots. He clears his throat. "Still doesn't seem to."

Cypress leans back and lightly taps some of the bags he had secured to both Cerberus's and Tess's saddles. "Never fear. Plenty more here."

I bite my bottom lip, wondering if the clear irritation is what

Cypress had in mind when he'd talked about Aiden's reaction back at the cafe. Surely not, since I can't imagine anyone looking forward to causing someone temper, although if there were such a person, it would be Cypress.

"It's so I can help," I add, trying to explain, and Aiden whips his head to stare at me as if I struck him.

"Help. With. What?" he says, voice low.

"Cypress. With his card games."

I had been attempting to reduce the tension crackling between the three of us, but apparently, I failed spectacularly.

"Absolutely not," Aiden snaps, reaching up to take me by the waist and pull me down off Tess's back. He doesn't release me once I'm on the ground as he usually does, his hands flexing at my sides. "You're not going anywhere near that."

"It's not up to you," I say back, my own hands balling into fists as I glare up at him. "If Cypress wants me there—"

"*No.*" His eyes drop to my mouth, and he shakes his head. "You don't know what you're getting into, Cora."

"Really? Why don't you explain it to me, then? Since you seem to know *everything*." Out of the corner of my eye, I see Cypress dismount, but I'm still focused on Aiden. "I am so *sick* of you telling me what to do."

"I wouldn't have to if you had a lick of sense," Aiden snarls back, stepping close enough that his body presses into mine. "I'm only trying to keep you safe."

"I *will* be safe. I'll be with Cypress. I don't need you to keep—I don't need you hovering over me one minute, only to disappear the next. I don't—" I shove at him, pushing him back so that I can breathe. I can't *breathe* when he gets this close. "I don't *need* you."

Aiden's jaw tenses, his eyes flicking between me and Cypress before he simply says, "Fine." Then he strides toward Helios.

My heart sinks, regret and guilt immediately swallowing me up. "Aiden, wait…"

He's already gone, taking off without looking back. I turn to Cypress, watching him watch him leave. "I'm so sorry. I didn't…"

"It's all right," he says, doing his best to give me a reassuring smile as he gives my hand a gentle squeeze. "I'll go after him." I nod, and within minutes, I'm watching Cypress leave, too. Hoping he will reappear as quickly as he vanishes into the landscape.

But he doesn't.

Hours later, I'm still waiting, back in my old clothes, huddled by the fire that Aiden started and that I have witnessed die down to embers. All I can think is, what if neither of them comes back? Surely both of them have had enough of the disruption I've caused, although logically I know they will at least have to come back for their wagon.

By the time the moon has risen overhead, I can't sit still anymore, and with nothing else to occupy my time, I finally get up and start wandering in the direction of the creek that Cypress led me to this morning to water the horses.

Dirt and thick brush crunch beneath my boots and tangle in my skirts as I walk, wondering why I said what I did to Aiden. Not only was it hurtful, but it was also untrue. I *do* need him. I know I do. And sometimes it scares me how much when he seems to need me so little in return. I feel worse the more I think about it. The more I wonder if I have already ruined the first thing in my life that has ever felt like it could be something more than what I've had.

That's when I hear their voices.

"I've already said my piece, Cy." Aiden's voice breaks through the darkness first, and I realize they must be just beyond the pocket of tall trees in front of me, down by the very water I'd been headed to myself. I creep closer until I can barely make them out before dropping down into the brush, not caring that I will likely be covered with fallen leaves and soil when I stand.

"Don't press me," Aiden continues after another moment, and I think I can tell which figure is which by the way they move, as if Aiden's ever-present hat isn't enough of an indication.

"*My wolf.*" I frown in confusion when I hear Cypress's voice, never having heard him refer to Aiden with that nickname. Nor have I ever heard the touch of tenderness in the way he says it. "Please reconsider the course you seem so intent to follow. All I'm asking you is to try to think about if—"

"I am right on this," Aiden interrupts, his back to Cypress. "Deep down, you know I am."

"No, afraid I am not inclined to agree."

There's a scrape and drag of boots in dirt as Aiden turns toward Cypress, stopping his advance close enough to Cypress that they are nearly touching. Then I'm waiting again, not daring to move, as the two of them square off, and I know I *should* go. Leave them to their conversation, but I've never seen them like this. And I want to.

"She can't stay with us," Aiden states at last, and I'm not even surprised to hear him say it out loud, even if it inspires something akin to grief in me. "She deserves better than what we can give her."

*You're wrong,* I think, wanting now to also hear his explanation for *why* he thinks that. For how he could ever say I deserve better than either of them.

"She deserves the choice," Cypress counters, and the emotion in his voice, spilling over on my behalf, makes my chest hurt. "You want her to end up kept as some other man's possession? Back in that city where you're so certain she'll be safer?"

"*No.* No, of course not. I can't…it's too much." Aiden's hand comes up to knead the back of his neck, then switches to sweep back his hair beneath his hat. "It's too much, Cy, and whatever price there will be for it, I don't want to pay it."

"Wolf…"

Aiden puts his back to him again, and after a few more moments, Cypress shakes his head and starts to turn away. I think that will be the end of it then, that they will both go their separate ways, and that I'll have to figure out how to get back to the camp without either of them seeing me, but then—

Aiden pivots, his hand reaching out and grabbing Cypress's arm to yank him back to him, and then his mouth is against his, a desperate kiss that is immediately accepted and returned as Cypress's hands fist in Aiden's shirt.

I gasp, burying my face in my sleeve to keep another sound from escaping, even if it can't suppress the *need* that I feel whipping through me as I start my retreat. Both of them too wrapped up in each other to watch me run.

The fire is all but gone by the time I reach camp again, but I hardly notice it when I already feel like I'm burning up from the inside out. I can't stop touching my fingers to my mouth, can't stop thinking about what it would feel like to have that with someone. To know without question how much you're *wanted*. My gaze keeps drifting their direction, a compass finding true north no matter which way my thoughts turn.

And I know, from that moment on, there's no going back.

# CHAPTER 20
## CORA

I dream about them. I think maybe I've *been* dreaming about them, only last night was so vivid that, now that I'm awake, I'm having trouble distinguishing reality from the dream.

One thing I know for certain is that I'd seen Aiden and Cypress collide last night while I was hiding in the dark. Seen the hunger, but also the immediate meeting of need, letting me know that hadn't been the first time they'd reached for each other like that.

Not the first. Nor would it be the last.

The way Aiden's hand grasped Cypress's arm. The way Cypress's fingers tangled in Aiden's shirt. The way their mouths met… I see it every time I close my eyes. Remember the way it made me feel.

I'd never seen two people kiss like that. Any affection between my parents had been limited to my mother's begrudging acceptance of my father's appeasing peck to her cheek. Any experience I'd had with boys my age had been limited to holding hands in secret on the walk home. A momentary and nervous brush of fingers that ended almost as soon as it started.

This was nothing like that.

All I keep thinking is that I want to know what it felt like. That I want to be the one Aiden grabbed for. To be the one Cypress pulled closer. To be caught in the middle of that storm. To figure out what it would do to that hum in my blood that I feel whenever I am near them.

And I am likely to go on wanting…

At my side, Cypress is once again riding with me into town, not a hair out of place on his pretty head, not a suggestion on his calm face that anything is amiss. Or that Aiden never came back last night.

Not long after I'd returned, I crawled into the wagon and into my bed. Unable to sleep as I listened for them, and it was nearly morning when I finally did hear someone approach, a single set of footsteps and a deep sigh signaling their arrival before the figure sank down by the spent campfire.

I don't think either of us slept, although neither of us would admit it when I emerged a few hours later, circled round, and climbed up to sit beside Cypress on the wagon bench. Leaning our shoulders against one another with our eyes on the horizon, and for the first time leaving so much left unsaid.

It's why I wasn't surprised when Cypress eventually suggested that afternoon that we go into town, apparently tired of pacing the same path in the dirt when entertainment could be found elsewhere. Needing the same, I'd been dressed and ready with Tess tacked in less than an hour.

As we arrive this time, I am certain that wearing my new green dress again makes me look more the part at Cypress's side, but after what I'd seen, I am even less convinced that the part is mine to play. Obviously, there is something between Aiden and Cypress, something that runs even deeper than the years-long partnership that I'd thought tethered them to one another. It isn't something I want to harm, to risk tarnishing when it clearly means so much to both of them…and when one of them also *clearly* does not want me around.

Nor, I'm fairly certain, does he want me in this saloon.

"Are you sure this is a good idea?" I mutter to Cypress as he leads me inside through the front doors, my hand tight on his arm.

"No," he says, bending to talk in my ear as the first wave of sound hits us. "I'm not sure it is."

"Then what are we doing?"

"Hoping history repeats," he says cryptically, inclining his head to people as we pass. "Stay close to me."

I tuck myself into his side, partly because it's what I want to do and partly because there's no other option. Inside, the tables are packed tight, a constant rotation of people coming and going from their seats as they find new sources of amusement, and I can understand now why Mrs. Jensen believed I would only find trouble in a place like this.

It's intoxicating. The lively music. The girls dancing in their bright dresses and flying skirts. The shouts and calls of people playing at cards and conversation.

"What do you think?" Cypress asks, undoubtedly sensing my excitement as I crane my neck this way and that for a better look.

"I like it," I say, smiling up at him.

He grins back. "I always have, too."

He finds us a table right in the center of all the activity, and he gives me the seat with the best view while positioning his own chair near to touching, his body leaning over mine in a way that feels as protective as it is practical. "Shall we go hunting, little bird?" he murmurs in my ear, and I nod, feeling my stomach tighten. "Tell me what you see."

I look everywhere at once, too easily swayed by a burst of movement to focus on any single detail. "I don't know," I say. "There's so much happening."

"Take it a piece at a time. A table at a time."

I start at the table nearest us, the group of friends there exchanging stories as well as laughs over drinks. Then I move to the next, to the smaller gathering of three gentlemen who look far more focused on business than pleasure. To the next, where an argument appears to be getting a little too animated. Sure enough, they're escorted out a few moments later when the first glass breaks.

It's while I'm following their exit that I see him. Tall, light gray hair, a bandana around his neck, and dark eyes under the wide brim of a hat that looks brand new. He's already engaged in a game of cards at his table, and given the large pile of money in front of him, I'd guess he's winning. Not that it seems to be improving his mood.

"Stupid girl," he's snapping at a young woman who is offering him a whiskey on a tray. "I said I wanted two fingers of whiskey. Does that look like two fingers to you? You trying to fucking cheat me?" She shakes her head, clearly apologetic as she backs away, but he yanks her back and smacks her thigh before loudly telling her that she'll have to make it up to him later. As soon as he lets her go, she hurries away.

"Him," I say, directing Cypress's gaze. "That one."

Cypress starts to observe him, his eyes drifting around the room here and there so that it isn't obvious, but always returning to the man at the table. Narrowing when the waitress returns with a new whiskey and receives similar treatment. "That one," he agrees.

# CHAPTER 21
## CORA

*"Gentlemen."* Cypress's voice booms as we approach the table, his expression all inviting smiles. "How are you this evening?"

The gray-haired gentleman looks up, eyes Cypress, then says, "This is a private game."

"Course, course it is," Cypress agrees, his words sounding almost slurred although I know he hasn't had a drop to drink. "But surely there's room for *one* more?"

"Piss off, would you?" the man replies.

"Oh, come now," Cypress pleads, placing a hand on the man's shoulder. "My money is good, I swear it. I can play."

The man knocks his hand away then stands up to his full height, and with the way Cypress is currently slouching as if cowed, the man at least gets to think he has the advantage in size. "I told you—"

"Sorry," I say, stepping out from behind Cypress and tugging at his arm with an embarrassed and apologetic grimace. "I'm so sorry. We'll go."

I start back toward the doors, dragging Cypress with me, but the man's arm shoots out to grab mine almost as soon as our backs are turned. I look up at Cypress and see his eyes narrow at the point of contact, temper flashing, but there's no trace of it left when we face the man again, especially once he offers, "We might have a spot after all. Two, if your girl will sit with us as well." The other men at the table seem less certain, but he's already waving over chairs and holding out his hand to shake. "Name's David. What's yours?"

David looks at me when he asks, but Cypress is the one to answer. "Cypress. And this lovely flower is my wife Cora." He gazes down at me with a soft smile. "Gorgeous, isn't she?"

I blush, not having to act when the affection in his gaze looks so genuine.

"Certainly is," David agrees, holding out a chair between him and Cypress for me to sit. "Hope you really are a betting man…Cinder, was it?"

Cypress nods cheerfully, not bothering to correct him as he fumbles to pull his pocketbook out of his coat. Every man at the table leans forward when they see the thick stack of money. "How much to deal me in?"

"Oh." David reaches forward and plucks several of the larger bills out before tossing them in the center. "That'll do for now." David's gaze turns to me, his eyes scanning me up and down, holding at the rouge on my mouth the same way that Cypress and Aiden did, although the feeling it inspires in me is entirely different. "We'll see where the night leads us," David says, running his thumb across his tongue before he picks up his cards. "Won't we?"

Beneath the table, Cypress's hand finds mine and gives it a quick squeeze. I squeeze back to let him know I'm fine as I smile and bat my eyes at the man on my other side the way Cynthia had mentioned yesterday. Judging by the way David chuckles and shakes his head, he seems to like it. *Interesting.*

Not long after the dealer brings Cypress in, the first hand gets played to its conclusion. And, as I expected he would, Cypress loses fantastically.

"Must be having an off night," he says, frowning at me in apology. "One more hand and then we'll go."

"What's the rush?" David asks, pulling in another sizable stack of winnings. "You have some place better to be?"

"Well…" Cypress glances at me. "It's supposed to be our honeymoon."

"That right? Well, she's having fun, aren't you, darlin'?"

*Aren't you, darlin'?* As soon as the words leave his mouth, I could swear they were in Jake's voice rather than David's, and I jerk away as the back of David's finger grazes my bare upper arm where he thinks Cypress can't see. The way he goes tense next to me tells me he does.

"Are you cold, little bird?" Cypress asks me, covering my reaction and deterring David at the same time by placing his arm around my shoulders as he bends his head close to my ear. "Do you want to go?"

I shake my head subtly, my smile back on my face so we look to everyone else like the two newlyweds we are pretending to be. Stealing a private conversation in a public place. "I'm fine. Besides, if we go now, you won't get your money back."

"I don't give a damn about the money, Cora. I could be losing ten times this sum and the question would be the same. Do you want to go?"

At my other side, David gives a grunt of impatience at us keeping him waiting. "Your turn, Cinder. Unless your *wife* is already bringing you to heel." He laughs, but given that the others at the table have already lost nearly the amount Cypress just mentioned, he's the only one.

Beneath the table, I find Cypress's hand and squeeze it again. Wordlessly letting him know that I'm still all right. That I still want to help, even if he seems to be having second thoughts. I also, now more than ever, want to see David lose.

"What do you do for work?" I ask him, leaning my elbow against the table and giving David what I hope is a sweet smile as Cypress plays his hand and the game resumes.

"Used to be in the oil business," he replies, chest swelling with pride.

I let my eyes go big as I say, "I can't think of anything more fitting for a man like you."

Next to me, Cypress coughs, turning away before coming back to his hand with a barely concealed smile. "How much to call?"

David gives him an annoyed look. "Thought you said you could play, ya fool. Barely seem to know how to hold your cards from where I'm sitting."

Cypress blinks at his hand, turning it front and back and flashing three of a kind in the process. "What's wrong with how I'm holding them?"

Needless to say, Cypress does not win that time either. Or the next. Or the next. In fact, we are on our sixth or seventh hand with a sizable pile in the center of the table when Cypress and David become the only two still remaining, along with the dealer.

"Raise you," Cypress says, tossing a few more bills from his pocketbook into the center in response to David's most recent bet. Something the man barely registers while he's busy tugging on one of the ringlets falling over the back of my chair.

I turn my head, pretending that it's to smile at him again when it's really to pull my hair free from his grasp. "It's your turn now, I believe," I say, making my voice unnaturally high. I'm getting the hang of this.

"Think you're right." David reaches for my hair again, not even bothering to look before pushing everything he has into the center. "Tell me something. What's that husband of yours going to do when he runs out of money, do you think?" I shrug, continuing to smile and fighting the urge to let my lip curl in disgust. "Might have to get creative with our wagers in the next round."

"Oh," I start to say, before my gaze catches on movement at a table in the back corner. I freeze, my voice hardly above a whisper as I finish saying, "I don't think it will come to that."

*Aiden.* He's there, nearly swallowed up by the shadowed corner, but I know without question that it's him. His broad shoulders are hunched as he sits with his elbows on the table, his dark eyes on me from under the brim of his hat. *How long has he been there? How did I not see him sooner?*

"All right, show your cards," the dealer says, but I don't even think to look, my eyes still on Aiden. He leans forward, and it's like I can feel the way he is following the path of David's wandering fingertips as they once again move up my arm, over my shoulder, along the side of my neck. Aiden stands.

Then everything explodes.

"The fuck is this?" David is shouting, jarring me back to the table. "The fuck did you get that hand?"

Next to me, Cypress has laid down a series of matching cards that I'm inclined to believe are good. *Very* good, based on the fact that he is now grinning like a cat who just ate every single one of David's canaries.

"Guess it was our turn to get lucky," Cypress tells him, laughing as he swiftly helps me up and tucks me behind him. A safe distance from David and a few other men from the saloon who have appeared at the first sign of an impending brawl.

"Think our friend here has had enough," Cypress informs them, tipping each handsomely with his winnings. "Perhaps you can help him find his way to his accommodations."

"You fucking *cheat*," David says, pointing a finger at Cypress as he's strong-armed out. "He's a fucking cheat!"

"Such a shame. Why gamble if you can't afford to lose?" Cypress asks of the remaining onlookers, their suspicion immediately evaporating the moment he offers, "How about I buy everyone a round of drinks? As an apology for the disturbance?"

He grins at me again when there is a deafening cheer, then leans down, cupping my face in his hands. He brushes the barest hint of a kiss against the corner of my mouth. "You did so well, Cora. Perfect girl," he murmurs. "Are you sure you're all right?"

I manage a nod.

"Would you do it again?"

"Yes," I say, smiling back at him and meaning every bit of it, because as much as being close to David had made my skin crawl at times, seeing him get his comeuppance made up for it. Would have made me *giddy* if not for…

When Cypress turns for the bar, I look once more at the back corner, my heart sinking when I find Aiden gone until the moment I catch sight of him heading toward the rear doors.

"*Cypress.*" I try to get his attention but he's too surrounded by hearty back slaps and words of thanks for me to break through. I hesitate for a fraction of a second, torn between staying and going after Aiden, but when I see him glance over his shoulder in my direction before disappearing through the door, my decision is made.

I move, weaving through the crowd of people clamoring for free drinks, barely able to take a breath until I'm out the door after him and into the alley behind the saloon.

"Aiden," I call, looking up and down the dark street. "*Aiden.*"

There's no response, and I'm about to head back inside, disappointed, when I finally see a figure appear. "There you are. I—" The figure comes closer, stepping into the low lantern light, and fear rips through me. I immediately turn, lunging for the door and yanking it open.

But David is faster. Rushing forward to slam a hand over my head to shut it again. The wood reverberates with a deafening smack as the sound from inside cuts off.

"If it isn't the thief's little wife," he says, leaning down close to my face. "Not so lucky after all, if you are out here on your own."

"She isn't," replies another deep voice, paired with the click of a pistol. The long shining barrel comes to rest neatly against the side of David's head. "You touch her again, and it'll be the last thing you do on this earth."

David puts his hands up, backing away and moving his glare from me to Aiden. "You don't look like the fella who cheated me at cards," he says. "What stake do you have in this?"

"One third," Aiden answers coolly. "Cora? Are you—"

"I'm not hurt," I reply, barely getting the sentence out before Cypress comes bursting out the back door.

He draws up short, takes one look at the assembled players, and raises his eyebrows. "Well, look at that, history does repeat."

"Cypress," Aiden barks. "Not a good time."

"Ah, I get it," David spits, still holding his arms up. "All three of you are in this together. Running a little scam, are ya? Well, I'm not going to be had by it. I want my fucking money back."

"You don't appear to be in a position to demand anything," Cypress points out. "Plus, I have about thirty witnesses in there that will say they saw me win fair and square."

"I'll bet," David says. "'Cause you fucking bribed them."

Cypress, ever the instigator, shrugs. "So?"

David lets loose a stream of curse words that would be enough to make a grown man blush, barely pausing when Cypress calmly warns him, "There is a lady present."

As if only now remembering I'm here, David rounds on me, and I take a step back, colliding with the alley wall made nearly smooth from years of compiling wanted posters. His gaze fixes on my face, then a spot behind me, his eyes widening and his mouth opening again to speak before he drops. Hitting the ground with a heavy thud after receiving a sharp blow to the back of his head from the butt of a pistol.

"Fucking perfect," Aiden mutters, stowing his gun away before toeing the unconscious man with the tip of his boot. David groans in response but doesn't get up.

"Still alive," Cypress points out.

Aiden glares at him. "Really astute observation there, Cy. Thank you."

"What are we going to do with him?" I ask, creeping closer myself.

"Leave him," Aiden says. "Someone inside will hear if we shoot him, and it's already fucking crowded enough back here." He looks at me. "You have your knife?"

I grimace, dreading to admit, "No."

"Course not." Aiden lifts his hat and gives the ends of his hair a firm tug. "Course not." He turns to Cypress. "How much did you take from him?"

Cypress tilts his head back and forth, considering. "Hardly anything."

"Would he agree?"

"Who's to say? Certainly not him now that he is concussed."

"You'd better *hope* he's concussed," Aiden says, pointing an accusatory finger at his partner. "We're going home."

"Aiden…" I start to say, and he doesn't even turn as he tells me, "Later."

"But—"

"*Cora*, trust me, I've things to say to you as well, but they're going to have to wait."

I press my lips together, not sure I want to hear whatever it is, but I still follow as he leads Cypress and me out of the alley. Then barely make a peep of protest when he lifts me up onto his horse instead of my own.

"Aiden," I say when he swings up behind me, his body surrounding mine as he reaches forward for the reins. "I'm sorry," I tell him softly, turning my head to try to see him, because I am sorry. I'm so sorry for all of it. "I'm…"

"Later," he says again, his forehead pressing temporarily against my temple. "Please, Cora, just—not here."

"Okay," I agree, leaning back into him once Helios starts to walk forward, unable to avoid it once we pick up the pace. The trail back stretches out in front of us, and knowing this could be the last time I get to be this close to him, all I can think is…I hope later never comes.

# CHAPTER 22
## AIDEN

*Well, look at that, history does repeat.*

God, I really fucking hate that he's right, that I'd thought the same when I stepped into that alley and saw Cora cornered.

The first time I'd seen Cypress, I'd been nursing a whiskey at the bar, watching him con a table full of men who thought they knew better. I couldn't take my eyes off him, couldn't understand why everyone else missed that he was playing them far more deftly than he was playing the cards.

More than once I thought I saw him look my direction, too. The slightest hesitation before he drew a card, a momentary delay before he raised a bet. I'll be the first to admit that I stayed there all night to see if he'd do it again, lingered to watch him finally play his winning hand. He'd looked at me one last time before he slipped out the front door, and I had followed.

I've been following ever since. And Cypress has been following me, too.

Last night, he came looking for me, another discussion that had turned into an argument until he started to walk away, and I'd panicked at the thought of losing him, too. Losing him because he doesn't understand…

The truth is, it's not that he doesn't understand. He does. He just understands it differently. And that hasn't changed. No matter how many times we've argued and no matter how many times that argument has ended with us pushing and pulling at each other in an entirely different way.

Last night, I let myself go, tried to spend all my frustration and my anxiety and my want. Tried to bury it until I had nothing left, only for Cypress to grasp me firmly by the back of the neck while my heart was still pounding, forcing my eyes to meet his.

"It's not selfish to want what is meant for you, Aiden," he'd told me, his tone commanding and insistent. "It's not *too much* to think that you might deserve it. She was ours before I ever stepped into that bar. And we were hers long before we ever found her in that town."

"Fate?" I jerked away from his grasp as I glared at him. Even as part of me wanted so badly to believe. "You're going to risk her life because you think it's fate? Fuck, Cy, what if you're wrong?"

He is wrong. He has to be. And I am, too, for wanting what I shouldn't. I already have Cypress. Already have more than I ever thought I'd get. How much more can I possibly take before God starts taking it back?

It's what I've been asking myself every morning. From the moment I start running as soon as there's enough light to see. Away from her. Away from him. Away from myself. I keep running in hopes that each morning will be different. That it will work.

It never does. I always end up stopping, shouting into my fists as I try to drown out the sound of my name on her tongue. *My* name. The one she murmurs every night while she sleeps. While she cries. Tossing and turning like something's still chasing her, and I'd protect her from it if only I could see it, too.

But I can't. All I can do is sit with her, because it seems to help her. Because it's what always seems to help Cypress. Because it's what used to help me.

Don't have to worry about the things waiting in the dark if you never sleep, and I'm not sure I have since that day I met her in Preston, since that first night after I heard her and crawled into the hayloft to find her huddled up alone and crying in her sleep on the floor. Since I started splitting my time between the stable and the boarding house, between the wagon and the campfire.

I know it's my fault. I know I'm the reason everyone is still holding back, keeping to their separate corners. But it's getting harder and harder to keep that line drawn in the sand without wanting to cross it.

I want things to be different. I want the reason my name is on her lips to be different. I want her to say it while I have my mouth on hers. While I have her close without having to let go. While she's next to me, under me. While I'm drinking down the sound of her *needing* me over and over even though she says she doesn't.

"*Aiden.*"

I open my eyes at the sound of her voice, not even really sure when we arrived back at camp, too lost in holding her while we rode to realize that the time had come again for me to let her go. And I'm too fucking weak to keep myself from taking one more deep breath of the scent of her hair and the feel of her soft body against mine before I do.

"I'm sorry," she's saying softly, her voice hitching over the words. "I'm so sorry, Aiden."

God, I want her so bad it aches. Want to know her. Want to touch her. Want to protect her so that she never has to be scared again. Never has to run again from things in the dark.

"Cora." I can feel her shaking, though she's trying not to. "Baby, please don't cry."

"I'm—I'm sorry. I'm sorry for what I said. I didn't mean it. I only wanted—please don't make me leave."

I should. Or I should find a way to convince her it's what's right, convince Cy and pray that someday he'll forgive me.

He's so sure. He's always so sure about everything. And I am always so...

"I don't want to leave," she's saying, so soft and quiet. "I want to stay with you. I want to stay with you and Cypress. Please, don't make me go."

I know if I look right now I'll see Cypress already standing on the ground, waiting for this to all play out, waiting to see if history really does repeat. God, I really hate that he gets to be right.

He'll never let me live it down.

My left hand reaches to cup her jaw, my thumb tracing the tear tracks along her cheek as I turn her face to look up at mine. "I don't want you to go," I murmur to her, brushing my mouth over her forehead as her eyes drift closed. "Don't cry, Cora, please. I fucking hate it."

She laughs softly, her hand coming up to cover mine as she sinks back into me even more, the smallest show of trust that I don't feel like I've come close to earning. "I hate it, too."

"I'm only trying to protect you," I tell her. "That's all I've been trying to do."

"I know." She sighs, her breath warm against my palm. "I know you are."

"I've never wanted you to go," I tell her, ready to hit my knees when she turns her head a bit, leaning the side of her face into my touch, and I can't stop myself. Can't help but drag my thumb across her full lower lip instead of her cheek. When it comes away red, I hope it fucking stains.

"I like this paint," I tell her, wondering if, as close as we're sitting, she can tell just how much I like it. "Looks pretty."

She smiles, and looks up at me with those green eyes that have possessed me since the first time I saw her. "Seemed like it made you angry when you first saw it."

"No, sweetheart." I'm leaning closer to her but telling myself there's still time to pull back. "I wasn't angry."

"Wrong emotion?" she says, and she almost sounds like she's teasing me now.

"Yeah, something like that." I drag my thumb through it again, smear it on her jaw, on the side of her neck, on all the places I can reach that I'd like to have my mouth on. "I don't want you to go, Cora."

Her eyes are fixed on my mouth, and we're close enough that all one of us would have to do is give in. "*Please*, Aiden, I…" Her gaze flicks away from me to find Cypress where he stands nearby, still waiting, still watching. Still so fucking satisfied with himself. God fucking damn him to hell. "I want you. I want…"

I chuckle, tipping her head back so she can keep her eyes on him as I press my lips to her racing pulse. "You want me, but you want him, too, Cora? That what you're trying to say?"

Her fingers find the fabric of my shirt, her lips parting on a soft whine.

"You want us both? You *need* us both?" I tangle my fingers in those long curls, bringing her focus back to me as my mouth hovers over hers. "Say it, Cora."

"I…" She tries to erase the distance between us, her eyes flashing when I don't give her what she wants, and I'm so close to saying, *Fuck it.* Likely would have already if I wasn't still trying to figure out how I ever thought I stood a fucking chance.

"Say it," I tell her again, grinning this time as I finally accept my fate. "Say it, Cora."

Her eyes meet Cypress's, then mine. "I want you both."

# CHAPTER 23
## CORA

Aiden's mouth crushes against mine. Nothing about the kiss gentle or soft or sweet. There's no hesitancy left in him now, no thought of retreat. Just a claim that manages to make me feel like he's giving me as much as he's taking.

"Dammit, Cora," he mutters against my mouth, his teeth nipping at my bottom lip to get me to gasp, to get me to open wider for him before he soothes the sting with his tongue. "Should've known you'd taste this fucking good."

I feel like I'm racing to keep up with him, to try to figure out the rhythm of what he's doing, the way he's moving with me, but it's all happening so fast. So fast, and at the same time, not nearly fast enough.

"Cy," Aiden groans, moving down my jaw and giving me my first true chance to catch my breath. "Take her."

Strong hands find my waist, Cypress immediately lifting me off

Helios's back and into his arms, not giving me a chance to mourn the loss of Aiden's touch before he's replaced it.

"Hello again, little bird," he murmurs with a smile, carrying me against his chest with my legs around his waist and my arms around his shoulders as he walks toward the ashes of last night's campfire. "How about you stay out here with us tonight, hm?"

I nod eagerly, content to never go back in the wagon again if that means I'll get more of this. More of Cypress's nose brushing against mine as he holds me to him and starts to kiss me, too, slow and deep as if I'm something for him to explore. One hand on my waist to hold me secure and one drifting over the fabric of my dress, his fingertips trailing slowly along my sides, my arms, my shoulders—like he's memorizing me. So different from the way Aiden touches me, but the intention feels the same.

"Put her down here," Aiden is saying, and I'm dimly aware of the way he's flattening out the bedrolls behind us, giving Cypress a place to lay me down just where he directed.

"So commanding," Cypress whispers in my ear as he settles us on the cushioned ground, making me laugh as he holds himself over me. Then he kisses his way down the side of my throat and teases, "As if I'm the one who makes him suffer."

"You are the one who makes me suffer, Cy," Aiden replies. "Don't act like you aren't."

Cypress lifts his head and grins. "Don't act like you don't enjoy it."

Aiden rolls his eyes, but then he's lying down and reaching for me, tugging me away from Cypress who is grinning when he turns onto his side to observe us better.

"So fucking pretty," Aiden tells me, one of his hands in my hair and one on my hip to pull me near so that I'm tight against him, and I can see him better now than I could when we were on horseback, see the way he's looking at me like he really doesn't have any plan of letting me go. "We'll go slow, all right?"

"What if I don't—" His mouth captures mine again, demanding in direct contrast to his words. "What if I don't want to go slow?"

He groans, kisses me harder. "Cora, I'm hanging on by a thread here. Have some fucking mercy."

"No," I say, still stumbling over how to kiss him back just as fiercely, still figuring out where he ends and I begin. "Don't want to do that either."

He almost laughs as his mouth moves to the curve of my neck, his teeth scraping against my skin in warning before digging in hard enough to leave a mark. This time my only response is a small moan as I try to drag him even closer.

"Our little bird," Cypress murmurs from my other side, smiling when I turn my face toward him and humming that same song he always does before his lips brush mine. "At last."

# CHAPTER 24
## CORA

It's still early when I wake, the morning light barely managing to illuminate my surroundings, and I smile happily as I take them in.

To my left, there's a head of perfectly styled black hair made messy by my fingers. A face accented with the occasional thin scar, a strong nose over a proud sinner's mouth. Intelligent eyes that are currently closed as he slumbers. *Cypress.*

The arm that I have across his chest as I lie on my side is rising and falling with each of his deep breaths, his left hand fully enveloping my right. Spread out on his back like he doesn't have a care in the world, and he probably doesn't.

To my right, there's a heated exhale into my hair, a strong well-muscled arm banding around my waist. I'm curling into the curve of his body as he surrounds me, protecting me even in his sleep. My fingers are tightly intertwined with his where they rest against my abdomen, as if afraid that if we don't hold on, one of us might slip away. *Aiden*.

I squeeze his hand, testing to be sure he really is still here, and he grunts, his voice low and gravelly as he mutters, "Morning, baby."

"Morning," I murmur back, the way his mustache scratches against the back of my neck as he shifts closer making me shiver. I stretch to try to hide it, pushing back into him in the process, and he groans.

"Sorry, did I hurt you?"

He's quiet for a moment before lifting up to kiss my cheek. "Not exactly." My brow furrows, and he chuckles. "Don't fuss. I'm all right." He catches my earlobe between his teeth, and I gasp.

"You're going to wake up Cypress," I warn.

"Not if you're good and quiet." Aiden lifts up on his forearms, dragging me beneath him, and I giggle as I stare up into his deep brown eyes. "Can you do that for me?"

"Neither of you can," Cypress growls from my other side, his eyes staying resolutely shut. "Clearly."

"Oh, good, you're up," Aiden says, already kissing what appears to be his preferred spot beneath my jaw. "Want you to listen to us and be jealous."

I flush, laughing again, and he smiles against my neck. I like him like this. So playful and relaxed.

"Trying to remember where we left off." His nose trails along my clavicle. "Right about here, I think." I arch into him when he moves lower. "Can't believe you fell asleep on us."

I bite my lip, covering my face with my hands in embarrassment. I hadn't been able to help it, not when their touch had turned so soothing, Cypress murmuring in my ear as I curled into his side, Aiden a comfortable blanket of heat at my back.

"Kissed into a stupor, I believe is the expression," Cypress chimes in and finally opens his eyes. "I require coffee."

"Mm-hmm," Aiden hums in agreement, lifting up to look at me. "You want some coffee, too?"

Coffee does sound perfect, but so is what he was doing just now. Fortunately, I don't really end up having to choose. They're both affectionate with me all throughout our new morning routine, placing a lingering touch as they move past, sneaking a kiss as they hand me a plate or a mug.

It really is perfect, except I keep waiting for them to be like that with each other, too. Keep waiting for a touch or a look that tells me what I saw hadn't been part of a dream after all. And it must be obvious that I'm watching them so eagerly, because Aiden catches me eventually and cocks his head in silent question.

"Sorry," I say quickly, flushing under his gaze when he walks over from his place by the horses to crouch in front of me.

"Don't be sorry." His mouth finds mine again. "There something on your mind?"

"Yes…" I tell him slowly. "You and Cypress."

"Can't say that bothers me," he says. "Anything in particular?"

"Um…"

Cypress chuckles from near the wagon, his eyes finding mine through his reflection in the mirror he hung up on the frame to shave, and I know immediately I've been caught by more than just Aiden. "She knows, wolf."

Aiden frowns and looks over his shoulder at him. "She knows?"

Cypress drags the straight razor along his skin with a soft *thwick*, though his eyes still manage to convey his amusement. "She does. Don't you, little bird?"

Aiden turns back to me, searching my face, and I go still, guilt for spying on them two nights ago clawing at me. "I…guessed?"

Cypress chuckles again and flicks the razor shut before drying his face with a towel and replying, "We really must teach you to cover your tracks."

*My tracks… Oh, God, he saw my tracks? He's known this whole time?* If the earth opened up and plunged me into hell at this exact moment, I wouldn't even scream. "I, um…" I wring my hands in my lap nervously, trying to find the right words to say. "I couldn't sleep when neither of you came back so…" I look at Aiden, and I'm not sure he's breathing even before I say, "I saw you kiss him."

"You saw me kiss him," he repeats. "You see…anything else?"

"No," I say quickly. "I didn't stay long. I mean, I *didn't* stay at all. I only meant to go down by the water, and then I heard you both arguing. You were saying that I couldn't stay. That it was too much and—"

Aiden pulls me to him, holding my face in his hands in much the same way he had last night. "I'm sorry, sweetheart. I was—*am* concerned about what it means for you to stay with us. It's not a life that a lot of people would choose."

"You did," I argue. "Cy did."

"We did," he agrees, glancing at Cypress. "But it's not…it's not a comfortable life, Cora, if that's what you're wanting."

"It's not," I reassure him. "That's not what I want."

He smiles softly, tucking a few strands of my hair behind my ear. "Yeah, beginning to think it isn't." His gaze goes to Cypress again, then falls back. "You only saw us kissin'?"

"Yes."

"Not what came after?"

"What came after?"

"Perhaps her next lesson?" Cypress says with a grin, stopping beside Aiden to grab a fistful of his hair, yank his head back, and kiss him soundly on the mouth before moving on as if nothing had happened. "Maybe tonight?"

Aiden looks after him, seeming slightly dazed before he yells, "We said we'd go slow."

"*You* said," Cypress throws back before climbing into the wagon to start organizing supplies. "Cora and I have a differing opinion."

Aiden's eyes close, muttering to himself something that sounds a lot like *Christ, help me* before he turns his attention fully back to me.

"Are you angry?" I ask him, even though I think I already know the answer.

"Wrong emotion," he confirms, smiling wryly as he brushes his knuckles across my cheek. "No, I'm glad you know."

"You are?"

"Was never meant to be a secret," he says, sounding a little sad. "Didn't used to be, but given how we make our living, it's become a habit. Figured out pretty quick that when people know you have a weakness, they'll try to hit it. Especially when they think it might get them back what they've lost."

"Someone hurt you?"

"They hurt Cy," he says lowly, like it still upsets him. "He took someone's money, and in return, they pulled a knife on me. Or at least, they tried to. Cypress stepped in the way. Fortunately, he's got nine lives, so he walked away with only a wound to his right shoulder. Took a long time for him to recover, though. As I'm sure you can guess, he's a pretty terrible patient."

I laugh, thinking of that scar and of Aiden trying to keep an injured Cypress at bay while it healed. Likely not an experience anyone would want to repeat. "So because of that you hide?"

"I hide, so if someone tries to hurt him, they won't see me coming," he says, the threat he poses clear in his voice though it only makes me burrow more firmly against him. "And they haven't ever since."

"Didn't yesterday," I agree, listening to his heartbeat as I rest my head against his chest. "Is that why you didn't want me going to the saloon? You were afraid it would happen again?"

He wraps his arms around me, rocking gently. "I don't want to lose him. Or you. I haven't…I haven't had a lot to call mine in my life, Cora."

I sigh. "I understand."

"I know you do." He leans back, tilting my chin up with his hand so I'll look at him. "I didn't even notice your tracks the other night…"

I smile. "You were distracted."

"I was," he replies, cocking his head to the side. "And what were you, Cora? Were you *distracted* watching us?"

"Yes." I blush. "Sorry."

"Don't be," he reassures me, kissing the tip of my nose. "You don't have to worry about being caught watching us."

"Why not?"

He grins, and for a moment, I can see precisely why Cypress calls him his wolf. "Because we like it."

# CHAPTER 25
## CYPRESS

It's midday by the time I pull Cerberus to a stop on the ridge, surveying the surrounding hills as they drift on and on and on. Endless and inviting.

"Which way is calling out to you this time, Cy?" Aiden asks, coming up next to me on Helios. Waiting on my answer, he already has an old map in one hand and is fishing a pencil out of his pocket with the other.

"Could go farther west," I suggest. "Was thinking Cora might be the type to want to see the ocean."

Aiden nods, the hint of a smile at the corner of his mouth. "Might be." He starts sketching a path of travel. "That what you're going to tell her we're heading for? The ocean, instead of the man who killed her father?"

"Who's to say we can't aim for both?"

"You're not being honest with yourself, Cy."

"Well if it isn't the pot calling the kettle."

"As if you aren't standing in a glass fucking house with that fucking kettle. Things have changed."

"Thanks be to God," I say with a grin as he glares at me. "Even so, she'll still be wanting justice."

"I told you what I found out," Aiden counters with a frustrated sigh. "He's a damn bounty hunter, Cy. And a particularly mean motherfucker to boot. My contact was certain of it. Frank Clancy. Said he's seen him come through near to a dozen times for one job or another."

"I still think a bounty hunter for a farmer seems excessive."

"Cora said her father was behind in his payments. Perhaps someone was hoping to collect?" He sighs. "But you can't collect from a dead man."

"You can," I refute. "More easily sometimes, too. What happened to their land after her father died?"

"I'm assuming it went to whomever he owed. Didn't pass to Cora. And she has no other family to speak of out here. Cora's never said who her father bought it from?"

I shake my head. "I don't think she knows. More like he came home one day and the deal was done."

"Bad deal to land them on a useless plot of land outside Preston." Aiden shifts in his saddle. "Doesn't ever seem to be much good that happens around there."

"Either the law there is ineffective…"

"Or involved," he finishes for me. "How do we even know that deputy was trying to help her at all with a bounty hunter? Hell, he could know Clancy. Would explain why they kept pushing her off."

"Sounds fairly nefarious. He seemed pleasant enough when I took his money."

"You think anyone who doesn't immediately try to kill you is *pleasant*."

"I don't usually have much else to go on." I frown, thinking over what all Aiden said. "Are you going to try to convince her to give it up?"

"I'm not saying that. I'm only saying…it may not be as simple as the man who pulled the trigger is the guilty one. And there's also the simple matter of geography." He drags a hand over the back of his neck. "Say we do find him and he was hired by someone out in Boston. We gonna follow him there?"

"I thought you believed it was best for her to go back to Boston," I remind him, arching an eyebrow in his direction.

"Things have changed," Aiden says again. "I don't want to find him only to end up losing her in the process."

I look away, hiding my smile at precisely how *much* has changed before I try to put his mind at ease. "We'll figure out a way not to lose her. And we'll also figure out a way to help her. Whatever she decides. Whether that be acceptance or vengeance."

"Right." He turns to look back in the direction of the wagon, staring like he thinks he'll actually be able to see all the way back to camp and the person we left there.

We had offered to bring Cora with us, but she decided to stay behind and pack up camp ahead of the next leg of our journey, not seeming to mind at all the prospect of another day spent traveling.

More than I could have ever hoped, she has clicked so neatly into our lives, into what Aiden and I have together. Finding her place as if it has always been saved for her.

Still, I suppose, there is wisdom in Aiden's decree that we take things slow with her, if for no other reason than her inexperience. But there's also part of me that rebels against the idea of another moment more of lost time. Of holding back. Of denying her anything… *God* forbid.

Feeling her move through layers of fabric last night had been a torment, imagining how it would feel instead to have my hands on her bare. To feel her tremble. Feel her skin grow damp with perspiration as I build her up, feel her get slick with need between her thighs. Feel her arch and hear her moan as I take her. As I watch Aiden step in while she is still falling to drive her back to that high so fast that—

"Cypress…" Aiden's voice is a warning at my side, and while I reluctantly leave my escalating thoughts to give my attention back to the present, my expression must still give me away. His eyes narrow. "Behave."

"Wouldn't dream of doing otherwise."

He's about to issue another retort when a gunshot echoes across the landscape, loud even with the distance and the overabundance of trees and rocks to deafen it. Before the sound fully dies, Aiden is already riding away, galloping toward camp at a breakneck pace with Cerberus and I right behind.

# CHAPTER 26
## CORA

I eye my bedroll as I stand by the remnants of the fire used to cook breakfast, thinking the three sleeping mats laid out together look unbelievably tempting, but if Cypress and Aiden can stay awake after last night then surely I can, too. Instead of crawling back into bed, I sigh and stretch, rising up on my tiptoes and extending my arms far above my head in hopes that it will remind my blood to keep flowing.

Admittedly, it's an awkward position to freeze in, but I do nonetheless when I hear a distinctly male presence clear his throat behind me. *Cypress or Aiden. Please be Cypress or Aiden.*

I already know it's not.

I turn slowly, calculating how many steps it will take to reach my gun where I'd placed it on the wagon bench, not thinking I would need it before we were on the move, until I see my visitor. Tall, light gray hair, a bandana around his neck, and his hat replaced with what appears to be a fresh bandage around his head.

"Hello, darlin'," David greets me, standing at the edge of camp. "Remember me?"

"Yes," I say slowly, trying to stay calm. "From the saloon. In Last Chance."

"That's right." He seems genuinely pleased to have made an impression, as if we didn't leave him unconscious in an alley. "You know, I've always wondered at the name of that town."

I take a step toward the wagon. "I think they're trying to set expectations."

"Perhaps they are." He laughs, but there's no humor in it. "Fortunately, it didn't apply to us, though. Even if you are an awfully hard woman to track down."

"Am I?" I reply, trying to keep my voice steady, almost bored-like in the way I've seen Cypress do. "You shouldn't have gone to the trouble then." I take another step toward the wagon, raising my hand as if I'm shielding my eyes from the sun instead of furtively checking to make sure he's alone.

"Was there something you wanted?" I ask, continuing to edge my way to my weapon as I scan the horizon for Aiden and Cypress. How long will it take them to come back? "I must confess, I thought our business over."

"'Fraid not," he says, taking a step closer while I take a step away. "No, after what I saw in that alley…" He grins. "I'll be getting my money back and then some. Now, you come over here nice and quiet-like. No reason for this to turn ugly."

"But it will if you don't leave…" I don't like the way he's looking at me, the way he's clearly sizing up how easy I'll be to grab. "My husband will be back any moment."

I risk a glance at the bench, and I can see the shining metal of the gun, but David is already moving closer, pausing over the exact spot where all three of our bedrolls are still positioned right next to each other, as near as Aiden could get them when just his and Cypress's hadn't been enough.

"Your husband?" David asks as he looks at them, too. "He the one who gave you that mark on your neck? Or was it the one that's so quick with his gun?" My stomach sinks as his mouth curves into a smile. "Maybe you let them take turns."

Only a few more feet. A few more feet and I'll be able to reach it.

"Guess it doesn't matter," he says, before he makes his move. "We'll be long gone either way."

# CHAPTER 27
## CORA

He hadn't thought I'd actually do it. Same as Jake and those men back at the stable, he hadn't even reached for his gun, because he really hadn't thought I'd do it.

Wonder what he thinks now.

I hear the hoofbeats, the shouts, then Aiden's voice, soothing as he comes to my side. "Cora, you can lower the gun. We've got him."

"*I've* got him," I say back through gritted teeth.

Cypress chuckles not far from my other side. Stepping forward into my line of vision, he has the long rifle from his saddle already drawn and pointed at the figure on the ground. "I do not recall inviting visitors."

David curses while holding his leg tight, trying in vain to stop the blood from flowing out of his upper thigh and into the soil. There's so much. So much that it feels like it will mark the earth forever.

"Cora," Aiden murmurs, and when he touches my shoulder, I startle even though I know it's him. "It's all right, sweetheart. You did good. We'll take it from here."

I force my eyes to find his face. His expression is confident, but I can see the worry in his eyes.

"He was going to make me leave," I try to explain. "He was going to take me with him."

"That's not going to happen," Aiden reassures me, his hand moving slowly down my arm until it's over mine on the gun. He nods, still holding my gaze, and at his silent direction, I finally let the weapon fall, releasing into his grip. "It's all right," he says again as I do. "No one is going to take you."

"No one is going to make you do anything, little bird," Cypress agrees. He's still standing over David, his next words for him. "That clear to you? I understand head injuries can make you confused. Which is how I presume you thought it prudent to come here."

"Fuck you," the man says, spitting at Cypress's feet. "That little bitch—" Cypress lifts his boot and presses the heel down on the man's leg, making a *tsk tsk* sound as the other man screams. I don't even realize I've shut my eyes until Aiden tucks me behind him, my arms wrapping around his middle as one of his hands comes to rest over mine and the other keeps hold of my gun.

"I've already warned you once that there is a lady present," I hear Cypress say. "Now, why are you here?"

"You fuckin' know *why*. I want the money."

"All things considered, you didn't lose a large amount yesterday. One could argue that you've lost more now. You'll be incredibly fortunate if you manage to keep that leg."

I think I hear the man whimper, and I peek out from behind Aiden to see the way he's still clutching his leg. His skin growing pale and waxy.

"Not just me you've robbed though, is it?" the man asks, laughing bitterly. "You think I'll be the only one who comes? There's others who will be looking."

"And I can assure you they will find a similar reception," Cypress tells him, bending so that his face is inches from David's. "Beginning to think you're going to lose more than your leg."

"You're a fucking devil," David shouts at him before looking to me and Aiden. "All three of you will burn for what you've done. Mark me. You'll find your way to the noose." His eyes lock with mine, his grip tightening on his leg. "And you'll find your way to far worse, you little *whor*—"

I shut my eyes again before the resounding *bang* reaches my ears, along with the accompanying thump of a body slumping over into the dirt.

"Dammit, Cy," Aiden mutters, and it takes me a second to realize he'd also had his gun—*my* gun—raised to fire.

Cypress turns toward us and shrugs. "I did tell him about his language."

"And I *told* you—"

"Hand slipped," Cypress says, cracking his rifle open and reloading from his belt. "Besides, we can't let the scales tip *too* far in your direction. Surprised he found us… Honestly, I didn't think he would have it in him."

Aiden shakes his head. "Must not have hit him as hard as I thought."

"Or he was simply more motivated than we thought." Cypress snaps the rifle closed again with one smooth jerk of his hand, then looks at me. "Are you all right, Cora?"

I nod, although the way I'm still clinging to Aiden likely isn't very convincing. I loosen my grip and step forward, surveying the man who now lies dead.

"He snuck up on me," I say. "All of a sudden he was there and I… He was by the bedrolls and…"

*Whore.* My mother's voice, rather than David's, echoes in my head, their twin convictions that I am already marked by sin. I look at Aiden and Cypress, and it feels as natural as breathing to want them both, but what if… "Have I done something wrong?"

"No." Aiden cups my cheek, and he bends down so that we're at eye level. "You did nothing wrong, Cora. It's my fault. I should have moved us last night. You did the right thing. You kept yourself safe. You did everything right." He kisses my forehead softly, and it feels so good that I don't have the heart to tell him that hadn't been what I was asking.

"Cy," he says, straightening back up. "Get us packed and get going. Make sure the tracks are hid. I'll bury the body and catch up in a while."

I half expect Cypress to argue, but he doesn't. For once, he only nods and steps forward, bringing me under his arm as Aiden whistles for Helios.

"Wait," I say when we're no more than a few steps away. "Shouldn't we help him?"

"No," Cypress replies, gently. "He'll want to sort through it on his own." We reach the wagon and he pivots me to face him, looking me over himself to make sure I'm not actually hurt. "You were magnificent, little bird," he says when his eyes land back on mine. "Truly."

I smile, wishing I was more convinced. "Thank you."

He helps me up into the wagon before gathering our last few things, and I try to focus on watching him rather than what Aiden is doing or, much later, why it's taking him so long to come back.

"Can I ask you something?" I say to Cypress just before dusk, standing at the edge of our relocated camp with my eyes on the path out of the pine tree grove. We'd taken a winding route to get here, changing direction more than once, disguising our efforts through streams and brush until we'd finally landed in this small valley. That had been hours ago though, and when I had grown anxious, Cypress joined me in keeping watch.

"Of course. You can ask me anything."

I turn to look at him, knowing that to an outside observer Cypress's moral code may not be without gray, but to him it tends to be quite black and white.

"You killed that man," I say, more of a statement than an accusation. "You didn't hesitate…"

"No, I didn't." He frowns. "Does it distress you? That I killed him?"

"Not really," I say. "But shouldn't it? Maybe that's… Do you think I'm wrong?"

His head cocks. "Wrong?"

"I mean, do you think it's wrong that it doesn't bother me? Or that… am I doing something wrong by wanting to stay with you both? I know it's not…typical."

He laughs. "What is *typical*? Show me a thousand different people and I will show you a thousand different definitions of that word."

"You know what I mean. It's not… I've never heard of someone having two people that they… Isn't it only supposed to be the one?"

Cypress shrugs. "Perhaps for some."

"But not for you?"

"Nor for you." He grins, stepping closer, and when he opens his arms, I gladly move into them, letting him gather me in as he murmurs,

"You should not dwell on anything that man had to say."

"Why not?"

"Well for one, he is dead, and I would prefer not to give him the opportunity to live on in our thoughts. Would practically undo all the hard work we did by shooting him." I roll my eyes at him, and Cypress smiles again before pressing a kiss to the tip of my nose. "And for another, I do not think we should allow a man who sneaks into the wilderness to kidnap a woman be our shining example of right and wrong."

I laugh. "No, I suppose not."

"Cora." His hands gently cradle my face. "You are not wrong to want who you want. You were meant to want us both, just as Aiden and I were both meant to want you in return."

My heart skips, those crystalline blue eyes staying on mine as I grip the dark fabric of his shirt. "You want me?" I murmur, and when he nods, I rise up on my tiptoes to kiss him, sighing against his mouth when he pulls me tight to him and lifts me higher.

With easy steps, he carries me back to the same sleeping mats that gave us away, unrolled and spread out again for the night, so that it's easy for him to set me down before he settles on his knees over me.

Keeping his eyes on mine, his hands brush against the fabric of my skirt over my thighs then back up my body, slanting inward across my shoulders and down my exposed collarbone. Before he goes farther, he gives me time to stop him, but I only arch into him, prompting him to continue his path. Almost reverently, his fingertips caress the bare skin on the tops of my breasts before his palms find and cup the weight of each one, making me gasp when his thumbs start to slowly circle the peaks through the bodice of my dress.

"There she is," he murmurs. "You like when I touch you, Cora?"

I nod.

"You want more?"

"Yes," I tell him, without really being sure what *more* entails, but I know there is a heady excitement in my veins when he leans down over me. Another gasp turning into a soft moan when his mouth finds those same peaks through the cotton.

He groans, switching to my other breast as his clever fingers take over the place his mouth had been. "So damn sensitive." He pinches lightly, studying my every reaction even as he's pulling me back up so that I'm straddling him as he kneels. "So damn perfect."

My head falls back, my eyes closing as I let him guide me where he wants, move me the way he wants, and God, the way it feels when his thigh rubs between my legs…

I rock my hips, moaning a little as I seek out the friction, and he chuckles, his mouth soft and sweet on my neck while his hands firmly grip my hips to encourage me. "Are you going to come for me if we keep this up, Cora? Let me see how pretty you look when you fall apart?"

My brow furrows, my eyes still shut. It's so hard to think when he's touching me. When this feels so much like last night but different, like that was kindling and this is a fire that wants to consume.

"That's it." He drags my mouth back down to his as my arms wrap around his shoulders, my fingers tangling in his dark hair, and I make an undeniable sound of pleasure when he shifts my position slightly, increasing the pressure, and it feels so *good*. So good that I keep moving as he bends so that his mouth can find my breast again. So good that it's a relief when I feel his fingers start to drag the bodice down to reveal more skin. So good that I— "*Wait.*"

Cypress stills immediately, and I listen to the sound of both of us breathing hard as everything begins to recede. Almost as soon as it does, I move to chase it, wanting it back. "*Wait,*" I say again, suddenly on the verge of frustrated tears. "I didn't—I've never felt—"

"Cora."

My eyes open to see Cypress searching my face, and the look in his eyes tells me that, as usual, he knows without me having to tell him. Still, he asks.

"Little bird"—he quiets my movements with one hand on my waist, another stroking my back—"if I were to ask you how you prefer to make yourself come…"

"I…" My cheeks redden, and I look down, trying to avoid his gaze.

He cradles my face in his hands again, pulling me back to him. Making me see that there's no judgment in his eyes, only a desire to understand.

"Tell me you'd know what I was asking."

# CHAPTER 28
## CYPRESS

She doesn't know. I already know she doesn't, and I'm taken aback by how much it bothers me that this is yet one more thing that's been kept from her. That's been shamed away.

I take one of her hands and kiss her palm before turning it so that my hand covers hers as I lead it lower, watching carefully for any sign of hesitation before I position it at the apex of her thighs. "Tell me you touch yourself, Cora."

She flushes, shifting in my lap, but I don't think it's only from nerves. "Of course," she replies, sounding a little indignant. "I bathe."

"I'm not talking about only when you *bathe*," I say, smiling and brushing my nose along her jaw as I breathe her in again. "Although, we will return to that topic at another time. I heard that you told Aiden once he could watch you."

"I did *not* tell him—I mean, I did, but I didn't mean—" Her eyes narrow, her hackles up now that she's forgotten to be embarrassed. "I *knew* he told you," she mutters, almost pouting, which gives me the perfect opportunity to tug at that bottom lip of hers with my teeth while I pull her closer, pressing a bit firmer where our hands are trapped between us.

"Cora, I need you to tell me you've played with what I just know is a torturously pretty cunt," I murmur in her ear. "I can't bear to think she's been so neglected."

She draws in a sharp breath, pulling her hand back up and squirming again in my lap in such a way that my cock is also starting to cry neglect.

"God, I cannot believe we are talking about this," she says, covering her face with both hands. "It's...*indecent*."

I encircle her wrists with my fingers. "Little bird, I must say I have far more *indecent* things in mind for us, although very few of them allow for this much talking."

"*Cypress*." I still can't see her face but I can hear that she's laughing before she takes a deep breath and asks, "Isn't that...isn't this a sin?"

"What did we just decide about adopting the morals of a man who—"

"It's not only him," she mutters, hands finally dropping. "He reminded me of...well, truthfully, of my mother. She always said it was wrong to—" She looks down at her lap. "She was quite clear that no one would want a girl who could forget that her service is to God and not to herself."

My teeth grind together. Why do so many people feel compelled to accept a version of a God that would wish to deny them everything? That would gift something as divine as a soul, only to declare every expression of it as a sin?

"She was trying to warn me, I think, in her way," Cora says quietly. "My parents had me out of wedlock. And they tried to cover it up with a quick wedding, but people still knew. People *talked*. Her parents never forgave her. She…she wasn't very happy."

"She took it out on you," I guess. "Made sure you were unhappy, too."

"I don't think she meant to. She worried that, because I was the product of sin, I was tainted by it. That I would be a sinner, too, if I didn't pray for forgiveness." She sighs. "Although, even if God forgave me, I'm not sure she ever would have."

"What happened to her? Something horrible, I hope."

Cora laughs before clasping a hand over her mouth. "That's terrible," she says, once she can nearly keep a straight face. "Actually, I don't really know what happened to her. She left after my father died. Took my sisters back to Boston."

"She left you behind?" I say, feeling a profound sense of sadness for her. "She abandoned you?"

"No," Cora says quickly. "No, not really. I'm the one who ran away, but…she was probably glad I did. She didn't really want me. Not like she wanted my sisters. There were rumors that— Let's just say they didn't remind her so much of my father. Or of me. She…she used to say I was half wild."

I smile slightly, even as I contemplate what I would do if I ever had a chance to meet this woman. "Only half?"

Cora lets out another huff of laughter, and I bend to kiss her again slowly, lingering over it as if in apology for having taken so long to find her.

"I love that you're a wild one, Cora," I murmur. "Don't you dare try to tame that to please someone who didn't deserve you." I stroke the loose hair away from her face, watching her eyes go glassy before she tucks her face into the crook of my neck. "Everyone's sins are their own," I tell her, resting my cheek on top of her head. "If you choose to believe in such a thing."

I can hear the disbelief in her voice when she responds, "You don't believe in sin?"

I consider the question for a while, liking the way she relaxes into me more and more. "No, I do not believe that I do."

"You don't think that people do terrible things?"

"I know they do. I've done a few of them myself. But I did not need a list of rules to tell me they were terrible. Cora, whatever mortal sins you think you've committed, I can assure you that finding the things that make you feel good aren't among them."

She sighs again, but it sounds happier. More content. "Are you sure?"

Rather than give her words, I slowly negotiate us both to standing, and with her hand in mine, I walk us to the wagon, selfishly satisfied at the way she still seems a bit unsteady on her feet while I start rummaging through my things. My hand finally lands on the small mirror that I use to shave in the mornings, and I pull it out before sitting on the ground again with my back against the wagon wheel.

Cora remains on her feet, staring at me with a mystified expression until I hold out my hand, adjusting my legs wide enough for her to fit between them. "Come sit with me for a while."

She hesitates momentarily, likely still worried over if she's wanting something that she shouldn't. But I see in her eyes the moment that the want wins out before she's settling herself between my legs, her back against my chest as I prop the mirror in front of us.

"Cypress." She's looking at us in the mirror as I do the same with my face next to hers over her shoulder. "What are you doing?"

"All these lessons we've been giving you," I reply, running my nose along her jaw and watching her eyelids flutter closed, "and all this time there's been something essential missing from your education."

I place my hands on the tops of her thighs, listening to her breathing stutter. "We don't have to do anything you don't want to do," I tell her, pressing a kiss to the side of her neck. "We can just sit here for a while if you'd rather."

I can practically feel her thinking, debating. "And if I said I want to…you'll…"

"Make you feel good," I reply, simply. "Well, actually, you're going to take care of that on your own. For the most part."

"But it will feel like when you and Aiden kiss me?"

"Better," I murmur, and she makes a small wistful sound, her head tipping back against my shoulder.

"I can't imagine that."

"Then we're going to have to work on your imagination, little bird," I say, certain I have her attention now. That curiosity is going to come out to play, and I love that quality about her as much as I really do love her wild.

She turns her face into me, nipping at my jaw. "I want to."

I think I simply love *her*.

I take a steadying breath in, doing my best to keep my own desire at bay so that I can keep it about her. My hands shift slightly to press between her thighs and guide her legs apart underneath her dress. As soon as I do, I can feel her tensing again, leaning her head back to seek my mouth for reassurance. I give her what she wants, kissing her until she relaxes into me and nods to keep going.

Only then do my hands bunch in the fabric of her skirts, easing it higher until the mere sight of her bare legs above those damn boots makes me dizzy. Too easy to picture them wrapped around my waist… on either side of my head. I bite back a groan when I reach her thighs, revealing the soft white fabric of her undergarments. "You can change your mind, little bird. Are you sure you want—"

"I want you to see me," she answers me, breathy and a little needy. "If you want to…"

To let her know just how much, my mouth presses against hers as I drag her skirts even higher. When I look again in the mirror, I can see them hiked up to her waist, and while women's clothing often has far too many layers for my liking, here at least, they excel. Exposing just enough of a tantalizing peek through the open seam of her undergarments to make a person want to see more—more of those soft curls between her thighs, more of that cunt that is just as gorgeous spread open for me as I thought it'd be.

"Look at yourself, Cora," I urge when I realize her eyes are shut, and I wait for her to open them before I take her hand and bring it to my mouth. I suck on two of her fingers, wetting them with my tongue, and keeping my eyes on her face in the mirror as she bites her lip and watches as I lower them between her legs.

Parting the seam of her undergarments wider, I lower the touch of those same two fingers to the sensitive little bud hidden at her apex. "Feel this?"

She nods, trembling slightly.

"I want you to move your fingers in a slow circle around this pretty clit, Cora. Drag them back and forth, circle and press until you figure out what makes your heart race."

She nods again, my fingers never leaving their place over hers as she starts to tentatively explore, slowly becoming less apprehensive and more intrigued by how her body is responding. Her other hand, still intertwined with mine in her upturned skirts, tightens as she does. Her head falling back against my shoulder again so that I can cover her throat with open-mouthed kisses in an attempt to soothe my own thirst.

I feel the moment she finds a rhythm that works for her, her chest beginning to rise and fall rapidly, and I watch what she's doing in the mirror, memorizing the pattern so that I can do it later with my own fingers. With my tongue. "That's it," I encourage her as her soft noises fill my head. "You're doing so well, Cora. Keep going."

She whimpers, and she's so close, but right as she's about to fall, her eyes close and she stops, pressing her legs back together and trapping my hand with hers in the soft heat of her thighs.

"It's all right." She's shaking as I kiss her, as I wait for her to settle again, and eventually she does. "You're all right."

"Sorry," she says, sounding upset. "I just—"

"You apologize too much, little bird. Try again."

She nods and reaches back to get my mouth on hers, demanding it in a way that makes me grin as her legs ease open again and her fingers pick up with the pattern she'd found. Building herself up faster this time after I guide her fingers lower briefly, letting her feel how wet she is.

She's so slick, practically dripping, and I so badly want to fuck her with my fingers, watch her fuck herself with her own, but better to do things this way the first time. Even if it kills me to still not have really touched her myself, I want her to do it, to know she can bring herself this feeling, to realize what her body is capable of all on its own.

Later, Aiden and I will have time to teach her what it's capable of with us.

"*Cy.*" She's panting against me, her face turning into my neck, on the brink of it if she'll only let herself go. "I—"

I release her other hand to take hold of her jaw to direct her focus back to the mirror. "Eyes on me, Cora." Her green eyes find mine just as she's told. "You keep your eyes on me. Don't stop. I've got you."

My gaze remains on hers right until her delicate fingers push her over the edge, and she shatters with a soft cry that nearly brings me with her. Her whole body tensing with the force of it, and I hold onto her as she rides it out.

"My wild one," I murmur in her ear, my eyes still on hers as she comes back down from the high. "I knew you'd be so very pretty when you come, but now that I've seen it for myself… You'll be lucky if you can still lift these pretty fingers by the time we're through."

She gasps, watching me bring them to my mouth so I can suck them clean of the taste of her as thoroughly as I wish I could between her legs. Savoring every bit of her and still wanting more. Always more, because it'll never be enough.

With her, just as it's always been with Aiden, it'll never be enough.

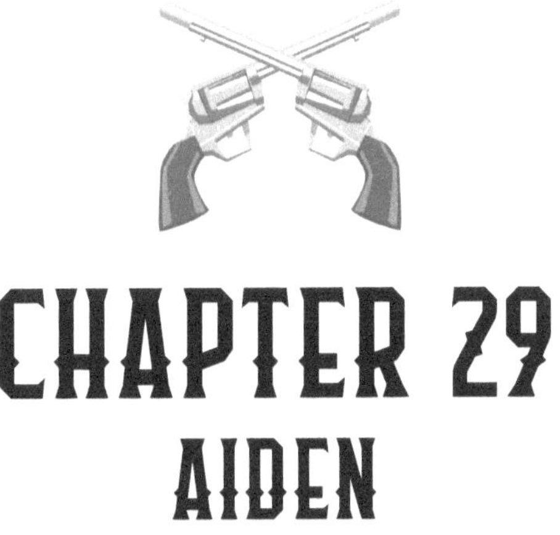

# CHAPTER 29
## AIDEN

I catch up to the wagon several hours later, a dead man's pocketbook in my vest and an ache in my bones that makes me want to turn in early. Then I take one look at the dazed expression on Cora's face before she spots me, and it's more than enough to have me yanking Cypress behind the wagon where she can't see.

"You've been busy in my absence," I mutter, keeping my voice low while I listen to Cora minding the fire. "Thought I asked you to behave."

"What makes you think I have not followed that advice?" he challenges, and I give him an even stare until he smiles. "I simply imparted some new skills, wolf."

I roll my eyes, lacking the patience for this. "Speak plainly."

"I may have given her some…overdue instruction on how to handle things on her own."

"Cy…"

"You know, the more I learn about her family, the more convinced I am that she is far better off with us. *Terrible* mother—"

"Cy…"

"—put all sorts of ideas in her head—"

"*Cypress.*" I crowd into him, let each word come out measured. "What did you do?"

"Me?" He arches an eyebrow as if confused. "*I* barely lifted a finger. Though getting to watch…"

I'm going to kill him.

"Did you fucking make her come while I was gone? Is that what you're telling me?"

He grins. *The bastard.* And I'm near to picking out a second burial spot for the day before the words sink in. "Wait, *instruction*? You *taught* her?"

Cypress nods, though some of the amusement in his expression fades as he studies me. "I know you still may have your reservations about us being able to give her the type of life she deserves, and after what happened this morning…"

"After what happened this morning, I think it's clear I was right to."

"Has it changed your—"

"No. It should but…" I let out a deep breath. "After coming that close to having her taken away, all I know is that I still want her with us. Her place is with us. You were right. I—"

Cypress is on me before I can finish, his hands on my vest to switch our positions so that my back is the one up against the wagon before his fingers fly to my belt.

"*Fuck.*" I'm already panting as my hands cover his. "Cy, hold on, we… *Christ*, of course me telling you that you're right gets you riled."

He chuckles, low and deep, then brings his mouth a whisper away from mine. "You would be admiring my restraint if you'd seen her. How gorgeous she is." His hands flex beneath mine as I groan at the picture he's putting in my head. "It's all I can see. I need—please, I need something."

Well, at least he's suffering for his behavior.

"You can fuck me, Cy," I croon in his ear after making him wait a bit longer. "I was only going to suggest we find a more private location. Don't want to scare her off already with how loud I can make you moan."

There's a flash in Cypress's eyes that shows he's taking my words as a challenge, which is precisely how I'd meant them.

"I'll meet you by the water, wolf."

# CHAPTER 30
## CORA

Aiden still seems to be in somewhat of a hurry when he finally appears and tells me that he and Cypress are going to go wash up before dinner, though he still takes the time to check in on me. As well as to check that my gun is safely at my side while I sit and mind the fire.

"You'll be all right by yourself?" he asks as he hovers. "After earlier?"

I nod, a little surprised that I mean it. That I am almost looking forward to having a few minutes alone again to collect myself after the day's events. Or, at the very least, to try to determine why I am having a harder time recovering my senses after what happened with Cypress by the wagon than I am from watching him gun a man down.

The way it had felt to have him holding me like that, to have him talk me through it… *Eyes on me, Cora.*

Before I can help it, I shiver, the flush in my cheeks likely making it clear that I'm not the least bit cold, but Aiden takes off his coat, crouches down, and wraps it around my shoulders anyway.

"Will have to find the one Cypress says you bought," he says, chuckling as he buttons it up. "Getting colder."

"He bought it, really," I confess. "Insisted."

"He does that," he says, the corner of his mouth lifting, and I think of Aiden's flashy gun and his watch. How I'd wondered about both of them before I'd even known them.

"You did good, Cora," Aiden continues, his eyes soft. "You held your own today."

"I knew you and Cypress would come back." My eyes drift shut when the back of his finger brushes my cheek. "I thought if I could just make it until then, I'd be okay, but then he tried to grab me and I—"

"You did good," he repeats, and I think I see a flicker of sadness in his expression before he leans forward and presses a kiss to my forehead. "You did so good, baby."

I sigh, wanting to wrap myself up in the praise the same way that I'm wrapped up in his coat, in his smell, in the way it feels when he tips my chin up so that his mouth can take mine. A small sound escaping me that he returns with something deeper, rougher. Something so distinctly *Aiden* that it makes me smile, and he returns that, too.

"You really are going to be trouble, aren't you?" he mutters. "Going to make me crazy."

"You seem to like that," I say back, thinking of Cypress again, and he laughs.

"Suppose I do." He lightly scrapes his scruffy mustache along my neck before placing one more kiss against my cheek. "You should get some rest."

"I'm not tired," I say, and it almost sounds like a plea.

His dark brown eyes meet mine before dropping to my mouth as he teases, "You will be."

He slowly stands and releases his hold on me, and I actually sway, the most movement I appear capable of until long after he's walked away and is no longer giving me those knowing looks over his shoulder as he goes.

Even after, I only huddle more firmly inside his coat, sticking my hands in the pockets. As the happy feeling in my chest threatens to spill over, I'm not even sure why I'm trying to hide the fact that I'm grinning like a fool when no one is here to see except the stars above.

Then my fingers graze a small slip of paper in his pocket, my first thought that it must be his list of supplies from town before I pull it out, recognizing it as I hold it up beneath those same stars to read. All that happiness dims.

One coach ticket.

One passenger.

One way.

Transportation to Boston.

# CHAPTER 31
## AIDEN

Cypress is waiting by the water just as he said he'd be. So clearly antsy that I have to bite the inside of my cheek to keep from laughing at his expense. Hard not to enjoy it, though. Very rarely do I see Cypress ruffled. Let alone in the type of mood to beg.

His head whips up when he hears a twig snap under my boot, the water behind him moving too slowly to drown out the sound.

"There you are." Cypress clears his throat and starts to pace near the bank. "It occurs to me that I forgot to ask about your outing earlier. Any trouble escorting our intruder to his final resting place?"

"Not especially." I circle right rather than walking straight to him, and Cypress's hand fists at his side, his frame rigid with tension. Suppose the generous thing would be to take pity on him, but seeing as how I am a bit irked to have missed out on his little lesson…

Firsts *are* firsts after all.

Cypress takes a step forward and I take a step back, winding him up with this little dance we're doing, and his eyes narrow. "Are you punishing me then, wolf?"

"I don't know what you mean, Cy," I reply, cocking my head to the side. "I already said you could fuck me."

The corner of Cypress's mouth curves into half of a smile, his light eyes glinting like the moon above him, and I know he knows that there was never really any question of me giving him what he needs. Just as it was the other night when I was the one who needed him beneath me, who needed teeth to meet straining muscled shoulders as my fingers held his claws to the dirt.

Cypress stalks forward, and I stand my ground, right up until his fingers twist into my hair, pulling my face close enough to his that his mouth brushes mine as he speaks. "My beautiful boy, shall we test that careful self-control?"

"Mine or yours, Cy?"

He grins, his other hand busy at my belt, and the heat building under my skin is almost unbearable already. Then he's moving to the buttons of my shirt, clothes coming off in quick succession until we're both bare in the moonlight.

At first, Cypress's movements are more hurried than usual, his mouth claiming mine only briefly before he's practically shoving me to the ground on all fours. So intent that I think this might be an occasion of quick relief for both of us. Then he drops behind me, hands tracing the planes of my back, kneading into my muscles in a way that would be soothing if I didn't know him so well.

"I *am* going to fuck you, wolf," he says, lifting up so that his chest is covering my back, his chin resting lazily against my shoulder as he adds, "But you are not allowed to come until I tell you to, understood?"

I don't reply at first, physically *can't* as my eyes squeeze shut. "Fuck's sake, Cypress…"

His hand tangles in my hair again, pulling my head back, exposing my neck for him to press a chaste kiss against my throat. "Tell me you understand, Aiden."

I growl an unintelligible answer at him, and I can feel him grin before he spits in his left hand and reaches between my legs to grip my already hard cock. I groan deeply, a sound he rewards by releasing his fistful of my hair and letting my head drop forward just before he squeezes hard at the base.

"*Fuck*." I'm trying to even out my breathing, but then he starts to move his hand in slow strokes. "Fuck, that feels—"

He stops, his touch turning featherlight before falling away completely. "I asked you a question, wolf."

"Fuck, *yes*, I understand."

"Wanted to be certain." He shifts back to kneeling, and I hear him spit again before I feel the slick drip of it down my ass, catching at my entrance as he starts to rub his thumb there, teasing until I'm groaning again. In response, he pushes in, just barely breaching me, and the next curse I'd been about to throw at him is lost in a low moan from the back of my throat. My resolve slipping the longer he holds there until I thrust into the other hand he still has wrapped around my length, because I need *something*.

"Easy, wolf."

Only once I'm still again does he start to ease his thumb in and out at a slow, deliberate pace, the same rhythm with which he's now stroking my cock. So much more than he was willing to give me before but not nearly enough. I need it harder, rougher. Need him to do it before I lose my mind.

"You should have seen her, wolf," Cypress mutters, barely increasing his pace. "So fucking perfect. I kept thinking…" Abruptly, he withdraws his thumb, and my arms nearly buckle before he replaces it with two thick fingers wet from his mouth. "Kept thinking what it would look like to see her head tipped back as you fuck her. About all the little sounds she would make for you."

The images are flashing through my mind now, just as he wants. Cora on the ground in front of me, ready to take me, *needing* me inside her because she feels so empty without it.

As if Cypress can see it, too, he murmurs, "You know what else I thought about?"

Even if I had air in my lungs to spare, I'm afraid to ask, afraid that anything else he puts in my head will make me break.

"I thought about the way her thighs would tremble so sweetly against your shoulders when you put that hungry mouth of yours on her, the way you'd grip her tighter because you're not sure how to stop, how to hold on yourself while you bury your tongue inside her. She tastes so good, wolf. She'd be so good for you while I take you…" He releases me, his fingers slipping away, and I let out a broken curse at the loss. "Just like this."

My fingers dig into the hard ground as I feel the tip of Cypress's cock at my entrance now, feel him pushing into me in slow increments, stretching me around the size of him until his hips are flush against my ass, and all I can do is try to adjust.

I could come apart right now. I could come right here if I wasn't so against giving him the satisfaction, because I can hear him panting, too. Can feel how hard he's gripping my hips. Not nearly as in control as he's pretending to be. But I never am either.

"Remember, wolf, not until I say," Cypress warns, his voice a little breathless when he finally starts to move in steady, deep thrusts. His moan deep when he changes the angle, leans down, and digs his teeth into the back of my shoulder, sharp and possessive.

My need to come keeps building, waiting at the base of my spine, and I know Cypress is getting close, too, when his hands dig in harder, when the constant stream of filth in that smooth voice tapers off to clipped urgent praise. "Just like that, wolf. Always take it so well. Always take me."

I'm not sure if the last part is a statement or a request, but it doesn't matter. I've been willing to take anything Cypress will offer me since before I stepped onto that street to see him surrounded, not even slowing my steps while I raised my gun.

He thrusts hard one last time, burying himself as much as he can before he comes, and it's all I can do not to join him.

I need to come. *Fuck*, I just need to come.

Cypress kisses me lightly between my shoulder blades as he pulls out, and I sway slightly, still seeking him, before he turns me onto my back. My still hard cock pressing against my lower abdomen as he crawls over me.

"Thank you, wolf." Cypress's mouth slants against mine as he kisses me, taking his fucking time with it.

"*Cy*—" He silences me with a sharp bite to my bottom lip before moving lower, the momentary pain enough to give me something to hang onto as I watch him.

"You'll have to forgive my greed," he murmurs against my skin, nuzzling affectionately at my stomach before moving down to take a long lick along the length of me. I jerk, oversensitive, and he smiles up at me before doing it again. "You taste so good when you're desperate."

"Cypress," I growl, "you sadistic—" My words briefly cut off on a moan when he takes me in his mouth. "How has no one fucking killed you yet?"

He pulls back, releasing me with a pronounced wet pop. "Because you kill them first when they try."

His head descends again, taking me down his throat, and my hands fist in his hair to try to take over the pace even though Cypress won't allow it. His hand pulses at the base of my cock while he only lets me fuck his mouth slowly, offering me enough to make me even more desperate but not enough to let me fall.

"Fuck, Cy." My hips thrust up, and he swallows with a groan. "*Please.*"

That word and all the power it provides is apparently what he's been waiting for because he rises up again, presses a kiss to my tip, and simply says, "Come."

And it's enough. Enough that as soon as he has me in his mouth again, I come hard until I'm spent, my chest still heaving when Cypress at last places a satisfied kiss on my inner thigh and crawls back up my body to collapse next to me on the solid earth.

It takes me a long time to be able to speak again, long moments where both of us are just staring up at the stars that have continued to come out above us. When I finally do, I know exactly what to say. "You are such an asshole."

He laughs, rich and rolling. And I can't help but laugh, too. "I know. But you love me despite it."

Another one of those statements that could also be a request. I turn my head to meet Cypress's gaze, already knowing it will be on me. "I do, Cy." My fingers trace his sharp jaw. "Just like you love me."

He nods, his eyes returning to the sky. "Was it too much?"

"Fuck no," I tell him, making him grin. "I needed it, too. Been…been an eventful few days." I pause before continuing, "Are you worried? That things will be different now? It won't be just the two of us anymore."

"We've shared partners before."

"This is different," I tell him. "This isn't just someone sharing our bed as we pass through town. This is someone sharing our *life*. Someone who has an equal stake in things."

"I know. I was simply confirming that our understanding is the same." A flicker of a smile plays across his face. "I'm not worried, wolf. I've been waiting for her, same as I was waiting for you." His hand grabs mine where it rests between us, fingers interlacing. "Are you worried?"

"Yes," I say quietly. "But not about us. More about…I worry about letting her in, only to lose her. About what could have happened if she hadn't been so quick with her pistol this morning."

"But she was."

"What if she hadn't been?"

"You could waste your whole life asking questions like that, Aiden. Wondering about what could have been instead of experiencing what did."

"I know." I let my eyes close, still sorting through things. "I think I've been waiting for her, too. Just didn't know it. And it's fucking terrifying to realize I know so little about what lies ahead." I sigh. "If she still wants this after everything that's happened, then I suppose she's made her choice."

"Suppose she has." Cypress is quiet for a time. Uncharacteristically so, until he says, "Do you ever wish you chose differently?"

I lift up on my elbow so I can see him better. "Chose differently?"

"Cora asked me earlier today if I believe in sin," he explains, gaze still on the stars as he frowns. "I told her that I don't. But you do. Believe enough in the balance sheet that…you could have chosen differently."

"Cy, look at me." He actually obeys, turning in my direction. "I'd choose you every time. I'd follow you every time. No matter where the road leads."

He nods, his smile returning and my mouth nearly touching his as he murmurs back, "No matter where the road leads."

# CHAPTER 32
## CYPRESS

She's not here.

Her bag and her bedroll are gone, as is Tess and her tack. Everything cleared so efficiently that it might have looked like she'd never been here at all had it not been for the remaining tidy pile of her new clothes and her knife. Left beside Aiden's coat on the wagon bench. Very likely intentional. Also likely not a great sign.

"*Cypress*," Aiden shouts as he comes around the other side of the wagon. "Do you see signs that she was taken? Signs of anyone else being here?"

He hasn't noticed the clothes yet, and I'm hesitant to mention them until I can make sense of it myself. A few hours ago, she shot a man for trying to make her leave…only to leave now of her own volition?

Aiden is already moving to tack up Helios with a determined set to his expression, and I'm only a step behind him as I ask, "Did she say anything to you before you left?"

He shakes his head. "She was content. Happy. Someone else must have come. Someone—"

"Aiden." I place a hand on his shoulder, trying to calm him even though I feel close to chaos myself. "Her things are on the wagon bench. I think she left."

"No." He looks at me, shakes his head again, before going over to check himself, climbing up to inspect her belongings before he goes alarmingly still.

"Wolf?"

Slowly, he reaches down and picks up the knife, holding it loosely in his left hand while his right grabs a small piece of paper I hadn't seen beneath it. When he only continues to stare at it after several moments, his worry worsening to obvious distress, I reach up and take both from him. "What is this?"

He doesn't look at me. "It's a ticket."

"I can see it's a ticket." I turn it over and note the destination as I tuck Cora's knife into my boot. "Why is it here?"

"It was hers," he says quickly. "I kept it." Regret stings his tone. "It was on the floor of the stable that night we took her, and I picked it up. I...I gave her my coat before I left. She must have found it in my pocket."

Understanding seeps in, then sadness. "And she must've thought..."

"*Fuck.*" Aiden smacks his hat against his leg, his fingers tugging at his hair. "Fuck, I should have given it to her sooner. Gotten rid of it. *Something.* I was just—I was half out of my mind trying not to want her, and every time I thought to return it to her..."

"She'll understand," I say, trying to reassure him even as a pit widens in my stomach. "You'll explain things when we find her."

He nods, a quick jerk of his head, and I already know he's being harder on himself than I could ever be.

"Aiden," I call after him when he gets down from the wagon and walks away to collect a couple lanterns set nearby. "We *will* find her."

He says nothing, just goes back to tacking up Helios as I do the same with Cerberus, although both of us opt to keep our feet on the ground as we head out of camp, only able to pick up a set of hoofprints headed south after about a half hour of searching in the dark.

We follow it for longer, eventually moving in the direction of that same stream we just left with lighter spirits. Based on her trail, she made a wide curve from camp to farther upstream, not daring to approach the water until she would have no risk of running into us by mistake.

"She could get lost out here," Aiden mutters after well over another hour has passed with barely any progress. "She could get hurt or even…"

He can't say it. Neither can I. But the knowledge of it is what keeps both of us searching into the night.

Finally, the water and her trail intersect, the current louder here. Faster, too, but not terribly deep. An easy crossing to make on horseback, and it appears Cora thought so as well.

Her horse's tracks disappear into the water only to…*not* appear on the other side.

Aiden lets loose a string of profanities, but something about her giving us the slip makes me grin. Perhaps it's seeing the way she had known to cover her tracks this time. Or perhaps it's that covering them at all shows that, despite the misunderstanding, part of her still believes we'll come after her.

How right she is.

# CHAPTER 33
## CORA

I had actually believed… It doesn't matter what I'd believed. The truth had been hidden in the pocket of a coat.

Have they gotten back to camp yet? Have they noticed I'm gone? Do they care? It had felt…God, it had *felt* like they cared. But maybe they'd only been pretending until the moment came when they could hand me that ticket and send me on my way.

They have each other. Why would they need me?

The even sound of Tess's hooves clomping over the ground is hardly enough to cover the crying I try to keep at bay, just as the burn in my chest is hardly enough to stave off the chill in the night air.

Honestly, I think the worst of it is being alone again, the endless promise of it stretching ahead of me the farther I go. Because while misery may love company, it will lie down just fine with loneliness.

I'd been rash to leave. I could've stayed, confronted Aiden about why he had the ticket, why he kept it, but what other explanation could there be than he was hoping at some point to use it?

Experience taught me even better than they could that the most likely possibility was that I'd fallen for another dream. Foolishly believed in the mirage when I *knew* better, knew that nothing so good waited for someone like me.

So why stay? Force myself to endure hearing his answer? Watch his expression slide into indifference? Even if it hadn't been today, the day would've come that they'd realize they didn't really want me. That I could be easily left behind. Again.

I'd rather leave than be left.

I dismount and walk beside Tess, guiding her back into the water for a little while before cutting back out. It feels warmer now than this morning when I'd stopped to rest and tried to wash away some of the fatigue. Careful to conceal our path afterward, just as Cypress had done the day before.

God, I wish I could stop missing them so much. Wish it would stop feeling like a gaping physical wound.

Maybe they'd come after me. Maybe they wouldn't. Maybe they would come for Cypress's gun at the very least, the knife I'd left nowhere close to replacing its value, but seeing as he still has my father's and I am no longer stupid enough to go out into the world unarmed…

All I can think about is how Aiden moved to protect me after I told him that David wanted to take me away. How Cypress sounded when he promised that no one would. How he'd held me when I told him about my mother. It had felt so *real*.

*It wasn't*, whispers the voice in my head. *You're nothing but a burden for them. Someone they feel like they have to take care of when they'd really rather be rid of you. They have each other. You don't mean anything to anyone. How many times do you have to learn the same lesson?*

When the sound of gunfire reaches my ears, I know that, out here, it could be anything or anyone. But I already know it's not. I bite the inside of my cheek to stifle another sob, swing back up into my saddle, and urge Tess forward. Determined not to make the same mistake again.

# CHAPTER 34
## AIDEN

I pick up Cora's trail again by midmorning, the thrill of discovery replacing some of the exhaustion that had been threatening to take over.

The last hours had been excruciatingly slow going, the water too wide to allow me to easily scan each side for her exit from the stream. Instead, I have been forced to practically crawl up one side and then the other in sections.

I hate to think how far behind I am. Not to mention the fact that I'm wet, tired, and downright pissed off. Mainly at myself.

I stopped only once for a few hours, and only because I could no longer make out the ground, let alone a trail. Reluctantly, I'd found a place to close my eyes, but I hadn't slept. Couldn't, knowing she was out here upset and alone. Knowing that we all are.

When her tracks first disappeared, Cypress and I decided to split up, him heading upstream while I headed down. Watching him walk away, even knowing it was temporary, hadn't been just an echo of Cora's absence, but an additional source of guilt.

Cypress hates being by himself, the quiet making him anxious and on edge. So much so that when we first started riding together, it had taken a long time for him to stop filling every silent moment with chatter. I hadn't minded. I'd already spent enough time in silence to last a lifetime.

The addition of Cora's company had been an unexpected balm on that old wound. The two of them able to ramble on well into the night while I pretended not to listen to the alternating melody of their voices. Pretended that I wasn't getting attached to hearing her laugh, to seeing her smile, as much as Cypress.

Now, I stare at her tracks as they move out of the water and along the bank, still heading in the same direction she left in. Resolve steels my spine as I stand from my crouch, raise my gun in the air, and fire twice in quick succession.

I manage to stay on her trail after that without misstep despite a few more solid attempts on her part to mislead us. I even gain some ground based on the still-warm embers from a fire that she'd tried to bury after she'd stopped to rest. The closer I get, the more I pick up the pace, pushing Helios faster. Calculating that if she keeps on this path long enough she'll hit another town, and I want to catch her before she does.

Some conversations are best left private, and this is one of them.

When I first see her in the distance, I'm almost too scared to hope. But I'm already leaning forward, digging my heels deeper into the stirrups as I give Helios his reins.

After all the mornings I've spent trying to run…let it be a chase now if it has to be.

# CHAPTER 35
## CORA

I don't spot him until he is already closer than he should be. Until I have no choice but to start flying, adrenaline coursing through my veins and exhilaration nipping at my heels. The only thing that feels faster than Tess and me is my heart as it thunders in my chest. And Aiden. He's gaining on me.

He's going to catch me or I'm going to fall and break my neck trying to outrun him, and it irritates me knowing the only reason either hasn't already occurred is because he really has taught me to be a better rider. Because he's taught me to be in control instead of just hanging on.

When I hear him shout my name behind me, my fingers wrap more firmly in Tess's reins and mane. Urging her on as she eats up terrain and churns up dust in our wake, so thick that when I dare look back I can't even see him.

But I know he's there. And I know I'm still not going as fast as he is.

Aiden shouts at me again a few moments later, only this time he's no longer behind me but drawing even. And I dare one more glance in his direction, seeing no less than complete command of the power beneath him. So captivating that when his hand reaches out to grab Tess's reins and pull us up, I almost let him.

At the last moment, I jerk away, Tess tossing her head in protest and my steady seat shifting precariously as I change direction. Aiden recovers quickly, faster than I do, pulling up alongside me again as both of our horses thunder toward a grove of trees.

"Dammit, Cora, *stop*," he yells, and I'm not sure if I can't or won't at this point. He makes another grab for my reins, and I pull away again, but this time, he anticipates it. And when Tess swings left again, faltering slightly, Aiden falls back only so he can shoot forward on my other side to cut us off.

Spooked by his sudden reappearance, Tess rears, but I keep my seat even as I hold onto her neck so that I'm not thrown. A vain effort, as it turns out, because my time in the saddle has apparently concluded regardless.

Aiden is already on the ground and reaching for me in an instant, pulling me off Tess's back to set me in front of him. "Are you out of your goddamn mind? Or just trying to get yourself fucking killed?"

He looks tired and windswept, his breathing heavy and his posture tight, and I must look the same as I struggle to remember how to speak. To remember that I'm upset with him instead of ready to fall into him.

"Answer me, Cora," he barks again. "What the hell were you thinking?"

"I was thinking—" I shove at him but he barely moves, massive and imposing while I snarl, "I was *thinking* that I was leaving."

"Because of this?" He pulls the ticket out of his pocket and holds it up in front of me. "This is why you up and left in the night?"

I stare at it, then back at him. Even the sight of it is enough to make me want to cry again. "I'm not going back," I shout at him, pushing more at his chest until he grabs my wrists to stop me. "I *won't* go back."

"Fuckin' right you won't." He jerks me forward, and I have just enough time for a surprised gasp before his mouth crashes against mine. The force of it—of him—enough to knock me backwards, but he holds me firm. "Don't you ever fucking run off again." His commands are quick, muttered between kisses and the type of desperation you can *feel*. "Don't you ever leave again."

I can't meet his frantic pace even though I'm trying. Even though I want to, right up until he breaks from me, his hand enveloping mine as he starts tugging me toward the trees. "Aiden." I grab at his arm, wanting him to face me again, but he keeps walking. "Aiden, *wait*." I dig my heels into the dirt and it's at least enough to get him to pivot back, although that, too, becomes fruitless when he simply bends and throws me over his shoulder.

"*Aiden*." I smack my hands against his back, resorting to using my nails when it doesn't make a bit of difference. "What are you *doing*?"

"We come back, and you're gone," he says as he keeps going. "Been looking for you all night. Been worried you were fucking *dead*. You couldn't have just waited."

I thump his back again with my fist before giving up with a huff, my energy temporarily spent. "What was I *supposed* to wait for? For you to come back so you could drag me to the coach yourself? Why does it matter how I leave if you want me gone?"

He deposits me back on the ground as abruptly as he'd removed me from it, my world spinning until I'm staring up at him again along with the unrestrained ferocity in his dark eyes. "I do *not* want you gone," he fumes. "I told you that's never been what I wanted. I wasn't lyin'."

"Then why keep the ticket?" I ask him.

"Because it was yours. And I thought at some point you might want it."

"Then why not put it with the rest of my things? You gave me back everything else. Why not that?"

"*Because*, Cora…" Aiden replies, crowding me with his size until my back presses against the wide base of a tree, its riot of fall leaves above us blocking out the blue sky. "Because I didn't *want* you to use it. Because no matter how hard I tried, I couldn't give you something that could take you away. Fuck, I *still* can't."

I bite my bottom lip, the hands that I have braced against his chest pushing at him less and pulling at him more. "You wouldn't have kept it if—"

He holds the ticket up in front of me again and rips it decisively into pieces, letting them fall into the dirt and crushing them beneath the heel of his boot.

"But—"

I stare at the torn pieces until I start to cry, then I *really* cry when he cups my face in his hands. "Cora, baby, what have I told you about these tears?"

I laugh but it comes out as a half-sob. "You hate them."

"I fucking *hate* them." He rests his forehead against mine. "I'm so sorry, sweetheart. I'm so sorry I made you think I wanted you anywhere but with us. I got so caught up in thinking that…that if I took what I wanted then maybe you wouldn't get what you needed."

"I need you," I say softly. "I need you and Cypress. I don't want a different life."

"I know." He places a gentle kiss over each of my eyelids as they flutter closed and brushes my tears away with the pads of his thumbs. "And you have us. We're yours, all right?"

My heart is still racing, my fingers gripping the material of his vest as his mouth drifts its way down my cheek. "Mine?"

"Yours, Cora." His mouth meets mine again. "Please stay with us, baby. No more runnin'. Either of us."

"Okay." I return his kiss with every bit of longing and pent-up emotion I can muster, and he groans when my tongue brushes with his. "Okay, no more running."

"Fuck, I missed you." He buries his hand in my hair so he can tilt my head back and travel down my neck. His lips skimming the mark he left before, as if reassuring himself it's still there.

"I missed you, too. I couldn't sleep. Where's Cypress?"

"He's on his way." Aiden smiles against my skin. "Not sure how much sleep I can promise you when he gets here, though."

His mouth returns to mine as his palms caress my sides, his fingertips pressing hard enough that they feel like they're directly on my skin even through the thin fabric of my old dress. "Can I touch you?" he asks, his nose brushing the shell of my ear. "Say I can."

A small, relieved sound escapes me as I nod, more than willing to let him do whatever he has in his mind to strip away any lingering doubt, and he grins, the kind of breathtaking smile I've seen so rarely from him. The kind I want to see again and again, but then his mouth slants over mine while his quick fingers drag up my dress. One of his hands slipping under the fabric, brushing the inside of my thighs through my undergarments, easing higher and higher.

"You're shaking, Cora. Do you want me to stop?"

"No," I answer forcefully. I don't think I'll survive if he does, so I tell him again, "Need you, Aiden."

His hand drifts higher until it's positioned at the apex of my thighs, and I gasp when I feel him touching me there, cupping me through the fabric before slipping his fingers through the seam. A deep rumbling moan reverberates through his chest as he turns his hand and brushes his knuckles over my curls, lower over my center. Then I watch as Aiden drops to his knees, his eyes never leaving mine as he places my skirts in my hands to hold them up for him.

When he does finally break my gaze, it's to grab the waistband of my undergarments, dragging them down while he places reverent kisses along every inch of skin he bares until I step out of them and he's able to toss them aside.

"The way I've wanted you," he murmurs, pressing another kiss to the inside of my thigh as he encourages my legs farther apart. Making me gasp again when he guides one of them over his shoulder and leaves me no choice but to rely on the tree at my back and his strong grip to keep my balance.

Standing like this, I'm completely exposed to him while he intimately examines me with his tongue against his bottom lip. While he cups me again, spreads me, drags his thumb through my center with such a slick, easy glide that I wonder if I should be embarrassed.

"Do you know how much I've fucking thought about this, Cora?"

he asks as I moan when he finds my clit. The spike of sensation from having *his* fingers there so different than when it had been my own, even with Cypress guiding me. "Do you know how many times I laid awake at night thinking about this sweet cunt?"

My breathing stutters, nerves replaced by an ache building low in my abdomen as I ask, "You did?"

He nods slowly then leans closer, inhaling my scent and pressing a soft kiss to my mound in a way that feels as filthy as the sound I make when he does it.

"You smell so fucking good." His gaze shifts back up to my face, two of his fingers going to his mouth before he places them back on my clit. "I already know Cy taught you some things yesterday, but I still have a few I can teach you, too."

I *need* so badly that I feel like I could cry again, and a broken sob does escape me when I next say his name. "*Aiden.*"

The corner of his mouth lifts, his warm eyes gone molten. "Now that type of crying I don't mind so much." His fingers move in slow circles, a moan on my lips that turns helpless the longer he does it. "So fucking pretty."

"Oh, *God.*" My eyes squeeze shut, the desperate grip I have on my skirt turning my fingers white as I try to find something to keep me grounded. Already about to fall apart before the pressure changes, and when I open my eyes again, Aiden's fingers are gone from me, replaced with his *mouth*. His tongue is warm and wide, my body jerking involuntarily when he wraps his lips around my clit and *sucks*.

"Be a good girl and hold still, Cora," he tells me, turning his head to nip my inner thigh in warning. When I yelp at the sharp sting before squirming again, unable to stop with how amazing this feels, he voices his disapproval by tightening his grip on the leg he still has over his shoulder, by placing his other forearm against my stomach so I can't move. Then his mouth is back on me, his grunt of satisfaction coursing into me, through me.

"Christ, that's it. You're fucking soaking me," Aiden mutters, the bridge of his nose rubbing against my clit as his tongue drags over me again and again. "Going to do this every day. Going to wake you up in the morning with my mouth on this cunt, you understand?"

I don't have it in me to respond, too busy careening over the edge I had only carefully approached the day before, my stability giving way to the point that Aiden has no choice but to catch me and put me on my back when my release slams into me hard enough that I see stars.

"Oh, God. Oh, *God*, that was—" I start to say, still panting, moving to press my thighs together to try to relieve the intensity, but Aiden's broad shoulders are already in the way as he settles back between my legs.

"Told you I had things to teach you, Cora, and you're about to learn I'm not nearly done," he says, smirking, the bottom half of his face still slick with me. "How many times do you think we can get you to come?"

"How many? What do you—" I gasp as he yanks me closer, rucks my skirt up again from where it had slipped down to cover me. Feeling even more sensitive now, as soon as his mouth finds me, my hands fly to fist in his hair, knocking his hat to the ground. With a cocky smile, he lifts up, grabbing it and placing it on my head instead.

"So the sun won't get in your eyes," he politely explains when I give him a questioning look as he lies back on the ground, already busy navigating both of my legs over his shoulders this time. "Want you to be comfortable, baby, since you're going to be on your back for a while. Isn't that right, Cypress?"

Surprised, I turn my head quickly, immediately encountering a pair of shined black boots coming up beside me, and I smile when I look up to see sharp blue eyes taking in Aiden and me with an expression of amusement. "*Cy*."

"Hello, Cora," he says in greeting, crouching and brushing his fingertips over my cheek and mouth. "I'd tell you how much we disliked your absence, little bird, but it seems Aiden is already set on making that clear." Cypress's gaze flicks down to his partner. "You know, *wolf*, it's customary to wait for all guests…" His eyes darken as he watches Aiden's thumb find my clit again, sees the way he drags his tongue over my entrance as I whimper. "It's *polite* to wait for all guests to arrive before *eating*."

Aiden scoffs, his heated breath passing over me in a way that makes me tremble before he raises his head. "You want to talk manners right now?" he asks, his thumb continuing its slow circles. "Really?"

"Well, I think it's only fai—"

"You *taught* her to make herself come while I was off burying someone."

There's a long pause, one that I also participate in given that I'm having a hard time thinking, let alone *speaking*, about anything other than what Aiden is currently doing.

"Fine," Cypress concedes. "Then we'll call it even."

"Nope," Aiden replies, and his thumb stops, but only so he can use both hands to adjust my legs wider, giving himself better access to me. "Firsts are firsts, Cypress. I'm owed at least two for that before you get to…*eat*."

"I don't recall that being written anywhere."

"Then find a damn pen."

"Are you two really arguing over—" I start to say, taking advantage of my temporary reprieve, but I stop, mouth still open as I watch Aiden spit right where he has me spread open beneath him. The clear liquid landing over my entrance so that he can use two of his fingers to spread it upward, gliding over my clit in a way that makes my back arch.

"All right, two," I hear Cypress say from nearby. "So we're even."

"No," Aiden says again. "I get three. *Then* we're even."

"How do you figure?"

"Because you're going to make her come when I'm done. And then you'll be ahead again."

"You—cannot—" I'm panting, already close to coming based on the way my thighs are starting to shake. "You cannot seriously be—"

Aiden's fingers slip lower, teasing my entrance, not quite pushing inside, and God, I'm about to *beg* him before he lowers his head and wraps his lips around my clit again. I come *hard*, moaning so loudly that I almost don't hear him tell me after, "Shh, baby, we're negotiating."

With some effort, I lift my head to glare at him. "Can't help but feel—" I look between him and Cypress. "Feel like I should get a say in this."

"Maybe if you hadn't left us in the middle of the night, sweetheart. Best take your punishment," Aiden replies, glaring back, but his expression softens before he asks, "You want us to stop?"

I plan to tell him that my heart is already pounding, that I'm already sure I'm not going to survive if they are *actually* serious about what they're *negotiating*, but all that comes out of my mouth is a breathy sounding, "No. Don't stop."

He grins. "Thought you'd say that. Really are meant for us, baby, aren't you?"

"She is," Cypress murmurs, and when I look back at him, he lifts my right hand to his mouth, kissing my palm and each of my fingertips in turn. "You know, I did warn you, Cora, about not being able to lift these lovely fingers by the time we are through." He looks at Aiden. "You said three to call, wolf?"

Aiden nods, still grinning, a mirror to the expression on Cypress's face as he keeps his eyes on me while asking him, "And what if I were to raise you?"

# CHAPTER 36
## CYPRESS

I wake believing I'm in a windowless room before I have a chance to see the stars, to see Aiden and Cora asleep beside me.

She looks beautiful…as well as thoroughly debauched with her kiss-swollen lips, mused hair, and rumpled clothes. Her bare legs intertwined with Aiden's as he sleeps wrapped around her, his face completely relaxed in a way it rarely is when he's awake.

His hand is outstretched in my direction, telling me that he had a hold of me, too, before I was jarred away from where Cora was curled against me.

Unable to stay put, I get to my feet, walking to the horses where they graze nearby and leading them back, trying to dispel the anxious feeling that still clings to me. Hating to wake either Aiden or Cora despite the feeling in my gut that it's time for us to move on.

I reach down and nudge Aiden awake first, and as usual, he's immediately at attention, his eyes searching and his body poised to act.

"It's all right," I reassure him. "But we should likely start heading back."

He nods, carefully disentangling himself from Cora before standing and stretching. I keep my face turned away so that he can't study it.

"Think maybe we wore her out?" he asks wryly, and I glance back at Cora still sleeping soundly, some of the tension easing from my frame as I laugh.

"For now. May your God help you, Aiden, when she learns to turn those talents you're teaching her back on you."

"Ought to start listening to your own warnings, Cy," he says, crouching to scoop her up before adding, "She can ride with me."

I murmur my agreement, knowing he's not yet ready to be separated from her as I move to tie Tess's reins to my saddle. Cora only stirs when I take hold of her long enough for Aiden to swing up on Helios.

"Go back to sleep," I murmur to her while she's cradled against my chest. "We're only heading back to camp."

She nods as I pass her up to Aiden and watch her settle against his chest while he places a gentle kiss against her hair.

"Mm, that's good," she mumbles. "Will be nice to be home."

I couldn't agree more.

# CHAPTER 37
## CORA

A beige sheet of paper stands stark against the side of a blood-red barn on the outskirts of town, the same one I'd apparently been heading for when Aiden had tracked me down yesterday.

Cypress spotted it first, riding alongside the wagon on Cerberus while I sat with Aiden to my left on the bench. Prompting both him and Aiden to dismount while the latter's request that I stay in the wagon fell on deaf ears.

One poster. Three portraits of three very different individuals. One of a fearsome-looking woman I don't recognize and two of menacing-looking men that I'd know anywhere. And above and below all of them? Fresh black script that boldly proclaims:

**WANTED**
**THE MIDNIGHT GANG**
**NOTORIOUS MURDERERS AND THIEVES**
**$1000 REWARD IF BROUGHT IN ALIVE**

*"The Midnight Gang…"* Cypress mutters as he draws up closer to the notice. "I quite like that. Not a bad likeness either for Aiden and myself." He turns to me as he adds, "They did not fully capture your beauty, little bird, but who could?"

"We're being charged as murderers?" I question, in shock even though I've been present or near present for five. "But—"

"Fucking hell," Aiden spits, looking around for anyone who may have spotted us, and not looking the least bit relieved even when he finds no one. "*Fuck*. We're going. Now."

I turn, following him toward the wagon, but I pause when I hear the sound of paper tearing behind us. I look back over my shoulder in time to see Cypress ripping down the notice, then carefully rolling it up before tucking it into the inside pocket of his coat.

"A keepsake," he says as he jogs to catch up, and the look Aiden gives him holds so much agitation that even Cypress seems to think twice about pushing him further. Unfortunately, I am still too stunned to feel the proper amount of danger.

"Wait," I say when Aiden moves to hoist me back up to the wagon bench. "We're really *wanted*? But it was self-defense."

"Apparently someone disagrees," he says back. "Please, get up in the wagon."

"But people are looking for us now? Because of what happened with that man in Last Chance?"

"It can't have been because of him. That was only a couple days ago, and these look like they've been up for at least a week or two…" Aiden trails off and lets go of me to pull out a pocketbook that isn't his from inside of his vest. Hurriedly, he starts rifling through it, and almost immediately, I see a piece of paper of the same shade tucked inside, my stomach sinking before he even has a chance to unfold it. "Fuck," he mutters, once he has the creased copy of the wanted poster in his hands. "Fuck, son of a bitch had it with him. That's why he tracked us down. He saw the poster and realized who we were. That's why he said more would come looking. *Fuck*, then that means…"

"Preston," I murmur, but he shakes his head, glancing at Cypress.

"There were four, you said," he argues. "I killed all of them."

"You're certain?" Cypress asks, frowning.

"For fuck's sake, I know what dead looks like, Cy." Aiden looks back at me. "Did you see anyone else there besides them? Before we got there?"

"No, it was just me and Tess and then… Hold on, you told me that you and Cypress came back to the stable for the horses, but Cerberus and Helios were already gone. I remember seeing them gone. Why did you come back to the stable that night?"

"For you, Cora," Aiden replies, sounding at his wit's end.

"You did?"

"Yes."

I can't help but smile. "Really?"

"Was I not clear yesterday when—never mind, can we please talk about this later?

"But—"

"Cora, we were both infatuated with you. Of course it was you that we came back for," Aiden snaps, his expression turning pleading. "Christ, I need to think."

"But if this is because of Preston…" I start to say, unable to stop myself. "Then it's my fault. You were protecting me."

Aiden shakes his head. "This isn't your fault. Wasn't then. Isn't now."

"But if not for me…" I feel Cypress's hand on my back, soothing as he strokes up and down. "The poster says *alive*. Does that mean they only want to bring us in to question us?" My conversation with the sheriff back in Preston comes to memory, how he said most bounty hunters would rather the simplicity of bringing someone in dead, but if the poster specifically says *alive*… "If someone else finds us, they won't want to kill us, because then they won't get the reward, right?"

"No one else is going to find us," Aiden reassures me, tugging me closer so he can hold me against his chest. "We're going to figure this out. We might just need to lie low for a while."

"Where?" I mutter, still thinking of the reward on the paper and about how many people like David would want to collect it. "It's so much money."

"Aiden's right. We have a place we can go. As it happens, this is hardly our first time on a wanted poster, little bird," Cypress says, still intending to be comforting but the look I give him must convey my surprise, because he adds, "Clerical errors can be so common."

"*Clerical errors?*" Aiden repeats, coughing over the words. "That's what you're going with right now?"

"Well…that's what we have always *gone* with. A couple hundred dollars in the right pocket, and this will all get cleared up."

I sniff, starting to feel a little hopeful if Cypress is so unconcerned. "It will?"

"Of course," Cypress says easily. "This is nothing."

"*Nothing?*" Aiden repeats again, sounding incredulous. "She's on a fucking wanted poster."

"A rite of passage. She's truly one of us now," Cypress replies, bending down to kiss me when I relax enough to look up at him.

"But who the fuck knows that? Cy, all *three* of us are on this poster. Who is still breathing that knows?" They exchange a look, and the anxiety that had so recently abated comes back at full force when I see the first flicker of uncertainty in Cypress's eyes. Then it doubles as I follow Aiden's gaze to the pair of riders who are now approaching over the crest of the horizon, still a long ways off.

"That was fast," Cypress mutters, swinging back up on Cerberus.

"What do we do?" I ask Aiden, going without hesitation this time as he helps me into the wagon and climbs up beside me. "Should we run?"

He doesn't remove his eyes from them, waiting for Cypress to come up on my other side beside the wagon before he urges Helios forward with Tess following behind. "If we run, they'll know we have something we're running from."

"They seem to be coming from outside of town. They may not have even seen the poster. Probably weary travelers just like us," Cypress suggests, but while Aiden seems to make a sound of agreement, he still adjusts his hands as we head their direction, moving the wagon reins to his left and slipping his pistol into his right, hiding it in the fabric of my skirt on the seat next to him.

"Do you have your gun?" he asks, and I nod, showing him the leather holster that Cypress had fitted over the right side of one of my new dresses this morning. All of my old clothes mysteriously vanished right around the time that he started a fire for breakfast. Though I can't say I miss them.

"Don't reach for it unless I say. Don't even act like you have one,"

Aiden says after giving me an approving nod, though apparently he's unable to keep himself from adding, "Should be easy for you."

"Very," I say, glaring at him. "In fact, I'll just go back to not carrying it once we make it through this, if that's what you'd prefer."

"*No*," he says, giving me a begrudging smile. "I prefer you armed and hostile."

"Funny, I thought you preferred me nake—"

"*Christ*, Cora, don't put that in my head right as we're approaching men who might want to kill us. Although, since we are about to die…"

"Wait, you don't *really* think we're about to die?"

"If you two are quite finished bickering," Cypress mutters, doing his best to suppress his amused grin as he stays close to the wagon. "I think it might not give off the foreboding air we are going for."

"Well, never thought I'd see this day," Aiden replies before putting his attention forward again, and despite our predicament, I also find myself trying not to laugh when he continues, "Cypress scolding someone for talking too much."

# CHAPTER 38
## CORA

It seems to take ages for the approaching riders to reach us, my stomach knotting in apprehension the closer we get while I try to give the appearance of disinterest.

The first thing I note is that they don't look at all like the weary travelers Cypress had hoped for. Their clothes are too clean, too freshly pressed, their faces recently shaven. The one on the left is young, round-faced, and sporting a self-assured grin. The one on the right is older, closer to Aiden and Cypress's age, his own smile more of a sneer as he pulls his horse up several yards out, directly in our path. When his younger companion does the same, we follow suit.

"Good morning," Cypress says in casual greeting, leaning forward with his hands draped over his saddle horn. Showing them clearly that he doesn't have hold of either his pistols or his rifle. "Is there something we can assist you with? Perhaps directions?"

"You know, there is something…" the older man says slowly. "Word came through a little while back that there's a mighty big reward being offered for the apprehension of a few criminals." His gaze lands on each of us in turn. "We've been riding from town to town hoping we'll get lucky."

"Well, in that case, happy hunting," Cypress says cheerfully, moving as if to spur Cerberus to walk on. And that's when the first gun is drawn, followed immediately by the second. Both riders point their rifles at Cypress, who still has yet to so much as blink in the direction of his own. He smiles, even as I jerk forward in panic, Aiden's left arm reaching across to settle me back in my seat. His right hand presses against my thigh, reminding me of the still hidden gun.

"I really would appreciate it if you would lower your weapons," Cypress says, this time dripping more venom than sugar. "It's not very polite."

"Polite?" the older man scoffs. "It considered good manners to murder innocent folk?"

"Depends on your definition of innocence."

"How about to rob a lawman?"

"To rob a lawman," Cypress repeats slowly, his eyes flicking to Aiden. "Now that's interesting. I don't recall robbing any lawmen. At least not recently."

"Not the way I hear it," the man replies, spitting a wad of tobacco from his cheek onto the ground. "The way I hear it, you robbed a deputy in Preston along with four of his men. Same four men you attacked and killed in cold blood before leaving town."

"They attacked me," I try to explain, failing to heed another one of Aiden's warnings. "Elliot and Jake—"

"So you do know them?" the man asks with a smile, and I bite the inside of my cheek, immediately recognizing my error.

"From what I hear," he goes on, "you seemed to know a lot of the men in that town pretty well…" He gives me a look that makes my hands tighten into fists. "Seduced those boys to their graves, didn't you? One of them a new father. Another one a reputable business owner who gave you shelter. People of that town took you in, and that is how you repay them?"

"That *new father* threw my head against the wall so hard that I was unconscious for days. They attacked me," I say again, and I can feel Aiden tense like lightning waiting to strike at my side. "They deserved what they got."

The older man shakes his head and looks to Cypress as if they're on the same side. "A real viper, this one. Probably planning to off you boys next."

"I should think not, since we don't plan on trying to harm her. Women can be so particular about such things," Cypress says with a warm smile that hardly conceals his malice. "Now, you *boys* on the other hand…"

"Cypress," Aiden murmurs in a low warning, then addresses the younger man first. "There doesn't need to be any trouble here. We can all pretend like we didn't see each other."

"Now how would that benefit me?" the older asks. "Can't collect a reward for someone I haven't seen."

"No, but you can keep your life," Aiden replies, appealing to the other again as he says, "You don't need to die for some money."

The youthful arrogance temporarily flickers, and he looks to his partner. "They do look a bit dang—"

The older man reaches over and cuffs him on the back of the head before snarling, "Let me handle this." He turns back to Cypress. "Tell you what…Cypress, is it? You look like a man who knows how to strike a deal. Hand her over, and we will look the other way when it comes to you and your partner here."

A cold wave of fear washes over me, even if I don't believe that Aiden or Cypress would do it. The suggestion is still enough, and I think it must be the same for Cypress because he cocks his head, staring the man down before he says, "Now why would I do that?"

"Word is that the deputy is real anxious to see her again. Wants her to explain herself, since it doesn't look too great the way she abused his generosity," the man continues. "Don't worry, I'll make sure she gets to him. As soon as I'm through with her." His eyes rake me up and down slowly. "I'll even split the reward money with you. What do you say?"

His answer comes in the form of a resounding *bang* of a gun, Aiden drawing and aiming his weapon so fast that I hadn't even seen it happen until the man was already falling. The last noise he makes is the smack of his body hitting the dirt, his horse spinning and taking off at a gallop in his wake. By the time his riding companion has time to blink, Cypress and Aiden both have their guns on him.

"Toss your weapon and get down," Aiden tells him in a voice that doesn't invite argument, but the young man still seems to consider it. His hands shake as he holds his rifle aloft, and Aiden cocks his gun again. "Get. Down."

He does, wisely throwing his rifle into the brush before he dismounts.

"All the way, kid," Aiden orders again and the young man hits his knees before lowering himself to the dirt and putting his hands behind his head.

Aiden jumps down from the wagon, his weapon still aimed and his boots crunching in the loose dirt as he strides over to collect the discarded weapon. After a quick once-over, he keeps it, as well as the one off the dead man, before stalking forward to stand over the man on the ground. Aiden places his boot in the center of the young man's back, and aims his pistol at his head.

"Don't kill me," he begs. "I never saw you. I'll swear it."

Aiden doesn't respond at first, just lets the silence hang over them like a second gun until he says, in a flat voice, "I'm assuming you either know your way to Preston or can figure it out?"

The young man fervently nods.

"Speak up," Aiden tells him, pressing his boot down harder.

"Yes, sir," the young man winces out.

"Good, because I want you to tell the deputy there that you saw me. You tell him I want the posters gone, and that if he comes after one of mine again, he'll find his way to an early grave. Very, *very* slowly." Aiden leans in even harder, and I suddenly feel like I'm the one who can't breathe. "That clear?"

"Yes, sir," he says again.

I can't move. I'm so transfixed by Aiden, by this version of him in front of me, that I almost don't notice Cypress has dismounted as well, moving to Aiden's side and placing a hand on his arm. Much like Aiden had for me when I'd stood over David.

Aiden turns his head to Cypress, the internal struggle clear on his face before he lets his weapon fall and once again speaks to the young man. "You don't do as I say and I'll find you." He eases off his boot. "Now go."

The youth scrambles to his feet, taking off on his horse within seconds.

"You think he'll do it?" I hear Cypress mutter.

Aiden nods. "He will. The upstanding deputy may not listen, but that boy won't want to spend his life looking over his shoulder."

All I can think is that is precisely what we are about to do.

# CHAPTER 39
## CORA

A week of hard riding passes by, our party stopping only long enough to rest the horses and ourselves before we move again. The path we take is jagged, full of backtracking and misdirection in the event that we should be followed again, which leaves plenty of time to think about what's chasing us. Although, that's not the part that has me most worried.

Aiden is.

He's barely spoken since the three of us rode away from that last town, a far-off look in his eyes whenever I sneak a glance at him. And it's as if all the progress we'd made only days ago has suddenly been lost.

I know Cypress is worried, too. I see him watching him, see the lines in his brow even as he tries to fill the quiet with his stories.

I want to ask Cypress what I can do, how I can help. But I don't trust the night to keep our secrets while Aiden paces so close.

Has he even slept? If he has, it's not been next to Cypress and me, his bedroll still cold and undisturbed when I go to sleep and when I wake.

I just want him back.

On the fifth night, I see them argue, reminding me of that evening I'd watched them by the water from my hiding place. There's nowhere to hide now, but I wouldn't even if I could.

Cypress's hands frame Aiden's face as they stand by the wagon, their voices low but their emotions high. Only this time, it's Aiden that shakes his head and walks away, and Cypress can't stop him even though he tries.

Two days later, the sun is still high when we reach our destination, a small log cabin tucked deep into the mountain woods.

To most, it would be nothing special. A cozy single room with three small windows and a fireplace along the back wall. A large woven rug in front of it. A stove, a table, and a few chairs on one side. But for all its simplicity, it's the item tucked into the back corner that makes it feel like a palace.

"Oh, God," I practically moan. "A bed."

Cypress chuckles softly beside me, putting his arm around me and nuzzling into my hair. "A *big* bed."

I grin, and I look back for Aiden, my short-lived smile fading as I see him already walking away into the woods with Cypress's rifle to hunt. My gaze returns to Cypress, his eyes thoughtful as he watches, too. When I turn to wrap my arms tight around him, I press my face into his shirt and inhale the spicy scent of pine and mint. No trace of leather and smoke.

"All right, Cypress," I say on the exhale. "Talk."

# CHAPTER 40
## CYPRESS

The first time I was here was after I'd gotten caught at the end of a knife blade, the sharp edge cutting into the curve of my right shoulder before I'd managed to twist away.

I'd lost a lot of blood before Aiden was able to patch me up, more than I'd wanted to admit until I'd nearly fallen from Cerberus as we fled. Aiden had grabbed my reins and swung up behind me without hesitation, holding me in place while I drifted in and out of consciousness. When I woke again, we were here.

"Cypress?"

I know I've stalled as long as I can when I hear Cora call me back to the present. I've already tried as many distractions as are available in the small cabin, the nearby creek where she could try to wash away the last few days proving to be the most successful.

When she came back I managed to slip around her questions again by slipping away to do the same before she could pin me down, but now she's standing across from me in the little room that feels even smaller with the way she's staring at me, hands on her hips and absolutely unwilling to be diverted again. At least, I don't think… "Little bird, did you see the be—"

"I saw the bed, Cypress. Tell me what's wrong with Aiden."

Well, I tried. Admirably, considering that I am struggling with my own attention span while also trying to redirect hers. Cora had interestingly failed to fully redress after she washed up, and is currently raising my blood in more ways than one, standing there comfortable and confident as can be in her white camisole and petticoat.

Not that I haven't seen her in less, memories that are burned into my brain as they burn me up, but there really is *something* about women's undergarments. Her mouth curves as she watches me study her.

She's doing this on purpose. Trying to throw me off. And it's working.

I wonder if she will let me buy her more things now. Because she would look so very lovely in something from Paris. Something with fine lace that she has no other reason to wear except to have Aiden and me take it off her with our teeth. Surely she'll let me. Let me get her whatever she wants now that she's firmly decided to throw her lot in with ours.

Clearly she has, otherwise she would have turned tail and ran a long time ago, and right now, Cora's refusing to budge.

No, my little bird is stubborn. Smart. Strong. My wild one. *Our* wild one. And for fuck's sake, she *needs* to be fucked. It's a crime she hasn't been, the only one I'd willingly plead guilty to as long as I get to do the honor myself. Well, and Aiden. Who also needs a hard fuck if he is to come out of the dark spell he's under, but who currently won't come closer than ten paces away.

"Cypress," she says again. "Now is not the time to go silent. Please, tell me."

I sigh, rolling my head from side to side as I try to find the right words. Scores and scores of them at my disposal, but none seem accurate to explain why someone might need to give up control to feel like they still have it.

"He's afraid," I say simply, not enough to satisfy either of us.

"Because of the wanted posters?"

"Yes. And because he already knows what it is to lose everything and is terrified it'll happen again." Her eyes soften, her brow creasing with sadness even before I ask, "Has he told you? About what happened with his family?"

She shakes her head. "Not in so many words. He said once that he hasn't had much to call his own."

"That's true," I acknowledge before looking around. "You know, this cabin is his. He built it himself once he had the means. Not that he spends much time here anymore. Afraid that's my doing."

"Cypress, tell me," she says again, and I sigh, relenting.

"He lost his parents when he was very young. Nine years old. A robbery that went too far."

"A robbery? But..."

"You're wondering how, in that case, he ended up with a thief?" I ask, and when she nods, I admit, "I think he used to ask himself the same. Especially in the beginning. I told you, Cora, I was not always so discerning with the people I sat down to cards with. Aiden was the one to first insist we apply rules. Well, only two really."

"Rules? About who you can con?"

"Yes. One is that they have to be sinners."

"You don't believe in sin."

"Aiden does. After he lost his parents, he was sent to an orphanage, lived there until he ran away at thirteen. He barely survived for a few years after. Slept in a lot of stables," I tell her, watching as the new information helps her see things in a new light. "As it happens, the orphanage neglected to teach him very much about how to live. Too busy teaching him all the ways he would be damned once he died. Ten, aren't there? In that set of rules? Always strikes me as odd that the one about killing is so far down on that list."

"It's sixth," she says, her eyes closing briefly. "Does Aiden believe he's damned? Because he's killed people?"

"He does."

"But he always wants to be the one to do it. I've seen him. He gets upset when you step in. I don't understand. If he believes it will damn him, and you don't, then why—"

"Because he'd rather our ledgers and our sentences read the same when and if the time comes that we stand before God. Just in case," I say to her, not at all surprised when she seems to struggle with that answer, and I smile softly. "You fall in love with a sinner and there's two ways it can go, little bird. You either raise them to salvation or you join them in damnation."

"And he chose the latter?" she asks.

"What do you think?"

"I don't believe it's that simple," she says, her eyes narrowing. "But what about you, Cy? What do you believe?"

# CHAPTER 41
## CORA

I'm quiet now, waiting for him to continue, because any subject that Cypress trips over must be one worth spending time on. He looks away, his hands tucked into his pockets in uncharacteristic nervousness.

"I believe…I believe that sometimes damnation and salvation are the same. You know, he thinks he's protecting me by being the one to do the killing," Cypress explains, before tacking on, "As if there's some invisible weight that a soul can withstand before it breaks." He pauses. "He doesn't see that I already made my choice long ago."

"What choice?"

"Survival for my soul."

Is that what he believes? That he doesn't have a soul? "Cypress—"

"I've never killed without reason. Even if that reason was simply to give myself a chance," he adds as a defense, perhaps misinterpreting the reason behind my disagreement. "But, I can't ignore the fact that I have killed more than most, and if there really is some kind of tally kept, I'm certain it's not counted in my favor."

"Then the count is wrong," I tell him resolutely, and he smiles, looking a bit more like himself again. "You said Aiden insisted on rules. That there are two. His is that they have to be sinners. What is yours?"

"That they think they're untouchable."

"Untouchable?" I almost laugh. "You want to ruin their pride?"

"No, little bird, I want to ruin their *life*."

There's anger in his tone, that same chilling voice he had when talking to the man who stopped us just outside of town. "Why?"

"Because I can."

"Because you can or because someone took that from you?" I guess. "Because Aiden isn't the only one who knows what it feels like to lose everything?"

He inhales, drawing himself up. "Very sharp, little bird."

"What happened?"

"That's a long story."

"Then tell me the beginning."

He shifts his stance, drifting closer to the window so he can look outside before he tells me, "My father died when I was young, even younger than Aiden was when he lost his. I don't really remember him."

"He was killed?" I guess, but he shakes his head.

"No, nothing so intentional," he replies. "One day he simply fell ill. And a few days later… It was only my mother and me for a long time after that."

"She was good to you," I say, able to tell by the way he mentions her. "You loved her."

"I did," he says. "She was…beautiful. Strong. And she loved me fiercely." He smiles softly. "Because it was only her and me, she had to work a lot, had no choice but to leave me home with mainly a stack of books to keep me company. She loved the classics, the old myths and fairy tales most of all. Whenever she got home, she would pick up wherever I had left off, and we would read together. So many times that I can still recite them from memory."

I think about the way Cypress likes to read by the fire, how delighted he seems whenever he has Aiden and me there to listen.

"As I got older, she started to worry that I would need someone to look up to. That I needed a father to guide me. I told her I didn't. She was more than enough, but she fretted over me, and when she met a wealthy and seemingly good man on the street one day, she thought perhaps he could be the one. That he could give us a better life, an easier one."

My chest starts to hurt, having a feeling where this is going, and I wish I could reach into the past and change the direction.

"The day after the wedding, he started hitting her, and I tried so many times to tell someone. Tried to get someone to help us, but he was well connected, had enough money to think he owned us both." Cypress sighs. "No one would do anything. So I did."

"Cy, how…how old were you?"

"Fourteen."

My eyes close as the picture of Aiden as a lonely child with his brown eyes and brown curls shifts to the image of Cypress as a lonely teenager. That dark hair and angular face and those startling blue eyes forced to watch someone hurt his loved one.

"I shot him," he says simply. "With the gun he kept displayed on his desk. The same one he used to boast had belonged to some general. Used to say it could have won the war if only he'd been there to wield it." He grins, eyes flashing when he looks back at me from his stance by the window. "It certainly won mine."

"You killed him?"

"I did. And then my mother told me to run." His shoulders fall slightly. "And I did that, too. I wish I'd… I sent her a letter once. I don't know if she ever received it. But I wanted to tell her that I was all right. That I had Aiden. That I was still looking for—" He lets out a soft *oof* as I collide into him, wrap my arms around his shoulders, and pull him to me so that I can kiss him as if that alone could grant him absolution.

Not that he needs it.

The man who saved the person who loved him, who stepped into that stable to save me, who took me in when I had no one and who had cared for me every day since—that man could never be condemned in my eyes.

He hums his familiar song, cupping my face as he kisses me back, looking at me again with such clear affection that I feel like I could sink into it forever, that I feel like I could tell him now that I love him, too, because I know that I do. Sinner or saint.

"Cy, I…" I start to say it, and I really *could* tell him. I *want* to. But it feels wrong without Aiden here. "I want you to tell me how to bring him back. How do I help him?"

Cypress frowns, wrapping his arms around me and swaying gently. "Aiden struggles sometimes. To not focus so much on what comes next because of what lies behind him. He keeps trying to protect himself from it. To protect us in any way he can."

"I know he does," I say softly. "You're both in this trouble because of me. He must blame me—"

"No," Cypress says firmly. "He does not hold you to blame for any of it. That's not why he's staying away. It's that he doesn't want to frighten you." Cypress presses his forehead to mine. "It's not just that he killed that man, it's also knowing how easily it could have ended another way. Knowing that it isn't over. Knowing that something went wrong in Preston that he thinks he should have prevented."

"But it's not his fault either." I shake my head. "Cypress, I just want to know how to help him. Help me understand."

He takes a deep breath, smiling a bit before asking, "What did you see that night by the water? When you followed us."

My cheeks heat. "I didn't mean to follow you."

His finger comes beneath my chin, keeping my eyes on his. "What did you see?"

I sigh. "I saw him grab you when you started to walk away. I saw him kiss you."

He nods. "Anything else?"

"No," I mumble. "I didn't want to intrude."

He grins and leans in to brush his lips over mine. "You should have."

"*Cypress.*"

He pulls back with a soft chuckle. "The first time we came here, he was like this, too. I was hurt, he felt responsible, and he was… brooding."

"*And,*" I press, "what did you do? To bring him back?"

"To take his mind off our brush with death?" Cypress smiles again, wicked enough to truly be the devil himself. "I reminded him that we were still very much alive."

# CHAPTER 42
## AIDEN

I keep my distance until the sun is about to set, walking up to set Cypress's rifle on the front porch before grabbing a change of clothes out of the wagon and heading for the creek.

I hadn't seen a single animal the entire time I'd been out hunting. The entire forest apparently also knowing well enough to give me a wide berth. Which is why…I just need some time to get out of my head.

That man needed to be killed. Deserved to die a lot worse than the death I gave him. He'd threatened Cora, threatened Cypress, believing I would simply sit there and allow him to take what's mine.

I can still feel the anger beneath my skin, dark and thick and…what the fuck is wrong with me that I'm standing on a creek bank, picturing killing a man that I've already killed once?

I can't go around Cora or Cypress. Not like this. But it's all I fucking want to do. A chant inside my brain that just gets louder the longer I refuse to heed it.

I should have let Cypress help me take the edge off as he offered, but neither he nor I had been willing to leave Cora unguarded again, and I had been unwilling to have her as a participant while I'm like this.

I don't want her to see me like this. Don't want to stain her innocence with my guilt.

I shake my head, trying to jar myself out of it with the motion, trying to strip away the fury in my brain as easily as I strip away my clothing.

When I can't, I wade in, the deepest part of the creek bed coming to just above my hip bones, and as good as the cool water feels on my skin, it still does nothing to abate the heat in my blood. I kneel, close my eyes, and dunk my head below the water before resurfacing.

I want to yell, to break something. I want to—

"*Hey!*"

My eyes fly back open as a voice snaps through the quiet, and I stand, ready to sprint for the bank and my weapon before I realize the identity of the intruder.

"Fucking Christ, woman," I spit out, panting as I try to slow my heart rate, but I swear again when I see that Cora is barely wearing any clothes as she stands with her arms crossed on the bank a few feet away. "What in God's name are you doing out here half-naked?"

I see the way her eyes travel over my bare chest and abdomen as she takes me in as well, the way they turn just a bit owlish, and a streak of male pride snakes down my spine right as she finally registers my words. She looks down at herself as if unsure what I could mean before she says back, "Little late for you to get proper again, Aiden, don't you think?"

My eyes narrow, knowing just as she does that there is nothing *proper* about the thoughts in my head. "Has Cypress seen you like this?"

Her eyes narrow right back. "Of course he has."

"Mm-hmm." *Of course he has. Fucking demon.* "And where is he now?"

She jerks her head back in the direction she came from. "Waiting back at the cabin."

"He send you out here?"

"I sent myself." The way she pulls herself up is downright stunning. "If I recall, I offered for you to watch me bathe once. Thought you might want to return the favor."

"That right? You stay out here like that, Cora, and you're much more likely to end up messy than clean." She arches an eyebrow at me, and I don't know why it fucking turns me on that she seems to enjoy sparring with me as much as I do her. I let my gaze rove over her once more. "You should go back to Cypress."

I turn away from her until I hear a splash of water behind me. *Fucking Christ.*

"*Don't,*" she snaps as she stops an easy arm's reach in front of me in the water. "Don't do this. What happened to no more running?"

My jaw tightens as I try to keep my eyes on her face instead of on the way the water is turning her undergarments goddamn *translucent.* "I'm not running."

"Oh, *yes,* you are," she argues. "Why do you keep punishing yourself like this? What happened in Preston isn't your fault."

"It is. I didn't—I missed something. *Again.* I keep making mistakes. What if the next one…" Jesus, she's starting to tremble from the cold, and every instinct in me is begging to reach for her. "Cora." My voice is low with warning. "Get back on the bank."

"No. You're allowed to make mistakes. I do. Cypress does. You forgive those but not your own. Why is that?"

"Get back on the bank, Cora."

"No. Not until you talk to me." She reaches out to shove at me with both hands, as she's so fond of doing, but I catch her by the wrists before she can connect with my chest, inadvertently bringing her even closer as she murmurs, "I know you're scared. I'm scared, too, but I'd rather be scared with you than alone."

"You're scared of me?" I ask her, hating that she would be but understanding—

"Not *of* you," she says, rolling her eyes at me. "Of *losing* you. Of losing Cypress. I'm so scared to lose either of you. I—God, Aiden, I'm so in—" She shakes her head. "I could never be scared of you."

"You should be."

"*Why?*" She keeps pushing me, tilting her face up to challenge me while also doing nothing to fight the physical hold I have on her. "You're a good man, Aiden."

"A *good* man? You watched me *kill* someone, remember?" I ask her, snagging both of her wrists together in my left hand while I rest my right at the base of her throat. Not squeezing, just resting. Her eyes widen, her pulse heightening as her lips part and her pupils dilate. Scared? No. She's excited. And getting increasingly more so as my thumb traces the side of her neck. "You also know it's not the first time. That *should* scare you."

She shakes her head, tilting her face down until she can brush my thumb against her mouth. "I watched you *protect* me." She kisses the tip of my thumb, traces it lightly with her tongue, and I groan. "I watched you keep us safe."

"Cora, I don't know if I—baby, you need to go." My thumb sweeps back to her nape, and she tilts her head into it, baring her throat in the prettiest display of willing submission even while she's being obstinate.

"I'm not going anywhere," she says. "Let me help you."

Because I'm just that fucking weak, I tug her to me so that her body is against mine, trapping her hands between us, and she gasps as she really feels me for the first time. A tremor racing over her skin as I savor the curves of her body, the soft swell of her abdomen pressing against my hard cock beneath the water where only a thin layer of soaked fabric separates her from me. So thin I could tear it with a flick of my wrist if I wanted to…and God, I do.

"You feel that?" I ask her, practically grinding myself against her, the temporary bliss calming that chanting in my brain while, at the same time, I hope like hell it'll be enough to make her come to her senses. "Do you understand now?"

Her breathing catches, uneven with every inhale. "Yes."

She tries to wriggle her wrists free, and I let her have her hands back, expecting her to run while I stay here and try not to chase her this time. Instead, her fingertips press into the planes of my chest as she drags them lower, ten separate searing points skating down my body, aided by the water's glide yet leaving fire in their wake. My chest, my ribcage, my stomach… She pauses at the dark trail of wiry hair visible above the water, seemingly fascinated by it, before she leans forward and presses her lips to my chest, right over my pounding heart.

"Aiden, let me help," she murmurs around another kiss, her tongue capturing the water on my skin. "You can have this. Have Cy. Have me."

"*Fuck*," I groan, my right hand catching her left and bringing it under the water, letting her feel my size. Her eyes widen again, and I bend my head to whisper in her ear even though there's no one else to hear. "You remember how it felt to have my mouth between your legs?"

She whimpers, and I nearly break right then before she gets out another quiet, "Yes."

"I wouldn't stop there this time." I dip my head, inhaling her scent just beneath her jaw, earth and rain and something else so devastatingly sweet that it makes me ache as she tentatively explores me, her fingers beneath my own as they stroke along my length. My hand squeezes over hers, showing her how to grip me the way I like. "I'd want to be inside you, too, baby. You understand that?"

She nods, nearly breathless, her chest rising and falling rapidly underneath the drenched bodice of her undergarments.

"Think about that and then think about how your hand can hardly close around the width of me. Cora, think…" My lips press against her pulse point, feeling it race. "Think about what I'd need you to take."

I guide her hand up and down, the sensation of her fingers *finally* being wrapped around me every bit as fucking perfect as I have pictured so many times. Her eyes find mine, half-lidded. "I can—I want to."

I kiss her, my teeth nipping at her bottom lip so that she'll gasp and let me in, so that she'll let me fuck her with deep strokes of my tongue into the heat of her mouth the same way I want to fuck her pretty cunt. "I shouldn't, Cora. Not like this," I tell her when I give us both the chance to breathe again. "You deserve someone who is gentle and slow with you that first time, sweetheart. You deserve—fuck, Cora, tell me to stop."

"No," she murmurs against my mouth, my jaw, getting bolder as she touches me. "I'm not scared of you, Aiden." I groan when her teeth graze my neck, when her hand squeezes me beneath the water. "I like when you teach me things. I like when you touch me. I like when it feels like you need me, too."

"I do need you, Cora," I admit. "Fuck, I need you."

"Then take whatever you need, Aiden," she tells me, placing a gentle kiss beneath my jaw. "*Please.*"

I move as fast now as when I'd drawn my gun a week ago. One moment, she's standing in the water with me, feeling me, begging me to take. Take what I need. Take what I want. Take *her*. The next, we're on the bank, cool ground at her back and the firm press of my body over hers. My fingers tangle in her hair as she arches into me and as my other hand digs into her thigh, wrapping it around my waist.

Her first moan rips free when my mouth closes over her breast through the drenched cotton of her camisole, quickly followed by my frustrated grunt and the sound and feel of ripping fabric. Then my lips, teeth, and tongue are back on her now bare skin.

"Aiden," she whimpers as I suck hard, her nails digging into my back, not to push me away but to pull me closer. "Aiden, we—"

"I know." I lift up, kneeling between her legs, releasing her only so that I can take two fistfuls of the fabric clinging to her leg and pull. It tears easily, and I make a satisfied sound at seeing more of her before I slip my right hand between her legs, cupping her firmly beneath the shredded fabric as she lets out an almost broken sob of my name.

"*Aiden*—" I tear the fabric up the other side, and her freed legs hug my waist before she looks down and sees what she'd only felt before. "Oh *fuck*."

I chuckle, both hearing her use that word and the honesty of her reaction breaking through enough to bring me a little more back to myself, to remind me where we are, who we are.

"It's all right, Cora," I murmur to her. "Not going to make you take it right away. Need to open up this tight cunt first." I roll my hips, not able to resist the friction of her against me, and she tries to mimic the movement only once before I grab her waist to still her. "Fuck, don't. Don't." My eyes squeeze shut tight. "You keep doing that and we're not going to make it back to the cabin."

She hums happily, her lips skimming my skin, seeking any part of me that she can reach as she mumbles, "*Cypress.*"

"I know, I want him, too," I tell her, groaning as I drag myself between her legs one more time, just to torture myself. "Should have brought him with you."

"I tried," she says, gasping when I pull her from the ground and into my arms. "But he…he said me showing up here without my dress on would be plenty effective."

# CHAPTER 43
## CYPRESS

I'm pacing in front of the fire, checking again and again how quickly the daylight is fading outside the windows. Maybe I shouldn't have let her go alone?

It's safe here. And if she's with Aiden, she is taken care of, but what if he hadn't gone to the creek as I thought? What if Cora is still out there looking for him in unfamiliar woods?

I'm about to grab my gun from the kitchen table when a loud thud slams into the front door and a much softer, surprised laugh follows. I cross quickly, jerking the door open, then have no choice but to jump right back out of the way as Aiden and Cora come tumbling into the room.

"There you are, wolf," I say with a grin, casually strolling over to the tangled heap now sprawled out on the rug in front of the fireplace.

The two of them are a state to behold. Aiden is beneath her without a stitch of clothing, skin wet and dirt-streaked as if he'd had a tussle getting out of the water. Which, judging by the drenched, mud-splattered, and torn clothing that hangs from Cora as she straddles Aiden's waist, I think that's likely correct.

"Fuck you, Cy," Aiden grunts, rapidly recovering and flipping her beneath him. "Make yourself fucking useful and help me get her naked."

I bend to pull Cora's knife from my boot, handing it over to him along my way to crouch by her head. "Hello again, little bird."

Her lust-clouded eyes blink up at me, her silky smile radiant even with dirt smearing her cheeks. "Brought him back."

"Of course you did," I say warmly, tracing her face with my fingers, my movements a slow counter to Aiden's rapid pace. The remaining fragments of her underclothes cut away with a deft efficiency as he tears through each strip, careful not to so much as scratch her skin in his haste. As he pulls them away, he tosses them into a sodden heap by the fire until she's left bare on the rug once he's done.

"*Cypress.*"

I look up at Aiden's call, take in the way his lips are parted, his eyes hot, as he points the blade in my direction.

"Strip," he orders, then drives the knife into the scarred floor and leaves it trembling there. His focus returns to Cora, his tongue resting on his bottom lip as he drags his palm over each peak and valley of her body. "Want to watch you fuck her first."

Only with Aiden. With Cora. Only with them have I ever been willing to even temporarily cede control. My past tells me that such a display of trust only ever preceded my near destruction, but here? Now? It only feels like deliverance.

I reach behind me, taking hold of my shirt before tugging it up and over my head. Tossing it to the side, I'm already moving to the button of my trousers when I hear Cora gasp.

*The scars.* I'd forgotten about them, my own view so clouded by building desire that I had neglected to realize how clear they'd be to her.

Aiden helps her up so she can get to me, her face holding so much worry as she looks at the ones that mark my chest as if each wound is still open.

"Do they hurt?" she asks, her fingertips reaching out to follow the one that runs along my side, her touch so healing that I half expect the ridge to be gone when I next examine it.

"No," I reassure her, letting her look. "They were a long time ago, little bird."

She nods, but there's fire in her eyes and a pang of need in my chest when she asks, "Who did this to you?"

My mouth dips to hers as I lift her up against me, close enough to whisper, "Ghosts."

# CHAPTER 44
## CORA

The three of us do finally make it to the bed. The *big* bed. The small distance quickly covered once Cypress started kissing me while I was in his arms, carrying me until he was at the edge of the bedframe and could lay me down in the middle of it. A mattress with soft sheets and a warm quilt at my back for the first time in months, and I hardly notice it…

Because Aiden is already waiting to drag me against him.

It's a smooth handoff, one I feel more due to the change in intensity than anything else. Aiden is still running like rapids, while Cypress is the calm, easy current when he joins us both a moment later, stripped down so that my eyes can greedily take in every uncovered detail.

He's leaner than Aiden, his wide shoulders and chest leading into tapered hips and long legs. Where Aiden is raw strength, Cypress is honed lethality. Everywhere I look he's marked, but there's a beauty in it.

In his survival. In the softness he's maintained even as life has done its best to harden him.

The words Cypress murmurs in my ear feel almost like a lullaby as my back fits against his chest while he sits with me in his lap, trembling and gasping as Aiden seeks me with bruising fingertips and an urgent mouth. The two of them heating my blood and quieting my cries in tandem.

I reach back and bury one of my hands in Cypress's hair, holding on while Aiden's mouth teases my nipples to hardened points, leaves a mark on the underside of my breast, making me shift and arch while Cypress's equally impressive length presses hard and insistent at my lower back. Oh, God, how am I going to be able to take them both? How is it all I want to do?

Cypress reaches down to circle my clit with the pads of his fingers, firm but slow, as Aiden sucks another mark into my inner thigh and soothes it with his tongue before he finds my center, licking in a long, hungry drag just below Cypress's persistent fingers. I gasp when Aiden's tongue pushes into me a few moments later, moaning when he doesn't stop.

"You're so fucking wet, Cora," he tells me, brushing the scruff of his beard against the inside of my thigh so I can feel it for myself. "So fucking perfect, rubbing your pretty cunt against my mouth like that."

I don't have it in me anymore to feel even the smallest amount of shame, too overwhelmed to do anything but tip my head back to meet Cypress's mouth when Aiden's thick finger replaces his tongue. He only eases it in at first, hardly to the first knuckle, but my mind goes blank to anything but the want to have him deeper.

"*Please*," I'm begging into Cypress's mouth, and he's humming to me gently, circling harder over my clit with one hand while his other kneads my breasts. "*Please*, I need…"

"Know what you need, sweetheart," Aiden mutters, lying on his stomach between my legs, easing my thigh to the side to open me wider as he pushes deeper. "Christ, you're so tight."

I'm panting as he lets me adjust to feeling more of him inside me before he starts thrusting his finger in and out. Waiting until I start chasing his movements before he adds another finger with the first, stretching me to take them. To take Cypress first just as he said.

"That's it. Just like that," he groans and presses another kiss to the inside of my thigh, driving his two fingers shallowly in and out, in and out, as I shift and moan and clench around them. The overwhelming feeling only intensifying when Cypress begins to roll my nipples between his fingers with one hand, rubbing my clit the exact way he helped me learn that I liked with the other. When at last Aiden picks up his pace, I can't help the whine that escapes me, immediately shaking my head when he stops.

"No, keep going. Feels—feels good."

"Then let me see you come, Cora. Be a good girl and come on my fingers," he grunts, and he pushes another finger in, curling them this time instead of only thrusting. Stroking some spot inside me that makes my back bow and my breath catch until I break, my world tilting so much that I hardly notice that I'm moving, too. I open my eyes to see Cypress beneath me now, grounding me with his hands on my thighs as I straddle him with Aiden at my back.

"You ready, baby?" Aiden asks me, guiding my hips as Cypress lines himself up beneath me. "Going to take him nice and slow."

"What if I—" My head falls forward when I feel the stretch of Cypress starting to press in, the scrape of Aiden's teeth at my nape, and for a moment, I really do wonder how I'm going to bear it. "What if I don't—" I nearly whimper. "What if I don't want to go slow?"

Aiden huffs at the familiar words, one of his hands back at the base of my neck. "What if one of you actually do as I say? For once?"

"Not…as fun." My voice shifts to a groan as I start to sink down, rolling my hips and working to take him deeper each time. My hands brace against Cypress's chest when he's halfway in, his thumb back on my clit to distract me, Aiden's hands still at my hips to help me know how to move. "Oh, *fuck*—"

Cypress clicks his tongue in mock admonishment. "Such language she's picked up." He arches his hips, pushing deeper and making me say it again. "Wonder from where?"

"Cy, if you ever stop running your goddamn mouth…" Aiden mutters, then moans, and I tip my head back to look at him, only to see him watching over my shoulder where Cypress and I are joined. "Fuck, baby, you look so perfect taking his cock. How does he feel?"

"So good," I moan back, adjusting again after the slight pinch. "Feels so *good*. I'm—feels so full."

"I know, it's a lot, sweetheart, but you can take more of him. I know you can," Aiden murmurs, still watching before Cypress leans up, fists his hand in Aiden's hair, and yanks him down so that he can kiss him deep. Pressing me firmly between them, and God, I want to stay just like this. Just like this.

"She can take us," Cypress encourages as he releases him and then brings his mouth to mine. "Was made for us. Just for us."

I nod, letting him kiss me as he eases out and drinks down my cry as he thrusts back in until I have all of him. Then he starts to move and I realize that there's so much *more*. So much more that I tumble off that cliff's edge again within moments, coming so hard around him that I'm left trembling and out of breath.

"*Fuck*," he says beneath me, sounding uncharacteristically close to breaking, too. "Aiden, she's… Need you to—" I'm lifted again before I've had a chance to come down, whining at the sudden emptiness until I open my eyes to see Aiden kneeling between my legs once he lays me out on my back, Cypress at my side while he takes himself in hand. They're so beautiful like this, Cypress's head tipping back as he groans and grips himself tighter, Aiden leaning over to press his mouth against his throat before he takes over, his hand stroking Cypress up and down until he comes with a low moan, painting my stomach with streaks of white.

As the tension leaves Cypress's body, Aiden's mouth goes back to his, their kiss still tinged with an edge that makes me wish I could press my legs together to soothe the quickly returning ache. I would, if Aiden wasn't still occupying the space there, holding himself over me now as he runs his fingers through the mess Cypress made, rubbing it into my skin and onto my bottom lip like rouge the way he had that night after the poker game.

"Would rather see this dripping out of you," Aiden murmurs as I taste it, almost transfixed by it. "But probably not wise to push our luck any further." His eyes meet mine as he brings his fingers to his mouth to suck them clean. "At least not tonight…"

I make a small sound of protest, frankly too far gone to consider consequences if it means feeling them inside me like that, but I'm also surprised by how little it scares me.

With them, everything feels different. Like they really are mine and I'm theirs. Like anything we made as a result would be a gift rather than a curse, which is how it always should have been.

"We've got time," Aiden murmurs, as if he can read my thoughts before he takes a firm grip of my thighs and pulls me toward him, positioning me just how he wants before he reaches down to notch himself at my entrance, his thumb gently stroking my already oversensitive clit in a way that makes my breathing pick right back up. His eyes find mine. "Deep breath, baby."

My brow creases in confusion, but then Aiden starts to push in and I understand, gasping at the stretch as my legs move to hug his waist the way they had on the bank. He bends down to kiss me, slow and easy, murmuring to me and surrounding me with his body, rocking only a little deeper into me each time. His breathing grows more labored the longer it takes to work himself inside, his chest heaving as he still fights to hold himself back despite everything that's happened since he carried me out of the water.

"It's okay," I tell him as my mouth grazes over his. "Aiden, take what you need."

"Can't," he argues, eyes squeezing shut as he pulls back and hesitates before pushing in again. "Fuck, I…I don't want to hurt you."

"You're not going to." I wrap my arms around his neck, my fingers in his hair as I hold him close. "You feel so good. So *good*. I love feeling you and Cy like this." The words are right there on the tip of my tongue. Three words I'm not sure I've ever heard, let alone said to another person. "Aiden, I—"

His forehead presses against mine before our gazes meet again, that unspoken understanding in his eyes that I had so often seen him share with Cypress now reflected back at me. "Say it, Cora," he says softly. "Please, say it."

And because he needs me to, I do. "I love you," I murmur to him. "I love you both. So much."

His eyes close, but this time his expression is relieved. "I love you, too. Scares the hell out of me." He looks to Cypress and I follow his gaze to where he lies next to us, a content and unworried smile on his face as if us ending up here was always inevitable. "Seems like too much to get to have you both. To get to love you both."

I smile, thinking of that night I'd unknowingly followed them. *Too much.* Aiden had said it was too much to have me with them, and it's hard to believe how the same words can sound so different. How everything can be so different now.

"Too much?" I repeat, smiling more broadly as he nods, and I lift my head to murmur in his ear, "You can take it."

Aiden is grinning when I pull away, shaking his head at me before addressing Cypress. "I still hate that you get to be right."

"I know you do, wolf," Cypress says, his fingers reaching out to brush my cheek and I tilt my face into his touch. As drawn to him now as the first time I saw him as he tells me, "I love you, little bird. Always have."

Aiden exhales, nodding before his arm hikes my right leg higher, and my eyes are on his again when he finally thrusts in deep. I roll my hips to meet him as he does it again. And again. Until we find our pace.

Aiden groans, feeling me grip him tighter. Tells me that he loves me again when I come and waits until the last moment to pull away, streaking my stomach with his release the same way Cypress had. Uses his thumb to rub it into my skin the same way, too, as Cypress watches. "No matter where the road leads, wolf."

Aiden smiles, kissing him and me before he lets himself settle down on the bed with me on one side and Cypress on the other. "No matter where the road leads."

# CHAPTER 45
## AIDEN

*How long?*

A few months have come and gone now while the three of us have been holed up in the four walls of that cabin. Weeks running by like a slow-moving river, the still water on the surface concealing a deep unrelenting current beneath.

I exhale, barely rustling the leaves and dusting of snow that lies on the log beside the long barrel of my rifle. My steadying breath the only movement I allow myself as I stretch out on the forest floor and watch the deer in the clearing ahead of me, its antler-laden head bent to search for food in much the same way my own had been while I followed its tracks here. Both of us in pursuit of enough to keep ourselves fed through the winter.

How much longer will we be here? How much longer before we can pack our things and move on? Take our chances in the world again and hope we haven't already run out of them?

For so long now, I've looked at the days ahead and wondered what they would bring, and I'm still adjusting to the idea that now I'm not just wary but also impatient for them. For their possibilities.

Which is why I keep reminding myself that moving on from this stalemate isn't a matter of *if* but *when*.

That's the way it's always been before. We get ourselves in too deep, hunker down, and wait for it to blow over before we resurface. Except, no matter how hard the wind blows this time, the posters are still posted whenever I dare venture into town, the reward on them only getting more enticing the longer the charges sit unanswered and the jail cells sit vacant.

Apparently, me sending that kid to Preston hadn't done a lick of good. Nor have the hours I've spent trying to figure out precisely what had gone wrong. I have my theory. No proof of it, but it is the only thing that makes sense in my mind…even if it is the worst of the options in terms of guaranteeing a quick path to resolution.

My jaw clenches tight at the thought, my eyes squeezing shut as I try to block out the anger and the sickening dread that always comes with the idea of either Cypress or Cora locked away. Instead, I force my mind back to the task at hand, demanding my body relax before I ready my shot.

It won't happen. I won't *let* it happen. We'll be okay. We'll find a way.

My finger moves to hover over the trigger only once I'm sure my kill will be clean, and a gentle squeeze of pressure is all that's left to precede the violent eruption of the bullet leaving its chamber. The sound still echoing through the trees for a few seconds after the deer has already collapsed to the soil.

In the immediate aftermath, I'm motionless as well, listening in the subsequent quiet for any sound that might suggest I'm not the only one who heard the shot.

With a half-day's hard ride from the nearest town of Troy's Hill and without a Navajo settlement nearby for trade, anyone else I might happen across today would either be out here with a purpose already in mind or would be just as likely to want to stay undiscovered. In either case, a scenario best left avoided.

*How long? How long can this last?*

There's no answer. Not that I expect one. The only other sound—welcome or unwelcome—that I encounter is my own grunt of discomfort when I eventually get to my feet, my stiff muscles slowly loosening as I walk toward my fallen quarry, returning Cypress's rifle to the sling at my back and brushing debris from my coat as I go.

When I reach the deer, I check to make sure my shot was indeed well placed before I drag a tired hand across the back of my neck, relieved to have something to show for my efforts though it had taken me a while longer than I was hoping it would.

I glance at the sky through the bare treetops, calculating that it must be past midday, then I bring my fingers to my mouth to produce a high-pitched whistle. The new noise not quite enough to overtake the sound of Cypress's deep cadence as it weaves its way back into my mind from a memory made just after dawn.

"You're going to the west ridge this time?" Cypress had asked me, confirming what he already knew as he sat in one of the rocking chairs on the porch, his mug of coffee in one hand and his unopened book in the other as he watched me tack up Helios.

I had nodded, lost in thought while I spooled a long length of rope around my saddle horn and took inventory of the contents in my saddle bags. Unease always swirls in my gut the closer I get to departure, even if I am confident that Cypress is every bit as capable of guiding any unfortunate intruder to their demise. Not to mention that Cora is getting handy enough with a pistol that she might just beat him to it.

Undeniably, the two of them can take care of themselves. But leaving still gnaws at me every time.

"About an hour's ride, then…" Cypress had continued, his voice low and contemplative. "Should put you back by…"

"Supper at the latest." That time my head had turned in Cypress's direction to respond, and my frown broke at the sight of him.

In the early morning sun, Cypress's sleep-mussed hair and the half-untucked shirt beneath his coat made him look akin to a self-satisfied barn cat who had found his ray of sun to lie in for the day. Perfectly at ease, with no trace of the claws that he concealed nor any of the concerns that might provoke him.

"You two will be all right?" I asked him anyway, absently starting to check my tack over once more to give myself a reason to linger.

"Of course," Cypress replied, giving me a crooked half-smile as he set his things to the side and stood. "We will have no trouble finding some sort of diversion to pass the time."

"I have no doubt," I clipped back, shooting Cypress a knowing look from beneath the brim of my hat. "You always do."

In response, Cypress's smile had grown into a full grin, and we both glanced at the cabin where Cora was still fast asleep, Cypress turning back just in time to catch me taking a half-step toward the front door before I snapped myself out of it and stayed by my horse instead.

"You're sure you wouldn't rather I go?" Cypress offered, causing me to pause once more.

"I'm sure," I reassured him, not wanting him to feel obligated to push himself. "You already did your turn a few days ago, and I probably should have gone yesterday. Our reserves are still lighter than I'd like them to be in case the weather turns. Especially if we get a good snow. Might need to go into town tomorrow."

He hadn't pushed me further on the topic, had even held up his hands in placation, though he might have given a much more convincing impression of surrender if he hadn't also started to close the distance between us. His keen eyes visibly assessing with each step, he had not stopped his advance until he was near enough to brush his nose against the whiskers along my jaw.

A low, pleased sound started at the back of Cypress's throat when I immediately angled my head to catch his mouth. Drinking in the strong taste of his morning coffee along with something sharper that was distinctly and maddeningly Cypress, an intoxicating combination that only grew more potent when I took the kiss deeper, not letting up until I was sure I'd never leave if I didn't.

"Don't fret. We will hardly make a move until you return," Cypress told me a few minutes later, remaining close as I, at last, swung up into my saddle. His attempts at innocent sounding assurances coming nowhere near to concealing the glint in his eye when I had given him his usual direction to behave.

In truth, I never really expect him to follow that order. Not nearly delusional enough to believe he will, since it has never happened before.

From a spot deeper back in the woods, Helios trots over in answer to my whistled call, and I move toward his saddle once the prickly mustang draws up next to me, reaching to grab my—

My fingers find only air, then the leather of my saddle horn, and my eyes flick to the spot to confirm what I've already gathered.

"He…" I look around at the ground as if the item will turn up, the corresponding shake of my head more at myself for not catching it sooner than at Cypress for doing it at all. "He fuckin' robbed me."

# CHAPTER 46
## CYPRESS

In my defense, I had originally intended to spend my morning on less… *lascivious* activities.

I had actually planned to spend a while letting my thoughts run across the pages of my book or allowing my hands to fiddle with some of the things that needed fixing around the cabin. I had even tried to do so and still might try again…once I've had a chance to burn through some of my energy and apprehension through other means.

Aiden will be fine. I trust enough in him and in fate to believe that she wouldn't be so cruel as to bring all three of us together only to separate us so soon. Still, that doesn't mean his absence doesn't tend to put me on edge…even more so than I already am these days.

I keep having those dreams at night. The ones where I'm back in that windowless room. Waiting again. Alone again. And I'm trying…I really am trying. Trying not to want to climb the walls the longer I sit in this cabin.

Can you die from boredom? Surely someone could, if not in body then certainly in mind with no real occupation to pass the hours.

I miss being on the move, miss having the stars above me as the only constant in my routine, and yet even they change night to night.

Of course, there are also things about our current arrangement I do find enjoyable—the comfortable bed waiting for me at the end of the day ranking high on that list, especially given its occupants. Still…I struggle with being idle in my own destiny. With waiting on someone else to determine what course I should take when I have grown so used to plotting it myself.

I want to take Cora to those places she finds on our maps, her fingers following the paths Aiden and I lay out for her on the kitchen table as we talk about a future, the crisscrossing and uneven lines cutting through a world that had been kept from her for far too long.

Aiden thinks we should wait the winter out. See if time might heal all wounds.

I think we should go to Preston. Finish what we didn't start.

And Cora, well…our little bird is currently refusing to take sides, offering herself up instead as neutral ground that will hear both arguments but give no judgment.

How adept she's already become at handling us both, I think with a grin, my gaze drifting over the rise and fall of her body beneath the quilt as she slumbers past her usual hour this morning. And I wonder what dream has her so under its spell, while at the same time wondering how I might best eclipse it.

At least for now, I decide to hang Aiden's *borrowed* length of rope around one of the bottom bedposts, even if I'm certain that she wouldn't object to being woken up bound. Her wrists tied to the headboard and her legs parted by Aiden's broad shoulders as he sates himself on her cunt before she's even opened her eyes.

Always does wake hungry, our wolf, and the fact that he had kept that hunger at bay this morning makes me think he has something on his mind. Something he's currently turning over out there in the trees and the quiet.

I had been able to taste it on him though. That hunger. Had felt it in the restrained flex of his muscle beneath my hands and in the impatient scrape of his stubbled jaw against mine. All of it an assurance that when Aiden does return, he might just be starving, and how neglectful would it be of me not to have something prepared?

With that thought burning away at me, I crawl into bed with Cora, carefully navigating over her sprawled-out form. I'm astounded that three bodies have managed to fit night after night in this space, given the way she is currently laying claim to it, on her stomach with one arm beneath her pillow and the other extending out to unconsciously seek Aiden and me.

Confident that I will be able to keep her warm on my own, I kneel over the backs of her thighs before I gently tug the quilt down from where I had pulled it over her before slipping from bed, following after Aiden who had woken her up just enough to kiss her goodbye but who had stayed sitting on the edge of the bed until she'd fallen back asleep against me.

"Gorgeous girl," I murmur as I slowly bare her soft skin, leaning forward and bracing myself over her so that my lips can play across her shoulder blades, her upper back, her cheek. She lets out a pleased sigh as I do it, though her eyes remain closed. I press a soft lingering kiss just below her hairline at the nape of her neck, feeling a profound satisfaction settling deep in my chest when she smiles.

"Good morning, Cy," she murmurs, her eyes fluttering open only once she's turned over onto her back beneath me. Not a shred of modesty to be found in her half-hooded gaze as she watches me look her over. "Are you coming back to bed?"

"I am, though I must confess not to sleep," I tell her, chuckling at her widening smile before I bend my head to kiss her until she's arching into me. Right now, my pace is kept slow, as if I have all the time in the world, and…I guess I do. "Can I have you for a while, little bird?"

She nods, too busy seeking my mouth back on hers to waste her breath on speech. Her hands span over my marked chest before skimming lower, sweeping up over my hips before dipping to seek the heavy weight of my cock where it rests against her abdomen.

"Patience, wild one." My hand captures her wrists before she can get to what she wants, guiding her arms above her head and keeping them there. I raise a brow at her when she narrows her eyes at me, her lower lip pouting. "What a terrible fiend we've created," I murmur to her, lowering my mouth to the valley between her breasts. "You are always so eager for it now, aren't you, Cora?"

"You…" She gasps as I take one of her nipples in my mouth and suck. "As if you and Aiden aren't—*fuck*—aren't the same way."

"Never said we weren't," I say, grinning, as I slide my free hand down between our bodies, feeling how slick she already is while she moans. "That's why you're so perfect for us, little bird. And why we're so perfect for you and your needy little cunt. Even let you fall asleep last night with my cock still hard inside you, and here you are again, aching for it."

"Mmm." She smiles dreamily as I touch her. "That was nice. Although it would be *nicer* if you'd also…"

"You know we can't, little bird," I tell her, some of the lightness falling from my tone due to my own regret. "If we got you pregnant… It's too much to risk right now. Aiden's right."

"I know," she says, sighing. Her gaze turns sly, her body arching and her long legs brushing my waist as I keep myself braced over her. "But think of how good it would feel. Think of how—"

My mouth lands back on hers, cutting off whatever she was about to say, because the truth is I've already thought about it.

"You think I don't want it, Cora? You think I wouldn't love to see you fucked full of me? Of Aiden? When the time comes…"

"Both," she suggests, making it sound innocent even as she continues. "I'll have you both. So you can feel him while you fuck me. So you can—"

I groan at the thought of her taking both of us at the same time, the hand I'd been teasing her with between her legs flying up to cover her mouth to stop her again. "What happened to that shy little thing that blushed and used to say my talk was *indecent*? If she could only see you now," I pretend to scold, feeling her smile against my palm. I grin back at her. "You're becoming downright dangerous to have around, little bird, you know that? How am I meant to focus on anything else now?"

"You crawled back into my bed, Cy," she reminds me when I pull my hand away.

"Ah, *your* bed is it?"

She nods, and as fetching as she looks in it, it's hard to argue with her. Not that I am interested in doing so at this moment.

"You know that I love you?"

She nods again.

"Good, keep that in mind for the next few…hours," I tell her, purposefully loosening my grip on her wrists and shifting back so that my weight rests on my knees again. My free hand frames the side of her face, my eyes on hers as I say, "You remember how this goes? You tell me to stop, and I will stop. Otherwise, I will fuck you until I am ready to stop."

A small sound escapes her, something between a whimper and a whine as her body trembles a bit at my words. A reaction I immensely appreciate but not the one I currently need.

"Cora," I say again, my tone carrying more authority this time. "You say stop, and—"

"I say stop, and you'll stop," she says, shifting impatiently beneath me for emphasis.

"Otherwise? Repeat all of it back to me so I can hear you say it," I prompt her again, dipping my head once more, this time so that I can take a deep inhale of the way she smells right along the column of her throat. Her scent always tangled up now with mine and Aiden's.

"You'll—" Her words catch as I start to kiss my way down her body. "You'll—you'll fuck me…"

I nod, letting the rare rough stubble on my cheek scratch against the soft surface of her abdomen. "Until?"

"Until…"

She takes a shaky breath in, and my right hand renews its grip on her wrists while my left dips between her legs, my index finger poised at her entrance. "Tell me, little bird."

She lifts her head, her brow pinched with impatience, and I know she wants to watch what I'm doing to her. What I *will* do as soon as she says…

"Until you're ready to stop."

# CHAPTER 47
## CORA

Everything is suspended.

My hands above my head as the rope keeps them in place, the words on my tongue, the thoughts in my head, the edge he's keeping me on… He won't allow me to come down, won't let me go high enough that I can fall on my own. At least, not yet.

"Doing so well, wild one," Cypress tells me, his voice rippling through me as he keeps his mouth close to my center. "Perfect girl."

He has two thick fingers inside me, shallowly thrusting in and out at a languid pace that he refuses to alter no matter how many times I cant my hips for more.

"Cypress," I plea with him again, longing to have my hands free so I can wrap my fingers in his hair and pull him to me. Tug hard on those few streaks of gray that are so much lighter than the rest. "Just let me—let me touch you."

He shakes his head, listening to me get closer and closer to truly begging, and for a moment, I think that maybe this time he will give in when his tongue starts to circle my clit. His lips closing around it and driving my desperation into a frenzy.

It's too much. Too much, but, God, I need more.

He enjoys me like that for a while longer, his fingers working inside me so that I can hear how wet I am for him. Feel the way I'm soaking his palm, and I whine at the slick stretch when he slips in a third finger to join the other two.

"That's it," he murmurs, placing a gentle kiss on my clit in encouragement. "I know you can withstand it a little longer for me."

I cry out as Cypress curls his fingers against that spot that makes my vision blur, pressing and stroking until I'm on the brink of bliss. Then he stops.

I practically shout my frustration at him, anguished to feel it slip away from me once more, tears pooling in the corners of my eyes before they streak down my cheeks. *"Please, please, please."*

He hushes me gently, pulling his fingers from me and bringing them up to circle around the peaks of each breast, each nipple now streaked with the proof of how long he's kept me needing him.

Whenever he takes one in his mouth, he sucks so gently that it's nearly comforting before his fingers are back inside me, thrusting deep, the pad of his thumb firmly circling my clit. Taking more so that he can do it again.

"I know, little bird, I know," he croons to me when I keen after he stops again, crawling back up my body to slant his mouth against mine once more. "But not yet."

The taste of myself on his tongue makes the want even worse, and encourages me to take advantage of the change in his position, wrap my legs around his narrow waist, and drag myself against him where his cock is hard on my inner thigh. When I do, he moans, presses his forehead against mine, and lets me tempt him. Lets me use him just as he uses me. Even as one of his hands falls to my hip, his fingertips gripping hard to lead my movements so that I'm more firmly pressed against him on each rotation. So that he is again setting the pace.

I don't think he's ever held off with me as long as he has this morning, made us both wait for it like this. Likely wouldn't if Aiden was here to intervene and compel us both to sense, but I like playing this game with him. Like seeing how close to delirium we both can drift.

"That's it," he mutters above me, a thrill shooting through me once I feel him reach between us to notch himself against my entrance. "I know, feeling so empty, aren't you, Cora? Not been enough to have us coming down your lovely throat, has it? Need so badly for us to fill you up right here?" He thrusts in deep, one of his hands spanning possessively over my abdomen as he does it. "One of these days we're going to fuck you until it takes, little bird. Take turns filling you until you can't take anymore, that what you want?"

I try to make my body convey my answer as I moan, letting myself indulge in the idea of it, trying to shift myself down to press him in again when he pulls out, but his hold on himself and on me remains tight. Strong enough that I trust him to never let go.

"Not yet," he tells me again, pushing forward just enough to let me feel the width of him and to hold me there until I cry half in relief and half in protest. "Not yet."

# CHAPTER 48
## AIDEN

I stalk toward the cabin from the creek, the change of clothes I pulled from the line clinging uncomfortably to my cool, damp skin after I had washed away the hunt, but I'm too distracted turning the same thought over and over to care.

So focused on it that by the time I finally reach the porch, I'm so anxious for it to be real that I don't even so much as slow my stride, my hand immediately twisting the knob to let myself in and whipping the door shut behind me with a resounding snap.

"And there would be my rope…" I say, coming to a stop in the middle of the room. "Here I was worried I'd misplaced it."

My eyes had gone straight to the bed where I already knew Cypress would have Cora bound and bare. Imagining it on my ride back had been one thing, but seeing it for myself… The way her wrists are fixed to the headboard while she kneels, her perfect round ass up while her chest lies flush with the bed and her hands hold fast to the rope. Cypress is positioned behind her, unmoving even as she shifts and whines, a remarkably calm smile on his face as he looks over his shoulder at me. *Fuck.*

"Afraid we had need of it," Cypress explains simply, his well-muscled form on display as his left hand runs up and down Cora's spine appreciatively, his right keeping a grip on her waist. "Challenging for her to stay still any other way. Isn't it, wild one?"

Her answer is half-curse and half-moan. No doubt partially due to the way Cypress times the question with a shallow push inside her, his strong hold and the rope enough to prevent her from taking him deeper even if she tried.

"Cypress," I say, trying to find the means to speak when my mouth has run dry. Wanting them both so bad that I can barely breathe. "How many?" I ask him with a note of disapproval. "How many times?"

How many times had he taken her to the brink only to pull her back? How many times had he left her wanting? Left her aching for him?

"I may have lost track." Cypress tilts his head, looking back down and taking a firm hold of Cora's hips, his fingertips digging into their plush weight while he considers the question. "But I suppose…"

She looks about to answer for him, but nearly as quick as he's able to draw a gun, Cypress flips Cora onto her back, the movement unexpected enough it makes me take a step forward, though Cypress is slow and methodical again when he leans over her to recheck the binding at her wrists. Testing to make sure the rope isn't hurting her before he tugs her down the bed, adjusting her body so that her arms are still raised above her and her legs are still spread with him kneeling in between.

"I suppose enough," Cypress says once he seems satisfied with her position, brushing her hair away from her face so he can see her eyes clearly as they plead with him in a way I would never be able to resist. "I suppose enough that she might justifiably seek retribution once I cut her loose, but…" He grins and arches a brow first at Cora and then at me. "Perhaps I can convince her to forgive me."

While he holds my gaze, he skims his hands over her, over every place I would like to have my own hands. Mapping her as he moves down her body slowly, pulling a moan from me as well as her when his right hand cups her at the apex of her thighs and he easily pushes three fingers inside her cunt while his thumb teases over her back entrance, getting her used to the sensation. One more thing we have to teach her as we continue to give her our lessons, as we introduce her to things in stages. Helps that both of us are so fucking addicted to her cunt that we haven't seen much reason to rush. Not that she would mind if we did. Never does want to go slow.

As Cypress touches her, Cora rolls her hips to fuck herself on his fingers, a blissful expression breaking across her face as she bites into her bottom lip and lets it wash over her. Her breathing gets quicker as my own grows shallower, my hand flexing at my side to reach for her as—

I close the distance in four strides at her frustrated cry, my hand at Cypress's throat with a pressure far lighter than the weight of my words as I bring my face within an inch of his.

"Thought you were seeking forgiveness," I say evenly, trying not to groan at the way his fingers are slick with her while his hands reflexively come up to grip my forearm. "Thought you said it was enough."

The Cypress that grins back at me is not the same one I left on the porch this morning. This one has the claws, the eyes that are more black than blue. This one provokes a memory.

One made in this same room years ago when we were both completely different yet much the same as we are now. When we were hiding from the trouble nipping at our heels but couldn't seem to hide from one another.

"Enough." My voice is low as I keep my hand on Cypress's throat, leaning forward so that my mouth brushes his. "Enough, Cy. I've got you."

# CHAPTER 49
## CYPRESS

I told Cora I would fuck her until I was ready to stop. But that moment hadn't come… I hadn't wanted to stop.

It had felt too good. *She* had felt too good, her body wound tight like a bowstring for me to pull and release. I had gotten lost in it. In pushing both of us to the point of desperation while still staying in control. I had been in control. Except I wasn't. And I certainly am not now.

Aiden's got me by the neck like an errant pup, those shoulders heaving as he looks at me with those deep brown eyes. Telling me that it's enough. My hands on his forearm loosen their grip, resting there as my body begins to relax. As I start to give myself over to a higher power.

Maybe I am religious after all. Maybe I really should ask for forgiveness since I'm already on my knees.

Aiden only lets me go for a moment to strip off his clothing, but Cora's already there. Her body fitting against mine without restraint once Aiden lets her free, her hands on my chest as she guides me to sit back on my heels so she can crawl into my lap.

I wrap an arm around her as she sinks down on me, so ready that she takes all of me in one smooth motion, and we both moan from the devastating relief of it at last. All I can do is hold her tight as she starts to rock, Aiden's right hand once more at the base of my throat now that he's crawled into bed behind me, angling my head back so that he can devour my mouth while Cora has everything else. Her lips fall against my neck as she tells me between kisses how good I feel, how good I am, how she never wants to stop.

I don't want to either. Even after she's lying on her back on the pillows with a satisfied smile as she drags her fingers through the mess I left on her chest and brings it to her mouth, then Aiden's. Murmuring to me when she cups my face while I brace myself over her, my forehead pressed to hers as Aiden takes what remains of my hunger in deep, measured thrusts.

Right before he comes, he pulls me back up with an arm across my chest, his teeth sinking in over the scar on my shoulder, and for a moment I think Aiden is the one trembling until I realize it's me. Too late to hide my tell.

Not that I ever could. Not with them.

# CHAPTER 50
## CORA

I want to stay in this moment forever. Listening to the sounds of the wind in the woods through the open windows, feeling the soft pressure of Cypress's hand on my thigh and the beat of Aiden's heart beneath my cheek.

He's tempting me back to sleep as he lies on his back with my head on his chest, but I'm too busy looking between him and Cypress where he sits against the headboard with my legs resting across his lap, his eyes on the nearest window and his discarded book on his bedside table.

I'm about to ask him a question about it when I notice the expression on Aiden's face, the deepening furrow in his brow as he also looks at Cypress, the worry that he tries to smooth away as soon as he catches me watching him.

*What's wrong?* I ask him silently, and he frowns, glancing again at Cypress before his eyes fall to Cypress's thumb *tap, tap, tapping* against my thigh. I watch it now, too, reminded of the way he'd been doing the same against his leg as he paced the first time I met him in that boarding house dining room. Feels like so long ago now. Feels like a different life.

I reach out and cover his hand with mine. "Cy?"

He jerks as if coming out of a trance. "Hm?"

"Are you all right?"

"Yes," he says quickly, turning his hand over to interlace our fingers. "I'm fine, little bird."

For the first time, I'm not sure if I believe him, and when I glance back at Aiden, it seems I'm not the only one.

"I've been thinking," Cypress continues. "Maybe I could be the one to go into town tomorrow. If we need supplies."

Aiden's eyes narrow slightly, but he nods. "Sure, if that's what you want. Perhaps one of us could go with—"

"No," Cypress replies, dismissing the thought before it's fully out of Aiden's mouth. "I'll go on my own."

"Sure," Aiden says again, but his frown deepens. "Just to supply and come back, right?"

"And to check for the posters," Cypress says, a fainter version of his usual grin appearing. "Want to see what they've done with our Cora."

I huff and roll my eyes. "Please don't bring back their latest attempt. I look more fearsome every time while the two of you only look more gorgeous. They're likely to give me fangs next."

"Do you not have them?" Cypress reaches toward my face as if to check, and I swat his hand away. He mutters, "Could have sworn one of those bites you gave me felt sharper than usual."

I sit up and press a soft kiss to his cheek before drifting down and scraping my teeth against his jaw. "You liked it," I murmur.

He grins, and this time, it feels more genuine. "I did."

He glances down at my hands and wrists, capturing them in his palm before brushing his thumb over each of the faint marks left by the rope. "Did you enjoy yourself, little bird?"

"Yes," I reassure him. "Plus…" I stretch before falling back against Aiden again. "It's so very attractive when Aiden gets to rescue me."

"From yourself more often than not," he grumbles, though there's humor in his tone, too.

"He does give a very good rescue," Cypress agrees. "Intensely commanding. Intensely…brooding."

"Fuck's sake," Aiden mutters, and I don't even have to look at him to know he's rolling his eyes. "Next time he has you tied up, we'll see if I save you."

"You will," I say, turning my head toward him, and he smiles affectionately at the warmth in my words before I add, "And you will look so *devastatingly* handsome while doing it."

"You know what?" Aiden grabs for me, and I let out a high-pitched peal of laughter as I try to fight him off before he drags me over him.

"I think I *saved* you too soon if you still have all that energy to make fun," he says, effortlessly positioning me so that I'm kneeling with his head between my legs, his mouth already working its way up my inner thigh and his hands making quick work of pushing up my nightdress. "Not sure why you even bother with clothes, sweetheart," he says when I start to muster a complaint at the distinctive sound of ripping fabric. "Fucking inconvenient."

He swats my now bare ass, not enough to hurt, but enough to startle me forward as I grip the headboard with one hand and his disheveled wavy hair with the other. "How many times are you going to come for me, Cora?"

"Oh, God, Aiden, I don't—I don't think I can after—" I gasp, feeling the first brush of his nose against my center as he breathes me in. "Oh, *God.*"

"No God out here, baby, just us," he murmurs, his fingertips digging into my hips as he leaves a gentle kiss on my clit. "Besides, this pretty little cunt needs me to look after her after Cy denied her for so long. Now be good for me and sit."

I start to protest again, but it turns into a moan when he pulls me firmly down against his mouth, his tongue dragging slowly from my entrance to my clit. My head falls back, my gaze half-lidded when it falls to where Cypress is observing us, anything but contrite. "If you're hoping to appeal to me for rescue now, little bird," he says, "you should already know you have the wrong man."

# CHAPTER 51
## AIDEN

It's midnight by the time I make it out on the porch, Cora fast asleep as I leave her to her dreams. Most nights, I stay up late just so I can watch her sleep, take comfort in the way she no longer cries, no longer runs from things I can't see.

I want to be able to say the same for Cypress. But I can't.

He's the reason I'm venturing outside into the chill instead of staying warm in bed, unable to fall asleep myself when I know he's out here on his own.

He doesn't acknowledge me as I take the chair next to him, too busy looking out into the dark woods around us. Never one to be cowed by anything that could be hiding out there, he rather seems to be comforted by it.

"Cy," I call to him after a time, hoping to bring him back. "It's bad again, isn't it?"

He doesn't say anything, that alone enough of a confirmation, but I can see the way his jaw tightens in the lantern light, can see the steady *tap, tap, tapping* he's doing with his hand against his leg. That he keeps doing once he gets up and starts pacing the porch.

"Why didn't you say anything?"

"Because I don't—" he starts to say, his tone agitated. "Because I don't want there to be anything *to* say. I'm fine. I *want* to be fine."

"I know you do," I say, not going to him yet, because I'm not sure it's what he wants. "I know you do. It's all right. I should've realized sooner. You've always done better here than anywhere else, but I was thinking even this morning. It's been too long…"

He shakes his head. "No, it's not… I don't… It's not for you to reckon with."

"It is," I argue, leaning forward in my chair with my elbows on my knees. "If it's you, Cy, then it is. And I know Cora would say the same. We both love you."

His shoulders hunch, his hands tucking into his pockets. "I know."

"Have you told her?"

"Have you told her about the bounty hunter?" he counters. "About what you think happened in Preston?" He's partially trying to dodge my question but he's also right to ask it. I do need to tell Cora what I know about the man who killed her father. What I think it means. But I hadn't wanted to add another element of hopelessness to our situation when, for the present, she seems so happy.

"I will," I say before I ask him my question again, never taking my eyes off him as he walks up and down the creaking floorboards. "Will you? Cypress, have you ever told her what happened to you? She asked that day we got here. About the scars."

"I told her the beginning," he says, a small smile at the corner of his mouth. "Perhaps you can tell her the middle."

"If you want me to."

"Seems right. That you should get to tell my story since I told her yours."

"My story isn't the same as yours."

"I know." He keeps moving, keeps tapping. "I know it's not, but… but maybe you can still tell her the middle, and I suppose we'll all simply have to keep reading to find out the ending."

"Cy." I stand, stepping into his path and pulling him to me. "It's okay."

He sags against my body, letting himself lean into me. "I keep finding myself there when I go to sleep. I keep having nightmares about it… I don't want to. I don't want to be there."

"I know," I tell him, wrapping my arms tighter around him as if that can hold all his pieces together. "It's okay. We'll leave. We'll start moving again."

"It's not time yet," he says, his forehead falling to my shoulder as his breathing starts to settle. "You're right. We need to wait until things are better, need to figure out something that doesn't require us to go into a town guns blazing."

I sigh. "Fuck, I know it's bad if you're thinking I'm right."

He chuckles, and the tightness in my chest loosens as I pull back to hold his face in my hands. "What do you need?"

"I think I just need…I think I need a change of scenery. Even if only for a day."

"That's why you want to go to town?"

"Yes."

"All right." I frown, searching his blue eyes. "I'm sorry for not letting you go out this morning. I just thought—I know you normally don't like to be on your own."

"Still don't, but I need to move. And people will be less suspicious seeing only me. Instead of the whole *Midnight Gang*." I scoff and he turns his head to kiss my palm. "I won't be on my own for long. I'll stretch my legs and then come back. Good as new."

"You'll be careful?"

He makes an attempt at a smile. "When am I not?"

"Cypress—"

"Yes, I'll be careful. No unnecessary risks." He smirks. "I do think I'll bring the new poster back, though. Once I have a chance to draw on some fangs."

# CHAPTER 52
## CYPRESS

I left at dawn.

Cora wearing an uncharacteristic amount of clothing for the current days as she and Aiden saw me off, although Aiden and I are also quite outside our norm.

Believing it to be a better disguise than my usual apparel, Aiden had insisted I wear some of his clothing into town, including his hat. Leaving his head of loose curls and his uncertain expression in full view as I held out my arms and asked them both how I looked.

Cora's tongue had tucked into her cheek as she tried not to laugh. "You look…well, you certainly don't look like a well-moneyed undertaker now."

"Do I look like a cowboy?" I asked, arching a brow and pivoting away from them as I drew both pistols. The guns another mismatch, since the one in my right is the one that belonged to Cora's father, still with only the single bullet in its chamber since I never have much cause to use anything except the pistol in my left and the rifle at my back. "Should I try to look more disgruntled?"

"All right," Aiden barked, gesturing toward where Cerberus waited nearby. "Get goin' so you can get back. Going to be pitch black on the return as it is."

Against instruction, I had walked over and kissed him hard, doing the same with Cora, though I'd added a dramatic dip to it that made her long hair brush the ground as she giggled. "Keep an eye on him," I told her before letting her back up. "You're in charge."

"I know," she said, her chin tipping up as she stood beside Aiden, and though he shook his head, neither of us could suppress a grin.

I'm still wearing it when I finally reach Troy's Hill, more and more secure in my decision that this was exactly what I needed to feel more myself again. To remember that this, too, will pass and that soon we will be back to our usual wandering.

Soon as that damn wanted poster fades.

I pass one posted to the first building on the outskirts of town and pass several more as I ride farther into town, keeping my head down beneath Aiden's hat and keeping Cerberus at my side once I dismount. Trying to determine which copy would be the easiest to grab without rousing suspicion, while also taking in how much the once sleepy town has continued to change into a small bustling city.

How long has it been since I was first here? Five years? Six? Every year more and more settlers find their way out here in pursuit of a better life, just as Cora had. Just as Aiden and I had. And exponentially more will continue to do so as the railroad expands west with an aggressiveness and violence that seems to far exceed any initial possibility of peaceful coexistence.

*Manifest destiny,* I am certain I've heard it called. The belief that it is not only America's right to inhabit but also her divine calling to conquer these lands. Regardless of the native people that have already been here, regardless of the destinies that they themselves believe in.

Never has sat right with me. Whether due to the influence my mother had encouraged by expanding my narrow world through her books or the influence my stepfather had exerted by attempting to close it right back down to anything but him, one person feeling a right to dominion over another has always made me want to bare my teeth, taken me back to places I'd rather not revisit but still feel trapped in even as I stand free in the middle of a crowded street.

I tie Cerberus to a nearby post and reach into the pocket of Aiden's coat to stop myself from fidgeting, understanding why, even after their initial misunderstanding, Cora remains fond of wearing it.

It *is* huge. Comforting. Smells like him and feels like him in a way that makes me breathe a little easier as I step into the general store for a few things that were deemed essential: coffee, flour, dry beans, and kerosene. And some that weren't: chocolate.

I wonder if Cora has ever had it as I take a bite from one of the bars while walking back out without finding trouble, loading up my saddle bags, and looking back in the direction from whence I came. But then my eyes land on the doors of the saloon across the street, and I debate the exact definition of unnecessary risk.

Surely, this doesn't count, I reason, when I walk through them a few moments later, having no intention of staying long, of sitting down to a game, or of indulging in a drink. I simply want to hear the noise, feel the bustle of activity and the thrum of possibility.

I linger right past the threshold, planning only to watch a little before I'm gone again. But then I see him.

*Tan hair. Short beard. Light eyes. A powder burn on his left arm.* I can hear Cora's voice in my head as she said it. As she described the man who killed her father.

He's sitting alone, two empty chairs down from me once I pick a seat at the bar, a half-finished drink in front of him as he waits…either for something or for someone.

Aiden's contacts back in Last Chance told him the man was a bounty hunter, and I suppose he has that look about him. Looks like someone who has spent a great deal of time facing down death. But then, I suppose, I do not sit in any position to judge.

He knocks back the rest of the whiskey in his glass and raps his knuckles against the bar top as a request for another. The bartender nods at him in acknowledgment, then looks to me in question and I hold two fingers up to tell him I'll have the same.

Cora's fugitive glances in my direction, and I've experienced it enough from both sides of the table to know exactly what it feels like when I'm being assessed. His eyes stay on me as the bartender pours his whiskey then mine, then he raises his glass in my direction before turning away.

"You from around here?" I ask him, hesitant to let the opening get away so easily. "Or just passing through?"

"Been here for a while," he says. "Longer than I planned."

"Know what you mean," I reply, my whiskey still sitting in front of me. "You heading out soon?"

"Today, seems like," he says, turning his head to look at me again. "And yourself?"

"Haven't decided yet."

He nods, takes another drink. "What type of business are you in?"

"Me? Cattle."

"Hear there's good money in that."

"Is there?" Frank. I think Aiden said his name is Frank. Frank Clancy. "Then I must be doing it wrong."

He chuckles. "Must be."

"How about yourself? What line of work are you in?"

I don't realize until he responds that I'd fully expected him to lie. "I'm a bounty hunter."

"Are you? That must make for an interesting line of work."

"Does sometimes." Frank knocks back the rest of his drink and raps his knuckles for another. "Other times, not so much."

"Take it this is one of those times?"

"Starting to get more interesting. This is a bit of an unusual job."

"How so?"

He looks away from me, watching the bartender pour. "Well, normally my job is finding people who don't want to be found. Usually pretty straightforward when you think about it."

"But not this time?"

"No, not this time," Frank confirms, his eyes flicking back to mine. "This time, there's someone trying to find me."

"That right?" I ask, another familiar sensation building in my gut, because while I know exactly what it feels like to be assessed, I also know exactly what it feels like to watch a trap you've laid spring shut. "Well, I wish you the best of luck with your endeavor."

"Luck, huh?" he mutters, a half-smile on his face. "That's your real line of business, isn't it, Cypress? Luck?"

"Cypress?" I finally lift my drink with my right hand as I reach for my pistol under the bar with my left. "Kind of a peculiar name. Think you must have me confused with someone else."

His eyes look over my shoulder, and I don't have time to turn around before I feel the knife at my back. "No," he says slowly. "No, I don't think I do."

# CHAPTER 53
## CORA

"Aiden?" I call his name as I step back out onto the porch, searching the front yard as if I don't already know the answer. "Any sign of him?"

Aiden shakes his head, still sitting in the same chair that he's kept watch in since long before nightfall. He reaches up to cover my hand with his when I rest it on his shoulder, but he never takes his eyes off the path through the trees. "Been too long," he says, not for the first time. "Should have been back by now."

"Maybe he stayed in town a little longer," I reply, trying to reassure myself, too. "Or maybe he's just taking things slower in the dark."

Aiden shakes his head again, then stands and removes his gun from its holster. He checks the chamber, making sure it's loaded before he puts it back at his belt. "Something's wrong. I can fucking feel it."

I don't try to argue with him. Don't try to stop him when he heads back inside the cabin, grabs the ammunition belt hanging on the back of a kitchen chair, and reaches for my knife on the table to tuck into his boot. Only, I've already got it in my hand.

"Where do you think you're going?" he asks, watching me straighten to check my own gun after concealing the knife.

I raise an eyebrow at him. "I'm going where you're going."

"The hell you are—"

I put a hand up to stop him. "Aiden, if you think for one moment that you are going to leave me here while you go look for him, then you must have lost the plot when I wasn't looking, because there's not a chance in hell that I'll be left behind here to wonder if either of the two people I love in this world won't be coming back." His eyes are dark, and he opens his mouth to reply before I add, "I feel it, too, okay? Something's wrong. But we'll have a better chance of making it right if we're together."

His mouth closes, his jaw tensing, but he finally says, "I'm sorry. Just…if something happened to you too—"

"We're both going. Make your peace with it," I tell him, stepping forward and wrapping my arms around him to give him a quick squeeze. "Besides, Cypress did say I'm in charge."

He snorts and gives me a squeeze back before letting me go and heading back outside. "Since when did that even need saying?"

I follow him, shutting the door to the cabin behind me without letting myself wonder if I'll see it again. "Will we head toward town?"

"Yes," he says over his shoulder, walking so fast toward the little lean-to shed where we keep the horses overnight that I practically have to run to keep pace with him. "He likely wouldn't have taken a straight path there. Wouldn't have wanted to make it easy for someone to follow him, so we'll have to track him as best we can. See if he got held up by something on the trail, then try for town and see what we find."

"Aiden." He's already reaching for Helios's tack when I stop him with a hand on his arm. "We *will* find him." His gaze meets mine, a look of surprise passing over his face that prompts me to ask, "What is it?"

He shakes his head, a torrent of emotion swirling in his brown eyes. "Nothing, just…history fucking repeats."

# CHAPTER 54
## AIDEN

I'm the one who sees the wanted poster this time from what seems like a quarter mile away. Seems that way because it takes me forever to walk up to it. To pull the knife free along with my hat and the note hidden beneath it over Cypress's sketch, both my and Cora's portraits serving as witness to the way their real-life counterparts stand together to read its contents.

*To the Midnight Gang:*
*I have your thief.*
*Bring the money to Under's Hollow at high noon on the 12th.*
*If I see that you're armed, I'll kill him.*

"The twelfth?" Cora repeats, taking the note from me as I stand over her and keep my eyes on our surroundings, watching to see if anyone is lying in wait for us to take it. "What day is it today?"

"It's the ninth of December," I mutter. "Fuck, it's…it's three days from now."

"Three *days*? Why would they make us wait so long?"

"Because they weren't sure how long it'd be before we'd come looking, and because they want us to bring the money, and they think we might need time to go get it," I assume, giving Cora a nudge in Tess's direction as I try to stave off my growing sense of dread. "C'mon, we can't stay here."

"But where even is the money?" she asks, swinging up into her saddle, so I can do the same. "I've never seen it."

"It's gone," I tell her as we move away from town back toward the cover of the treeline. "Apart from what's in Cypress's pocketbook and mine."

"Gone?" I know she's thinking of the large pile she saw Cypress win at the saloon in Last Chance, about how she hasn't seen him spend a dollar of it since. "Where does it all go?"

"Usually? He burns it."

"He *burns* it?" She comes nearly level with me as I urge Helios into a brisk trot, the understandable shock evident on her face. "Cypress *burns* the money he wins?"

"Well, he keeps some for us to get by, some for…*clerical errors*, and some for amusement, but the majority…" I look at her to gauge her reaction. "It's never been about the money for him. It's about—"

"Making them pay," she finishes, and I nod before she looks away, keeping her eyes on what's ahead until I cut us off into the first pocket of trees, weaving back deeper and deeper until we won't be easily spotted.

"We need to talk about a few things," I say as we dismount again and lead the horses farther into the woods. "Things we should've talked about a while ago. So that you know everything."

"Everything about what?"

I pause and face her, wanting her to see that I mean it when I say, "There are things I should have told you sooner. Was planning on it, but then with everything that's happened…didn't seem like there was much we could do about it at present. And…you've seemed happy."

"I have been happy," she says, her brows drawing together. "What things haven't you told me?"

I frown, feeling deserved guilt as I tell her, "I learned some information about the man who I believe shot your father. Before we left Last Chance."

"You did?" she asks, clearly caught off guard.

"My contacts there said he's a bounty hunter by the name of Frank Clancy. He doesn't exactly play nice with others, so they didn't know much more, but they were pretty certain it was him based on the description."

"That doesn't make sense. Why would a bounty hunter have gone after my father? He wasn't guilty of anything."

"Not all criminals have wanted posters." I cross my arms against my chest, hating to ask but needing to anyway. "You're *sure* your father wasn't mixed up in anything he shouldn't have been? Maybe he wasn't who you thought?"

"No, he wasn't the type of man to get caught on the wrong side of the law." She looks at me, then chews on her bottom lip. "Well, not to say… You understand what I mean. He wasn't one to be on the wrong side of the law so much as he was one to be taken advantage of by those who are."

"That's my worry," I admit. "That it wasn't actually someone on the wrong side of the law but…*was* the law."

"I don't follow."

"The deputy back in Preston," I say, cutting to the point. "What if it was Zeke?"

"Zeke? You think *Zeke* killed my father? But he's not the one I saw."

"I think he may have hired someone."

"Why would he have done that? My father was innocent apart from the debt he owed. He knew that."

"So were you," I remind her. "Didn't seem to help you either. Cora, how much did you know about Preston? While you were there?"

"How much is there to know?" She shrugs. "It's a small town."

"Shouldn't be. There's enough business passing through there that it should be bigger."

"But it isn't because…"

"Because it's pretty common that people end up having a pretty hard time there. No one tends to linger on account of the fact that a lot of robberies go unsolved. Lot of murders, too. That's why Cypress and I were there in the first place."

"Lot of sinners," Cora mutters under her breath.

I nod. "It's got a reputation. And it's not a good one."

"That's why you warned me. When we first met. Not to go wandering by myself. Why didn't you just say so then?"

"I was trying not to get too…*involved*."

She smirks. "Missed the mark there a bit."

"A bit." I roll my eyes, but give her a begrudging smile all the same before I continue, "We assumed the law there was just incompetent.

Couldn't be bothered. But the more I think about it, the more I think that maybe the law there isn't *just* looking the other way…"

"You really think Zeke is *involved* in what happened to my father?"

"Yes, I think he might be. Was your farm resold after your father died?"

"We didn't—I don't know. There wasn't anyone when I went back to visit the grave. My mother did try to sell it, but couldn't. Everyone around Preston knew that plot was useless."

"Which is why they need people who aren't from around Preston. Someone must run things here. Collect payments. Keep an eye on things while someone else finds takers out east for when the previous owners give up. Or for when the money runs out."

"But my father didn't give up," she says softly, the lingering guilt clear. "He wanted to, but I wouldn't let him. I kept pushing him, and that day, he had a meeting in town."

"With who?"

"He didn't say." She frowns. "But he was close to the sheriff's office when he was shot. That's why I couldn't understand why they wouldn't help. It happened right in front of them."

"What if his meeting was with Zeke and that's why he was so close to the office? You said Zeke worked with the bounty hunters, which means he could have easily given one a job himself. And if he knew your father was going to be in town…I know you said he was getting you a bounty hunter, but…"

"He wasn't. Not really."

My eyes narrow. "What do you mean?"

"I didn't tell you all of it either," she says, sighing. "The last time I saw Zeke he gave me that ticket you found. He told me he knew I didn't have any money, and that I should just leave town. That it would be better for everyone. He also said he knew I was staying in the stable. That other people knew, too. That people *talk*, and then that night… I'm sorry." Her eyes fall. "He was trying to warn me like you were, and I didn't listen."

I feel a fresh snap of anger. "He was trying to *warn* you or he was trying to *threaten* you?"

"No," she says immediately, but then seems to rethink it as she continues to stare at the ground. "No, he…he's the one who told them. Elliot kept saying Zeke told them not to hurt me."

"He told them not to hurt you but then he put you on a wanted poster?"

"Because he thinks I was involved with Jake and Elliot and the others getting killed. And I was, but he doesn't realize you saved me. He wasn't there to see—"

"I'm not so sure about that." Her eyes lift back to mine. "Cora, I've thought about this every which way and the only time all three of us were together was the night we took you. And for him to put all three of us on that poster… Cypress and I were never seen together, and I didn't speak to another soul while we were in town."

"You spoke to me."

"That's different," I tell her, and a hint of a smile tugs at her mouth. "Apart from when it came to you, we were careful. Not to mention that so many people come and go through that town that unless someone saw me at the stable that night, I doubt they would have known I was even a person of interest. Let alone that I was with you and Cy. Someone else had to have been there that I missed…" I confess, trying again to rethink through every detail. I'd been so sure that no one had come after

I'd killed them, but if someone had already been there…had hidden as I killed the others... "I didn't think to look for anyone else besides the four at the stable. Cypress only saw the four of them, too, but Zeke was with them at the saloon that night."

"He could have seen you leave together?"

"No. As I said we were careful. After Cy won, he took off out of town like always, but I stayed. Zeke and the others remained, too, talking for a little. Zeke stayed in his seat with a drink when the others took off, but they didn't get too far. Stood out front arguing for a bit until Jake and one of the others left in the same direction as Cypress. I followed them but then they turned around. I figured they were heading back to the saloon or home. Never thought any of 'em would go to the stable."

"But they did. And you think Zeke did, too?"

"Knowing now that you heard them say he talked to them about you, knowing he told you to leave town… What did you say to him when he told you to go?"

"I said I wasn't."

"Thought as much." I find myself smiling, in spite of everything. "And how did he take that?"

"He said there was a coach leaving in the morning, and I needed to be on it. I told him I wouldn't be, and he said he really hoped I would change my mind—" She presses a hand to her temple. "Oh, God, he did threaten me. How did I not see that?"

Sadness steps alongside my anger for her, knowing she'd been that alone, and in need of help, that even a threat had seemed like a kindness. "You wanted to believe he was on your side. You needed to."

"But he—" Her breathing is starting to pick up as she buries her face in her hands. "If he was there, then he *does* know what happened. He *knows* why you killed them."

"Depends on how much he saw, but…no matter. He would know you weren't involved in the way he depicts on that poster. And he still did it."

"But why? If he wanted me gone, then why would he try to hunt me down now?"

"Because he thinks it will help him get his money back. You read that ransom note same as I did. *Bring the money.* Zeke lost a fair amount that night."

"But the money's gone now…" Her hands drop from her face, only to clench over her stomach. "And if he has Cypress…" Her gaze meets mine again. "You should have told me sooner that you thought Zeke was involved."

"I didn't know for sure. I *wanted* to be sure. And I didn't want to make you relive it if—"

"I'm reliving it now," she interrupts. "*Cypress* could be reliving it now."

I wince, not only because of what she's saying but because she doesn't even realize how true it is when it comes to Cypress.

"You can't protect us from everything, Aiden. You can't keep taking everything on yourself," she continues, her next words an echo of the last conversation I'd had with Cypress. "You don't have to when there's the three of us to work through things. You should have told me sooner."

"I know. I'm sorry." I sigh. "Cy told you. About my family."

She nods. "That day we got to the cabin."

"Then you know that I know what it is to want revenge. I know what it is to think it'll be the thing that will bring you peace, but it doesn't.

Because even if the one who did it is gone, you're still alone."

She's silent for a few moments before she asks, "Did you kill him? The man who killed your parents?"

"I did. He…he wasn't much to speak of by then, practically an old man. I thought it would make me feel like I could breathe again, but it didn't. Only made me feel like I lost more of myself. It won't bring you peace."

"I don't need it to." She comes closer, resting her forehead against my chest before wrapping her arms around me. "How do we get him back?"

I exhale, running my fingers through her hair and feeling some of my tension release the tighter she holds on. "I know Under's Hollow. It's about a day's ride away. If they're planning on bringing him there then that means they have him stashed somewhere already. Near enough to the meeting place that they aren't going to be out in the open with a captive for too long. They'll have the advantage once they're in the hollow, though. Only one way in and out."

"So we need to find him before then…" She turns her head so that her cheek is resting over my heartbeat. "No more runnin' *and* no more secrets, okay?"

"No more secrets," I agree, bending down to press my mouth against the crown of her head before I tell her our last one.

# CHAPTER 55
## CYPRESS

*I'm in a windowless room.*

*I have been for days. Maybe even weeks. Hard to tell when there's no sky.*

*I like when it's dark because that means they're gone. That means that, for a little while at least, I can try to sleep. Can try to remember the words in the stories my mother used to read to me when I can't. Say them over and over again because that voice feels stronger than my own.*

*I think she'd be proud of me still. She always was. I think she'd forgive me still. She always did.*

*I hadn't known what I was signing up for. Had liked the idea of causing a little destruction, of taking something that didn't belong to me but didn't belong to them either. I liked the idea of not being alone anymore.*

*How long has it been? Two years since I ran away from home, and I still wonder sometimes if I can run back.*

*Everything hurts. Everything hurts so much, but at least it means I'm alive.*

They think they're punishing me, teaching me my place by keeping me locked up in here, making me crack with every line they carve into my skin. And I think it frustrates them when every time that I answer, it's the same as before. Even when I'm screaming it.

"Where did you take them?"

"Away."

"Where did you take them?"

"Away."

I know it pisses them off. And I like that.

I hadn't minded when we were only stealing things. Stealing money from pockets and stagecoaches and trains. I minded a lot when they started stealing people. Stealing lives. Started thinking that it was right to drag them away like they were also just another piece of property.

I really, really hadn't cared for that.

There's water somewhere in this room but I can't reach it. Can only hear its tap, tap, tapping as it falls onto the hard ground. At least it's something. At least it's some company until I can finally fall asleep and see them again.

Whenever I fall asleep, I'm not alone anymore. I'm back outside. I'm back under the stars, sitting in an open field as I watch them. They're so vivid that it never feels like a dream. Feels less like one than when I'm in this room.

The wolf appeared first. Tall and menacing looking as he sat in the field, too. Staring at me with his head tilted to the side as if he's also trying to figure out why I'm here. As if he's not sure why he is either, but now that he is, he won't leave my side.

The bird appeared second. Little and quick. Racing through the sky as she sings a song I like to hum back to her, flying up into the stars before finding her way back. The wolf likes to watch her as much as I do, even likes it when she *stops and settles herself in his thick fur with no concern for his teeth.*

*I seem to see them more and more now. Seem to be able to stay asleep longer, and sometimes I think I'd like to just stay here entirely. But, I think that maybe if I do, they'll be trapped, too*

*The wolf bares his teeth and growls, the little bird diving toward me with a sharp cry right before I'm pulled away again. A long sharp pain running down my side, over my ribs, but I don't even flinch. I only wait.*

*"Think he's dead."*

*"Is he? Good fuckin' riddance."*

*"You wanna go tell the boss?"*

*"Everyone's sleepin'."*

*"Well, go check."*

*The door opens again, then closes, leaving us with only the light of his lantern. Easily extinguished with a well-placed kick from a supposed corpse before everything is plunged into darkness. He screams, but I don't. Not anymore.*

*I must nick my wrist when I finally manage to cut the ropes free. Hard to tell when there's already so much blood. When everything already hurts. Means I'm still alive. Humming a bird's song as I walk out into the night with a dead man's pistol.*

*Means I'm still alive.*

*And they're all dead.*

# CHAPTER 56
## CYPRESS

"Would you fucking *stop* that humming?"

A fist cracks across my cheekbone, the pain making me temporarily see stars but not the ones I prefer. Good arm on him, that Frank Clancy. Though I think Aiden's is better.

"Take his gag out. Maybe now he's ready to talk," says another voice, the one that's been keeping its distance, although how far exactly I can't really tell with the blindfold.

Blindfolded. Gagged. Hands and ankles tied. Almost as if they're scared of me. Good.

"He's *been* talking. He's just not saying anything useful. That's *why* we gagged him, remember?"

"I don't have time for this. What he had on him isn't enough. I need him to tell us where the rest is."

Blessedly, the rag gets pulled from my mouth, and I work my jaw to ease the strain as I tilt my head against the wall at my back. "Thanks so much," I mutter, then I go back to humming as I wait.

"Fuck's *sake*," Frank says, applying a hard pressure to the side of my head, cold and unforgiving in the way only a gun can be. "Stop *humming*."

"Do *not* shoot him. He hasn't told us where the money is," says the other one, and I'm almost positive I know that voice. That Aiden was right. He usually is, although not always about the things he thinks.

The other one comes closer this time, almost within spitting distance, and the thought does occur to me. But considering I haven't had water in at least a day or two, I'm not sure that's wise.

"Where is the money?" he asks again. "Tell us, and we won't kill you."

"I already told you where it is," I remind him. "It's in the ground."

"*Where* in the ground? Where did you bury it?"

"Who says I buried it?"

"You said it's in *the ground*. Tell me *where*."

He sounds like he's so close to losing his mind. So *very* close. "Could be anywhere by now." I shrug. "Depending on the wind."

I receive another crack against my head, but this fist aims too high, and I'm pretty sure I hear the sound of bone crunching as well as a slight whimper of pain when it connects with my skull. I sigh, rolling my head left then right to abate the dull throb. "Not used to beating people yourself, are you, Deputy?" I ask. "Prefer to hire that out typically?"

There's a moment of silence and then he rips my blindfold off, bright light flooding in as I open my eyes to see that I'm on the dirty floor of an old mining shack. Practically the lap of luxury compared to the last place I was held in. At least this one has a window.

"Where is my money?" Zeke is asking again, and I turn my head to look at him. Smiling when I see his disheveled blond hair, his sunken eyes, and his several days' worth of stubble. Not nearly as shined up as the last time I saw him, but then, I'm likely not either. Pretty sure I'm still prettier though.

"Been a rough few months, has it?" I ask.

He turns to look at Frank where he stands in the corner, a table with my rifle and my pistols to his left. "Do *something*."

"What do you want me to do?" Frank asks. "I've already offered to kill him."

"If we kill him, then we can't use him as leverage, and whatever they bring tomorrow won't be all of it. I need to know where *all of it* is. I need him to tell us where it is and have them confirm it, so we know he's telling the truth. Do something. That's why I hired you."

"You seem to have quite a few needs, Zeke," I tell him, swallowing to try to get the stale taste of the rag out of my mouth. "Happen to make more than one bet you couldn't afford recently?"

"Shut up," he snaps, eyes looking marvelously unhinged. Must be difficult. Suddenly not getting your way when you have all your life. Too bad he won't have time to adjust. "You're going to give me back the money you stole—"

"Technically," I interrupt, "you *lost* it."

"I did not *lose*," he argues, holding a finger in my face like *I* am the petulant child. "You cheated on that last hand."

"No, not on the last hand," I say, giving him a sympathetic frown. "Now, I *may* not have played my best on the earlier hands so that you could win. Which you don't seem to be complaining about. Hard to recall since you keep striking me in the head."

Zeke leans closer in a fruitless attempt to be intimidating. "I'm going to do a lot worse to you if you don't tell me where my money is."

"I already told you, it's—"

"If you say *in the ground* one more time…" Zeke pivots away from me back to his bounty hunter. "I want you to hurt him."

"Hurt him?" Frank repeats.

"Yes, get the information out of him."

"Ah, you mean that you want me to torture him."

"Yes."

"No."

"Why the fuck not?"

Frank takes a knife out of its sheath at his hip, but uses it to start cleaning under his nails instead of stabbing me, which I do appreciate. "You didn't pay me for that."

"What?"

"You did not pay me to torture someone. You paid me to find someone. Which I did."

"Because I *told* you how to do it. Because they have that girl with them. I told you she would be looking for you. *I* am the one that said she wasn't going to let it go and that you could use it to your advantage."

"Doesn't matter whose thought it was. What matters is that one of the three of 'em was found. As far as I'm concerned our contract is finished, and I'm due the rest of my pay so I can get out of this shithole."

"You can't go now." Zeke gestures in my direction as if to prove his point. "And you *just* hit him, so why not—"

"That was for me." Frank's eyes flick to mine. "He's really fucking irritating."

"Then hit him again because he's irritating."

"No, anything else you have to pay for."

I nod in a show of support. "Always good to know your worth when negotiating compensation with an employer."

"Would you shut *the fuck* up?" Frank says. *Well*, see if I take his side again. "Besides, I don't think torturing him is going to work."

Zeke turns back to me, and I tilt my face up to the light shining through the window so he can see the scars. Even hold up my arms so he can see the ones visible on my forearms beneath my rolled-up shirt—*Aiden's* rolled-up shirt. I smile as Zeke registers them, registers their meaning, but he doesn't appear ready to accept it yet.

"I'll pay you. I'll give you a cut of the money," Zeke says to Frank. "Just make him tell you where it is."

Frank seems to consider it for a while before at last he says, "You're not asking him the right questions. He's not getting it. Those two that were with 'im…" He looks at me, assessing again. "What are they to you?"

"Ah, well…history will say we were friends."

He walks forward and kicks me hard enough in the side to make me wheeze before he crouches down and does a much better job at looking intimidating than Zeke did. "You really don't know when to stop running your mouth."

"I've…" I try to suck in a breath, but the sharpness to it tells me he's cracked at least one rib. "I've been told that before."

"You ever been told that your *friends* are dead because you wouldn't shut it?" He tilts his head as he smiles. "How sure are you that they'll even come for you at all? Guessing they are the ones that have the money. And they have each other. Maybe they don't need you."

I meet his gaze. "Still not getting it, Frank."

"I'll spell it out for you then. Hear that girl you have traveling with you is a pretty little thing. If I were your partner, I'd be wanting her all to myself."

I say nothing, and he grins, thinking he's found a weak point.

"Don't tell me that it hasn't crossed your mind. I know she must mean something to you. You bellied up to that bar just because she thinks I shot her daddy, right?"

"You didn't?"

"Oh, no, I did. Well at least, Zeke here says I did. I don't really remember it myself. They all kind of blur together after a while. Another dollar. Another day. You get what it's like."

"Of course. I, too, have trouble remembering all the unarmed farmers I shoot as they're crossing the street."

He laughs, then shrugs. "Everyone has to make a living. You think you have some superior moral code?"

"Moral? No. Superior? Yes."

"Rich talk coming from a thief."

"We all have our hobbies. Besides, taking money is not the same as taking a life."

"Isn't it?"

I tilt my head, studying him. "You know, you remind me of someone."

"Do I? Who's that?"

I smile at him the same way he just did at me. "A dead man."

He shakes his head. "Full of it, aren't ya? Do you know how I knew to be sitting at that particular bar in the first place? Do you know how I managed to track you down?"

"I'm sure you're going to tell me."

"Because of *you*, Cypress. I've been going town to town for months and the thing is, you have a tendency to make quite an impression. All those scars on your face that you showed off just now…people remember seeing something like that. So much so that they remember you coming and going through Troy's Hill for *years*. Remember your partner, too. Quiet sort, right? Only place that you both seem to visit frequently, which likely means you call somewhere around here home."

"Here specifically?" I frown. "No."

"You lie."

"Rarely."

"You're lyin' about this, which I'll bet means they're right close by and will still never spare you another thought." He smirks. "I'll bet your partner is already counting his blessings to be rid of you. Bet he's enjoying *your* money and *your* girl without a thought about coming after you. Bet he's wondering how he ever put up with you for so long. Bet he can't wait to never see you again."

"I'll take that bet."

"Awfully confident, aren't you?"

"Absolutely."

"Mind if I ask why?"

I meet his gaze, unflinching as I tell him, "Because in this lifetime and in any that follow, I would wager everything I own on them, including my last breath." I smile. "Including yours."

The knife he's holding comes up to my throat, the flat edge just beneath my jaw, and I keep my eyes on him as I lean into the pressure of it. Watching as his eyes widen slightly when I say to him, "Getting it now, Frank?"

344

# CHAPTER 57
## CORA

Aiden and I lie on our stomachs on the ridge, overlooking a small shack situated on the side of another rocky hill below. It's taken us a day and a half to find, a little longer to be certain until we see they have Cerberus tied up along with two more horses. The black stallion looks almost as irked about his containment as I'm sure his owner is.

It had been Aiden's direction to start at the hollow and work our way out. Get to the highest ground we could and search in sections. At the time, it had felt tedious, but as it also gave us better odds than a frantic search through the Arizona mountains, we had little choice. Even if every moment that Cypress is gone feels like a moment too long.

We almost missed the shack on our first pass, nearly hidden in the landscape with its sun-faded gray sides, but I spotted the faint smoke from the stove and then the movement at the door. The first of two men that have each only appeared once.

At this distance and with their coats and hats, it was hard to make out their features when they stepped outside, especially in the dwindling daylight, but we're as sure as we're going to be that they're the only ones here besides Cypress.

"We could wait until they move him in the morning," Aiden is saying, his voice low as we wait for one of the men to appear again. "Might be easiest."

"And leave Cypress in there another night?"

He doesn't answer, and he doesn't have to. There is little chance of Aiden being able to stand that idea either. Ever since he told me about what happened to Cypress with the group he'd joined as a youth, I can't get it out of my mind. Can't stop thinking about him alone and in pain. Just as he could be now.

I want him out of there. I want him back with us where he belongs.

"There's a window," I mutter. "We could go down and shoot through it."

"It's too high up. We wouldn't be able to aim properly. We could hit Cypress."

"What if we draw them out?"

"Draw them out how?"

"We could make a lot of noise. Make them think there's a whole posse of us."

"That won't work either."

"Why not?"

"Because no one actually falls for that."

"Fine. What would Cypress do if he were here?"

"Probably walk through the fucking front door." There's a pause, and he looks at me. "We are not doing that."

"Maybe we should."

"Why? *Why* in God's name would we do that?"

"Remember what that man said? The one you killed in front of me."

"Thank you for specifying."

"He said Zeke wanted to talk to me. If you're right, then one of those men could be Zeke. Maybe we give him the chance?"

"And if I'm wrong? Also, a chance at *what*? What are you gonna do, walk up to the door and say we need to talk?"

"What other options do we have?"

"*Anything* but that one."

"Fine," I huff.

Aiden lets out a long breath and fixates on the shack again for a time. "We could cover the stove pipe on the roof. Smoke them out."

"What about Cypress? He'll still be in there."

"If it gets him out, I'm sure he'll forgive us." Aiden glances around, looking for the best route down. "You'll have to be the one to go up on the roof. Could climb up using that overhang on the west side. But you'll have to be careful not to fall through. It looks old. And you'll have to be quiet. Can't sound like a flustered animal."

"Maybe if I do it'll scare them out faster."

"Or maybe they'll shoot you. Christ, maybe I should be the one to go up there."

"If you're worried about the roof with me up there, then it's not going to be any better with you. You're too big."

"Thought you liked that about me."

I roll my eyes. "Are we doing this or not?"

"I don't like it."

"It was your idea."

"I didn't say it was a bad idea, I just said I didn't like it." He looks at me, the worry clear in his eyes. "But I think it's our best chance to get him."

I nod. "So we take it."

# CHAPTER 58
## CORA

We wrap around the back, moving as quietly and as quickly as possible with guns drawn until we are flush with the side of the building. Careful to avoid being seen on our descent and even more careful now as Aiden cups his hand and hoists me up onto the overhang just as we discussed.

The roof is indeed old but still holds as I crawl low across it, heading for the small stovepipe that juts out. I toss my coat over the top, the thick and long black fabric put to a use I had never imagined when Cypress purchased it for me back in Last Chance.

As soon as it's over I start to ease back, knowing we won't have a lot of time before all hell breaks loose, and sure enough I drop off the side and into Aiden's arms just as we hear the first sounds of a commotion from inside.

Someone's yelling. More than one someone before there's the distinct sound of the window shattering as they attempt to let the fresh air in.

Not enough it would seem, because someone also fires toward the roof, inches from the spot I'd just vacated.

"Told you," Aiden mutters, looking over his shoulder at me with his gun drawn. "Christ, here we go. You hold until I give the signal, all right?"

I nod, and a second later the wood on the front door splinters as someone shouts, *"Don't."* The command goes unfollowed as the door bursts open and someone stumbles out, hacking and coughing in the billowing smoke as their knees hit the ground.

The fallen figure raises their gun, gesturing wildly from side to side to try to find their attacker. *"Come out. Come out now, you—"*

Aiden steps out from the side of the building, only far enough to aim and shoot, hitting the man in the arm so that his gun goes flying. He screams, trying to scramble for it before Aiden shoots him again, and he slumps backward into the dirt.

I resist the urge to move forward, waiting as Aiden keeps his left arm across me. "We've got you surrounded," he calls in the direction of the broken front door. "Best to show yourself."

"Thought you said that doesn't work," I mutter, rolling my eyes.

When the silence only lengthens, he gets to once again mutter back, "Told you." Peering around the corner, he yells, *"I'm coming in if you don't come out."*

"I wouldn't," says a voice back. "I'm not as stupid as that fella you already gunned down. Nor as weak. Going to take more than a bit of smoke and some threats to work on me. Not sure I can say the same for your friend, though."

*Cypress.* My stomach clenches, and I almost move forward again before I catch myself.

"My money is on him more than it's on you," Aiden replies, but despite how calm his voice sounds, I know he's fighting just as hard not to run in.

"Thought he was the only one who placed the bets," the voice says back.

"Family affair," Aiden counters.

The voice laughs. "You know, he said you'd come. Been adamant about it no matter how many times I suggested otherwise. Never gave up hope. Right to the end."

*The end.* I look to Aiden, my chest feeling like it's going to crack in two. "No," I say softly. "No, can't be…" *Too late. We can't be too late.*

Aiden shakes his head, his fingers tightening around the handle of his gun. "That shit isn't going to work on me either. Hand him over and I'll let you live."

"Not so sure about that. Not while you got that girl with you."

Aiden glances at me and motions for me to stay quiet. "You think I'm that much of a fool to bring her, Frank?"

The voice chuckles, further confirming Aiden's assumption as he replies, "Women make fools of us all; I know she's with you. And I know you'll kill me because she is. So I guess we better finish this right here."

Aiden's eyes close for a second before he looks around, searching for something to get us out of this.

"The window," I remind him.

"It's too high," he murmurs back.

"Not to throw something through it. It'll distract him."

Aiden's mouth presses into a tight line, but after another moment passes, he nods. Before I can turn away, he bends down and kisses me, just once. Just in case.

"You still out there?" yells the voice. "Or did you two decide it's better to go home after all? Wouldn't blame you."

"Still here," Aiden says back as I start to creep around the side of the building, grabbing a large rock along my way. "I'm not leaving without him."

"How sweet," the voice croons. "I'm sure he would have appreciated that."

*He's not gone,* I keep telling myself as I move. *He's not gone. I would know.* If either of them were truly gone, I would feel it.

They keep talking, exchanging spars that are meant to push Aiden into a rash act, and by the time I finally reach the other side, I wonder how close it is to working. And that's even before I see him.

Though too high for a clean shot just as Aiden said, the window is still low enough for me to see inside the small hazy room. The stove now extinguished in the corner while one man hovers near the door and the other…

Cypress is sitting on the floor against the wall, hands and feet tied, head lolling back, and even wearing Aiden's burgundy clothes, I can still see the spots on his clothing where the red is too dark. He's so still. So quiet. And even though I still believe, even though I know I would feel it—

The figure near the door pivots as he seems to feel me, too, and right before he aims his gun, I see his face, the spark of recognition lighting faster than the spark of his pistol.

I drop to the ground, broken glass and shards of wood raining down over me as he shoots once. Then twice. Only the second time, there's no explosion. No connection. At least not one by me.

"*Cora*," Aiden shouts. "Are you hurt?"

"No," I yell back. "Are you?"

"No," he says. "I got him. He's down."

I scramble to my feet, running for the door, and as soon as I enter the room, I know I hadn't imagined it.

My father's killer is there in the lingering fog of smoke. Tan hair. Short beard. Light eyes. A powder burn on his left arm. Lying on the ground with a shot to his chest. Blood pooling beneath him, reminding me so much of the way I'd found my father that day in the street. The day my whole world had stopped.

But I don't even pause now.

"Is he—" I sprint across the room to Cypress, dropping to my knees beside Aiden who's already there. "Please tell me he's—"

"He's alive," Aiden says, his head down as he keeps his fingers on Cypress's pulse. "He's alive." Aiden's breathing is shaky, the emotion obvious in his voice as he mutters, "It's faint, but… Cy, please don't do this to me. Please, baby, don't… I swear to God, if you die on us, I'll bring you back just to kill you myself."

There's a long silence, but then finally there's also a low chuckle that's taken over by a cough. "Seems…seems a shame to…to pay the ferryman twice."

"Thank God," Aiden says, leaning forward to press his forehead against Cypress's. "Fuck, thank fuckin' God you really do have nine lives."

I laugh, smiling as I cup Cypress's face in my hands after Aiden pulls away, brushing my thumbs gently over the bruises and the scratches that fade away as soon as he opens his eyes. "You're okay," I tell him. "It's okay now. We're here."

"Always were," he murmurs, smiling even as he takes in an uneven breath. "Thank you for the rescue, little bird." His gaze shifts to Aiden. "And you, wolf. Told him you'd come."

"Was never a question," Aiden agrees, holding his gaze as Cypress continues.

"You know...you really do look very handsome when you're being heroic."

Aiden shakes his head but grins all the same. "Thought you might have missed it."

"I got the gist," Cypress mutters back, wincing slightly in pain as my hands move from his face to his neck to his chest, unable to stop checking him over. "But perhaps we could reenact it later?"

"Later," Aiden agrees, and I know his eyes are watering from more than the lingering smoke as he sees the same wounds I do. "For now, let's just get you out of here."

He ducks his head, pulling the same knife from his boot that they'd used to hold the ransom note and cutting through the bindings at Cypress's wrists as I reach for my own knife to do the same at his feet. Anger rises in my chest when I see how tight they'd made them, and I take painstaking care not to inflict further damage.

"His technique could have used improvement," Cypress mutters, seeing me struggle with the knot. "I did offer him a few pointers."

Aiden snorts, and I can't help but laugh again, too, as he remarks, "Only you, Cypress. Only you would tell your captor that he wasn't tying your restraints correctly. I'm sure he really appreciated—"

Cypress's hands come free just in time for him to reach for Aiden's gun, pulling it from the holster with lightning speed and aiming toward the open door when we all hear a noise from outside. However, he drops it again just as quickly, the effort too much when it's clear even from here that the source poses no threat. That he can't even reach his own gun.

Aiden looks to me, an understanding passing between us before I stand slowly, grab my father's gun from the table by the door, and walk outside, whistling a familiar tune as I take the final ten paces that leave me standing over another face I already know.

"*Please*," Zeke says as he looks up at me. "*You have to help me*."

Judging by the state of him, Aiden shot him in the stomach after he'd shot him in the arm. A slower, more painful wound than the one he'd granted the bounty hunter, but a death sentence all the same.

"*Please*," Zeke says again. "Please help."

"You seem to be quite outside your jurisdiction, Deputy," I say to him, and when he only blinks up at me, I continue on. "But since you're here, perhaps you can finally answer some questions for me. Let's start with…did you arrange to have my father killed?"

He doesn't answer. Not until I press my boot to the wound on his arm. He screams but he starts talking.

"Yes, yes, I did. I had to. You don't understand—"

"Oh, I think I do." I press harder with my heel, but let up so he can answer after I ask, "Did you know they were going to come to the stable?"

"Wasn't—wasn't supposed to be… Was only supposed to be Elliot—supposed to frighten you so…so you'd decide to leave."

"You wanted me gone bad enough that you sent Elliot to *scare* me. Because I wouldn't give up?"

"You—you were—said you were still going to the farm and…you couldn't be there. When the… Needed you to be gone when the new owners came. They—they wanted me to kill you."

God, Aiden was right. He was right about all of it. "Who are *they*?"

"The men that…sold the land to your family. They're dangerous people. Criminals."

"So if they wanted you to kill me, then why didn't you?"

He actually has the nerve to look insulted. "Kill a woman? I'm—I'm not a monster."

I stare at him, long enough to still see the prince of Preston I'd known before. "You look like one to me. How many people? How many lives have you ruined to line your own pockets, Zeke?"

"You don't—you don't understand how it is…out here. There's no stopping it."

"I'll bet you didn't try that hard."

"You have to… *Please*, help me. I tried to help you."

"You had my father killed. You sent men to attack me. You tried to take one of the people that I love from me. How exactly were you trying to help me?"

"He took—he's a thief. He took money from me. Money I owed them. They'll kill me—"

"What was that you said about my father, Zeke? That he should have understood the *risks?*"

"No, I—you don't understand. I was…I was only trying to get you to go home. You don't belong out here."

"I know exactly where I belong," I tell him. "When did you get to the stable that night? Did you get there in time to see what your men did to me? What they were *going* to do? Did you know when you put us on your poster?"

He's silent. And that's answer enough as I raise the gun and he flinches away.

"Don't—don't do this," he begs me. "It was only supposed to be— Jake wasn't supposed to… He was supposed to go after the thief. But when I left the saloon, I saw him heading there and I—"

"And you hid like a coward while I was attacked, didn't you? You hid while your friends were killed."

"I—there was nothing." He raises his hand toward me, sees it painted in his own blood. "*Please.* Your father…I knew him. Before he died. I'm sorry for what happened to him. He was a good man. He wouldn't want this for you. He wouldn't have wanted you to…to end up with them."

"Unfortunately for you, it's not his choice. Or yours. It's mine."

I look back at Aiden and Cypress, see them watching me as I remember another question I'd asked that day we arrived at the cabin. About why Aiden would be the one to kill, why he wouldn't let Cypress do it if he believed it would damn him. I've never gotten the chance to ask him myself.

But I don't need to. I already know.

Better to be damned than be alone in this life. In the next. Better to be damned because sometimes damnation and salvation are the same.

"You know, Zeke, maybe you have helped me after all," I tell him, watching him frown in confusion. "In a way, you helped me get where I needed to be in this life. And now, maybe you'll help me in the next. One last question," I say, aiming right at his chest with both eyes open. "What is my name?" He stares at me, mouth open but no sound comes out, and I smile as I pull the hammer back until it clicks, as I let my finger hover over the trigger. "It's Cora. Please, tell the devil who sent you."

I squeeze, not even flinching as the gun kicks back and hits its target for the first time. I let it fall to the ground as the sound falls away along with the last of Zeke's life, and Aiden was right again. It doesn't bring me peace. But I was right, too. I already have it.

Then Aiden shouts my name.

# CHAPTER 59
## CORA

*One Year Later*

I say goodbye on a hill.

A peaceful spot beneath the open desert sky on a spring day. A bundle of white flowers and a book in my hand that I lay on a grave of stone. Still fighting back tears even though more than a year has passed.

I'm still not sure exactly what to say—thought I might by the time I was standing here—but I still don't. Don't know how to apologize for the things that brought me here while also feeling grateful for them at the same time.

If we'd never come here then my father never would have been killed. But I also never would have met them.

Aiden and Cypress stand together a few paces behind me, giving me the space to say my goodbyes while Aiden keeps a watchful eye on the world around us. While Cypress continues to be the most suitably dressed to attend a service.

His head tilts when he sees me looking at him, a soft smile on his face as he interprets it as an invitation to take his place by my side.

"I would say that I wish I could have met him, but I'm not sure he would have felt the same," he says, looking at the Bible and the flowers that I laid down. "I don't imagine many fathers dream of having their daughter end up with a pair of outlaws."

"Maybe not," I say back, teasing him, though I don't miss the way his eyes sharpen a bit when I suggest, "Perhaps you'll find out someday."

"Perhaps," he repeats, smiling more broadly before he wraps an arm around my shoulders. I lean into his right side, the same one where Aiden had discovered a deep wound almost too late. The same one where, whenever I touch it, I still look at his face to see if it pains him even though I know he's now healed. No more worse for wear than a few new scars.

We hadn't been sure that would be the case when Aiden put me on Cerberus with a fading Cypress all those months ago. When he'd told me to ride for the doctor in town as fast as I could and I'd fought for the strength to hold Cypress and myself steady over uneven ground, hoping his boast that Cerberus had yet to be caught would remain when racing against death itself. Hoping it would be enough as I sat in the parlor all those hours later and waited for the doctor. As I told Aiden when he arrived that I'd tried as best as I could.

"I know you did, sweetheart," he murmured, holding me against his chest as I wept out days of worry and fear. "You did good."

Later that night, he told me both the good and the bad of what he'd done. How he'd covered our tracks, how he'd dragged Zeke inside and made sure the shack burned to the ground, made sure this time that no one could follow before coming to find us.

After that, all we had to do was wait. Until at long last, the doctor emerged to tell us both what we already knew.

Which is that Cypress is a terrible patient, and that there was not enough money in the world to convince him to keep him under his care any longer than was strictly necessary.

Not that Cypress would have allowed it in any case. After three days spent as a captive and several weeks more spent recovering, keeping him there any longer seemed likely only to result in yet another building being set ablaze.

"Can you imagine Aiden as a father?" Cypress murmurs at my side now, proving again that he is very much recovered as his eyes spark with mischief. "Waiting on the porch after some poor soul came courting? After someone thinks to take one of his babies from us?"

"They'd have to find us first," Aiden grumbles out.

Cypress easily responds, "That will be their test." He grins at me. "To see if they're a hunter, too. Imagine if any of the children brought home someone *reputable*."

"God *forbid*," I mutter. "Also, *children*? How many are we talking about, Cy?"

Cypress tilts his head, considering. "We will need a few with their mother's green eyes. At least a couple with Aiden's stoic intensity. I think…a dozen should be sufficient."

"A *dozen*?" I nearly choke, Aiden laughing behind me as I say, "Absolutely not. I've things to do. Plus, with our luck, the first one will end up being your spitting image, and it'll take all three of us to keep them out of trouble."

Cypress shrugs, then laughs, too. "A dozen, one, none…I suppose fate will decide."

"Not entirely fate, is it?" Aiden chimes in. "Considering how many times we fu—"

The end of his sentence is cut off when I rush over to clamp my hand over his mouth, though I can still see the grin in his brown eyes before I nod in the direction of the grave. "Quite a first impression you're making," I tell him before he kisses my palm and eases my hand away. He keeps the smile and my hand in his as he walks with me to stand where Cypress and I had just been, then bows his head as he stands between us, both in presumed apology and possible prayer.

"What did you say?" I ask him as the three of us walk down the hill a few moments later, curious to know which hymn he chose.

"That we love you," Aiden says, matter-of-factly. "That we will keep you safe. Make sure you are happy. Gave him my word."

"I love you, too," I say, giving both their hands a squeeze and smiling not only because, of course, that is what Aiden would think to say, but also because it's what I would say if it were his family I was promising to. If it were Cypress's. Chances that will never come, but I like to think they still know.

We keep walking, the horses following behind us once we collect them at the bottom of the hill, and I know we're almost to the house when Tess's head perks up. Still hoping for hay at the end of the trail even though this isn't where we're stopping. Not for long anyway.

We see the house a few moments later, and I'm struck by how

much shorter the journey had been from the hill now that I'm no longer walking it alone. How much less afraid I feel to approach the threshold. Even when there is currently a gun being pointed at me from the other side of it.

"Stop right there," says the woman in the doorway. Her long blonde hair is plaited into a braid and her expression is determined as she stands her ground with her rifle. "Don't come any closer."

Cypress, Aiden, and I all stop, and I can sense that Aiden likes this idea even less now than he had before. Still not a fan of walking right up to the front door, and I suppose I can see his point.

"We aren't here to take anything, I promise," I tell her. "I know the people who used to live here."

"Well, we live here now," she says back. "So I suggest you keep moving before I shoot you and your two fellas there."

"There's no need for that," I try to reassure her, temporarily distracted when I spot three small faces peeking out from behind her skirt.

She sees me see them, and shoots a round in the air in reply. "Last chance."

"We're not here to take anything," I tell her again. "We're here to *give* you money."

She doesn't lower her weapon, but I can see her hesitate, clearly surprised by my reply. "Why would you do something like that?"

"Someone lied to you, right?" Slowly, I reach for the bag at my hip, keeping it clear I'm not going for a weapon. "To get you to buy the land?"

She frowns. "How do you—"

"Happened to the last family, too. But it won't happen again. We made sure of it."

She stares at me, then at Aiden and Cypress. They both nod in confirmation, and eventually, she lowers her weapon. "They're really gone?"

"They're gone," I repeat, watching as the three children press forward, crowding around their mama as she hugs each of them in turn. Three girls. The oldest, who couldn't be more than eleven, remains after the other two run back inside to play. Their interest no longer held now that the danger appears to have passed.

"My husband is out in the fields. He's not going to believe when I tell him…" the woman says, still wary. "This isn't a trick?"

"It's not," I say, stepping forward and holding out the small leather bag. "This is for you."

"What is it?" she says automatically. "We don't need charity."

I keep my hand out anyway. "I'm not offering you anything that isn't yours. They took your money. We took it back."

She eyes it. "That looks heavier than what we paid. I'm not trading one loan for another."

"It's not a loan. It's yours. You can choose to do what you like with it. Go home. Find a new place. It's up to you."

The woman shakes her head. "Why would you do this?"

"So history doesn't repeat," I tell her. "If you don't take it, we'll just get rid of it."

"Get rid of it?"

I jerk my head in Cypress's direction. "He likes to burn it."

"To *burn* it?" She snaps it from my hand, now giving Cypress a wary look and I don't have to see Aiden to be able to picture the smile he's fighting to hide. "Why would you burn it?"

"We have what we need," I tell her. "Now you will, too."

She glances between all of us again before she focuses back on me. "I heard some things about the family that used to live here. Heard the father was killed. And the mother took the two little ones back east." Her gaze never wavers from mine. "Heard the oldest daughter turned outlaw."

I smile, adjusting my hat before smoothing the green dress with black trim I'm wearing. "People do love to talk."

"Indeed they do." She smirks. "You ever see her, you tell her she might want to pass through Preston. The former sheriff might still be a bit sore about his son going missing, but others there are pretty grateful for the way things are going now. Might like to thank her." She looks at Aiden and Cypress again. "And her outlaws."

"I'll tell her," I say. "Should our paths happen to cross."

The woman looks down at the bag in her hand. "I shouldn't accept this. If they really are gone, then you've already done enough. And surely you…"

"He actually will burn it," I reassure her, and that seems to put an end to it as we say one more set of goodbyes, leaving them to their future as we walk into ours.

"I think I like Cora's rule the best," Cypress says after a time, all of us back on horseback as we head farther west toward the setting sun and the spot where we left the wagon. "Makes me feel almost…saintly."

"*Almost* being the crucial word," Aiden says. "But I agree. Was a good addition." He rolls his shoulders, relaxing the farther away we get without being shot. "Not that we need to be in a hurry to use it again anytime soon now that the rest of Zeke's partners are taken care of."

Cypress glances my direction, and I have to bite the inside of my cheek when he says, "Cora and I have a differing opinion."

"Why does that not surprise me?" Aiden replies, letting out a deep sigh. "Which is?"

"We want to go into town," I say.

Aiden whips his head in my direction. "Why in God's name—"

"We practically received an invitation just now," Cypress replies. "The sheriff has been replaced, and you said yourself that the wanted posters are gone. Already buried beneath new criminals that are not nearly as pretty to look at."

Aiden looks like he wants to argue, but he can't for more than one reason. One being that, as Cypress mentioned, he himself checked around town for the wanted posters late last night. The other being that he also thinks we're pretty.

"A quick stop on our way to the Pacific?" Cypress encourages. "Would only be sensible to resupply. Cora is out of chocolate."

I raise my eyebrows at him. "*I* am out of chocolate?"

Aiden shakes his head. "I'm not listening to this debate again. We can go into town. Cora, I know you want to leave something at the boarding house, but we're not getting into anything else. We go, do what needs doing, and we leave. No thieving."

"Why are you only looking at me when you say that?" Cypress asks. "You know, I could win just as easily without any of the…"

"Theatrics?" I pipe in helpfully, and he nods.

"Yes, I could win without *theatrics*. Far less enjoyable that way, though."

Aiden tilts his head, eyes narrowing. "You're tellin' me that you think you can win playin' it fair?"

"You doubt my abilities as a card player?"

"As a card player? No. As a harbinger of chaos? Yes."

Cypress grins. "Care to wager on it?"

"What are the stakes?"

"If I play and I win the dull way…"

"Then…?"

"Then you and Cora both have to join me at the table on the next game."

"Both of us? You want both of us at the table? Don't you think that will be…distracting for you?"

"As much as it is for you."

Aiden rolls his eyes and mutters, "Sadist."

"Masochist," Cypress replies, grinning. "I said I would win without the games. Not that I wouldn't have fun."

I look at Aiden, the corner of my mouth lifting as I see him think it over. "It *would* be fun, don't you think?"

He sighs, and without ever having to sit down at the table, it's clear Cypress has already won. We all have.

"Okay, Cy," Aiden says, eyes moving to him rather than the horizon. "Lead the way."

The Midnight Gang will return in

# PROVIDENCE

# ACKNOWLEDGEMENTS

Several years ago now, I had a thought that wouldn't leave me alone about a smart-mouthed cowboy with an enthusiasm for chaos. Unbridled internal desires all dressed in black, riding from town to town with twin pistols and a complete lack of regard for his own safety. Which is where his partner came in.

This other cowboy was all worries, the sharp brake before they careened off a cliff, the one who made sure they lived to tell the tale. The one who was scared, but who did it anyway, because he would rather be afraid sometimes than always alone. Because he loved him, too.

My gambler. My gunslinger. And of course, my girl they stole, who came to me last but who the picture could not be complete without. Who is for all of the wild ones looking for the place they belong.

To Cypress, Aiden, and Cora. Loves of my cowgirl heart. Thank you for being my companions for all these years and for sticking with me until I had the time to tell your story. Thank you for reminding me to love fiercely, to keep fighting, and to have some fuckin' fun.

To my readers, whether you found me new or followed me from

my fandom roots, I'm so glad you're here! Thank you for supporting me and for taking these adventures with me. I appreciate it more than I can ever say.

To all the people who helped me put this book together. To Makenna, who gets me and my book babies, and who also thinks Aiden striding into the stable was the fuckin' hottest thing. To Rachel, who designed me the cover of my dreams, of BEYOND my dreams. To Reid, who always finds a way to bring my babies to life in the most beautiful way. To Lemmy, who brought me into the Luna fam. To Phoebe and Anna, who helped make me amazing content to share so I could keep focusing on writing.

To all the people who helped keep me sane. To Kelli, who I started writing this story as a love letter to so she would be the western wife of my life. AND it worked. To CiCi, my bestie and forever parachute buddy, who talks me off the cliffs while also telling me to keep climbing them because I *can* do it and you know what? She's right, damn it. To Kirby and Bee and our unhinged group chat with its unhinged name.

To my family. To Kat, who read this book in its early stages and sent me escalating chats about her love for Cypress. Who is always one of my loudest supporters and my favorite people. To Kayla, who jumped right in with me with both feet and matching outfits. To my wonderful parents, who continue to support me in lots of little ways and in big ones, too. To my amazing in-laws, who have done the same. It truly does take a village, and I've been truly lucky in mine.

To my mom, who took me to the library every week, who always signed me up for Book It, and who instilled in me a lifelong love of reading. Who always had and continues to be a diehard romantic with more romance books around than she has time to read. Who could not have been prouder when I started writing my own.

To my grandfather, who was obsessed with westerns. Who always had a cowboy on the TV whenever I came home from school and who lifted me up into a saddle on more occasions than I can count. To both him and my grandmother, who never stopped paying for lessons so he could watch me be a cowgirl, who bought me my first pair of black chaps and my first black hat so that I, too, could look like a well-moneyed undertaker.

To my babies, who think it's pretty neat that Mommy writes books. Who point to bows in stores and say "Look, *The Crush!*" You are, without question, the best thing I will ever create.

To my husband Kyle, who makes all this possible. Who shows up for me every single day and who I'd choose over and over again in every lifetime. Who I'd follow no matter where the road leads. I love you

# ABOUT THE AUTHOR

**Ren Browne** is a lifelong romantic, cowboy enthusiast, and rumored woodland spirit. When not reading or writing, she can be found spending time with her husband, who is the living embodiment of Ron Swanson, their two outdoor-loving children, their silly dog, and a growing flock of chickens.

**Other Books by Ren Browne:**

Providence

The Crush

For updates on future releases, including bonus content, consider signing up for her newsletter at RenBrowne.com or following her on:

**Instagram: @renbrownewrites**

**TikTok: @renbrownewrites**

**Threads: @renbrownewrites**